WILLIAM S RUSSELL

The Guardian of Carlsbad Caverns

Newhouse Creative Group

Names: Russell, William. | Traynor, Daniel, Cover.

Title: The Guardian of Carlsbad Caverns / by William S Russell

Description: Orlando, FL :AimHi Press, 2019. | Summary: When a baby bird is caught in a plastic bag on a tree branch, Luna and her friends are on a mission to save him!

Identifiers: LCCN 2019953305 (print) | ISBN 978-1-945493-19-5 (paperback)

Subjects: CYAC: Environment. | Ecology. |Animals. | Wildlife. | Planet.

Classification: LCC PZ7.1.R87 Gua 2019(print)

LC record available at https://lccn.loc.gov/2019953305

First edition

ISBN: 978-1-945493-19-5

This book was professionally typeset on Reedsy.
Find out more at reedsy.com

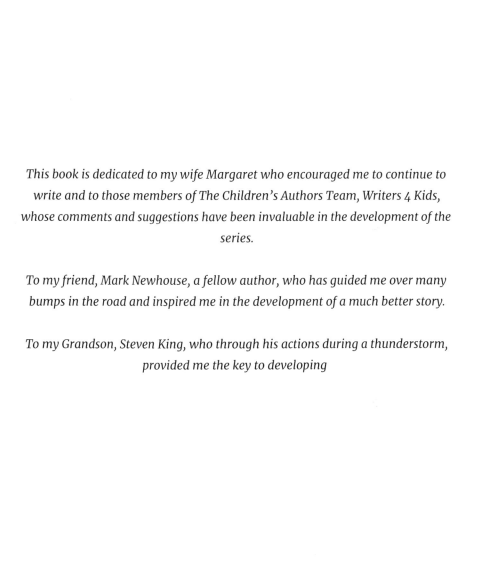

This book is dedicated to my wife Margaret who encouraged me to continue to write and to those members of The Children's Authors Team, Writers 4 Kids, whose comments and suggestions have been invaluable in the development of the series.

To my friend, Mark Newhouse, a fellow author, who has guided me over many bumps in the road and inspired me in the development of a much better story.

To my Grandson, Steven King, who through his actions during a thunderstorm, provided me the key to developing

Chapter 1

Steven closed his eyes and whispered. "My God, we're home." He ran his hand through his hair. It was still moist. "We did it. We're safe and the Portal's closed. I gotta skedaddle upstairs. Aunt Celia will be up soon, and she's not about to buy another excuse about where I've been."

Steven dropped his backpack in the chair, clutched Morag, his scaled-down dragon, in his arms, and hurried up the cellar stairs into the kitchen. He tip-toed, hoping his aunt would still be asleep.

He was too late.

Aunt Celia was leaning against the counter, a cup of coffee in her hand, yawning. "Steven, I know you weren't out walking the beach again. Did you spend another night in your parents' lab?" She looked closer. "What's that in your arms?" She stared in horror. "Get that lizard out of the house! Right now, young man."

Morag, startled, leaped from Steven's arms. The size of the dragon doubled as she hit the air. Landing on the kitchen table, her body redoubled in size and weight.

Steven didn't realize what was happening until he found himself pushed out of the kitchen by Morag's hind legs.

The thunderous sound of the kitchen table smashing to the floor was drowned out by his aunt's screaming.

Morag was now so large her head was pressed against the cathedral ceiling and her long spiny tail extended out of the kitchen and down the cellar stairs.

Steven, shoved into the hallway, got to his feet, straining to see his aunt over Morag's body.

Bastet, Steven's Egyptian cat, strolled over. *I think we are in big trouble,* she said telepathically and jumped on Morag's tail. *Maybe, I can calm your dragon down.* She ran up along Morag's back to the dragon's head. *Morag,* she called, but the dragon was in no mood to listen.

Steven heard Aunt Celia's terrified screams, but couldn't see her.

"Aunt Celia, calm down," Steven shouted, trying to be heard over all the noise.

Bastet was rubbing Morag's head. It was starting to soothe the panic-stricken dragon. *I'm a cat. I should know how to make a dragon purr,* she said.

Feeling much calmer, Morag looked down at Aunt Celia. *Is She all right?* Morag asked, still pressing Aunt Celia between the cabinets.

Aunt Celia looked up into Morag's looming eyes, an empty coffee cup still clutched tightly in her hand and bellowed, "Get me out of here!"

Steven called back, "You'll be all right. Morag won't harm you. She's a friend."

"She's no friend of mine," Aunt Celia shouted. "Get this thing out of my kitchen!"

Bastet kept rubbing Morag's head, and the dragon, looking a bit sleepy, began to revert to her smaller size.

Steven almost wished Morag wasn't shrinking. *How will I explain this? What will she say when she learns about The Seeker and my mission to save the Earth?*

Chapter 2

Steven saw the shocked look on Aunt Celia's face, her coffee cup dangling from her fingers. His aunt's body was still wedged tightly between the cabinets. He sighed. *Why did she have to find out about Morag this way?*

"Aunt Celia," he said, as he reached her after wading through the wrecked kitchen.

The terror of seeing the head of a dragon inches in front of her eyes was etched across his aunt's face. "Steven. Is this...is this *a dragon? It can't be! Can it?*"

Morag, now perched on the windowsill, bowed her head in shame at the wreckage she caused.

Bastet sat in silence; paws pressed together as if praying. *Oops! The cat is out of the bag,* she said telepathically.

What cat? Asked Morag, sending her own telepathic message.

You! Bastet said and burst into laughter.

I'm not a cat, Morag replied, *I'm a dragon, remember?*

It's a human expression, Bastet explained. *Oh, never mind. I don't know why I bother trying to teach anything to you.*

Steven glanced at the broken kitchen light dangling by a single wire from the ceiling. Next to the shattered chairs lay the mangled steel pot rack, torn from the kitchen ceiling. Aunt Celia's pots and pans were scattered across the floor like a minefield.

"Whaaaat happened?" Aunt Celia asked, not daring to move.

"You startled Morag," Steven said.

"Morag? Who is, Morag?"

I am Morag, said the dragon, opening her wings, and leaping onto the kitchen counter.

"No!" Aunt Celia screeched, trying to press herself against the wall, far out of reach of whatever this creature might be.

The miniaturized dragon folded her wings and rested on her haunches on the counter, eyes studying Steven's frightened aunt. *Please tell your aunt I am sorry. I did not mean to make such a mess, but she frightened me with her screams.*

"Morag said she is sorry," Steven said. "You frightened her."

"I frightened her?" Aunt Celia looked at Steven, then back at the dragon. Grabbing the edges of the cabinets, she pulled herself out from between them. Still shaking, she hesitated, before shuffling cautiously toward Steven, hugging the wall all the way.

Morag stood on her hind legs, unfolding her wings in case she had to make a speedy getaway.

"Beautiful, isn't she?" Steven asked, moving closer to Morag.

Aunt Celia, still frightened, looked at Steven, then back at the dragon, then again at Steven. Her hands were shaking. "Beautiful? Steven, she's a d-r-a-g-o-n."

"I know. Isn't she amazing? She won't hurt you," Steven said, stroking Morag's back and watching hopefully, as his aunt appeared to be calming down.

Morag purred.

"You see, she's like a big cat," Steven said.

She's nothing like me, Bastet replied, glaring at Steven.

"What did you call her?" Aunt Celia asked, still staring with fear at the dragon.

"Morag," Steven replied. "She's really nice."

"If I move, she won't bite me, will she?" Aunt Celia asked in a quivering voice.

"Yes," Steven replied, then, realized he should have answered, "no."

Aunt Celia shivered. "She will bite me?"

"No. I mean, yes, you can move closer."

Aunt Celia stepped cautiously toward Morag. She eyed the creature with suspicion.

Steven smiled. "Let her have your hand?"

"I will not," Aunt Celia said, protecting her hands.

"I mean let her sniff it. She'll get used to you and not be afraid of you anymore."

"Afraid of me?" Aunt Celia shook her head then she extended her hand, palm up as if approaching a friend's dog. "If my eyes weren't seeing this dragon, I'd never believed it's real." She shot a look at her nephew. "How is it possible that I'm looking at a mythological creature right here, in my kitchen?" She looked back at Morag. "Nice dragon. Nice dragon."

Steven, not eager to answer questions, moved closer to his aunt. "Are you hurt, Aunt Celia?"

"Scared out of my wits," she said breathlessly. "I want to know what just happened. Why do you have a dragon in my kitchen?"

I can't talk *my way out of this, Steven thought.* He took a deep breath. "You see, it's kind of a long story—"

Steven, Morag interrupted, *I must feed tonight.*

What again, Bastet asked.

I'm a growing dragon, Morag replied.

"Let's discuss food later," *Steven shot at the dragon.*

Aunt Celia watched in amazement as there was some sort of discussion going on between Steven and the dragon, but only Steven's side of the conversation was audible to her. "Well, are you going to tell me what's going on?" she asked, aware that she was indeed facing a dragon, right here, in her kitchen... her wrecked kitchen! "Look what she did to my kitchen! You tell me right now what this is all about, young man!"

"I guess I'd better," Steven muttered. Although he hoped this day would never come, he realized that he had no choice but to tell her everything, well, at least some things. If he told her everything, he knew she would have a 'cow,' and he'd never be allowed to fulfill the prophecy. The consequences of that would be terrible for everyone on Earth. "Before I explain what happened,"

Steven said, "I think we should move to another room since the kitchen is...not as comfortable as usual."

"What part of the house would you like to wreck next?" Aunt Celia asked glaring at the mess the dragon had made of her kitchen.

Steven gulped. "Can you meet me in my parents' lab in fifteen minutes? And, oh yes, please bring a change of clothes, passport, money, your warmest jacket, and best walking shoes?" Steven started for the kitchen door, hoping to escape before she stopped him with her questions.

"Wait one minute, you!"

Aunt Celia's voice stopped him cold.

"What do you mean, bring clothes and a passport? Just exactly where do you think we are going?"

"Scotland." Steven ran out of the kitchen, promptly followed by Bastet and Morag.

"Steven, you come back here! I want some answers, now, young man!"

Steven headed for the stairs.

Aunt Celia watched helplessly as the trio disappeared up the stairs. "I can't believe any of this," she mumbled, standing alone in the kitchen, staring at the crushed table and chairs scattered all over the floor, trying to grasp what she had just experienced. "I wonder what that boy is up to?" She turned to the stairs leading to the basement lab, and a chill ran down her spine.

Chapter 3

Steven made sure to arrive in the lab before Aunt Celia. He was checking the coordinates on his smartphone and talking to Bastet when she entered. He had already spread out on the rectangular lab table the contents from two backpacks he and his aunt had taken on a previous 'normal' camping trip.

"Steven, you will explain to me immediately why we are supposedly going to Scotland. I want to know exactly where and why you think we are going to where?"

"Glencoe, right below the Highland mountains," Steven interrupted, still checking coordinates. "Morag needs to feed tonight. She must eat at least every four or five days, or she gets a bit bad-tempered. Not a good thing in a dragon."

Aunt Celia stared morosely at Morag. "On that, I can agree with you after seeing what she did to my kitchen. But why, Scotland?"

"Scotland, with its vast hills, mountains, and low population above Glencoe, will ensure she is not seen by anyone. Just imagine what would happen if people knew about her?"

"I can imagine. Are we camping?" asked Aunt Celia, seeing the camping gear on the table.

"Yes. I thought we might enjoy the night sky. The stars put on a good show this time of year; don't you think?"

"All this is so you can feed this dragon and enjoy the night sky?" Aunt Celia shook her head. "I don't think so."

She doesn't believe you, Steven, Bastet said. *Wait until she hears the real story.*

"You're right," Steven said with a sigh, knowing Aunt Celia would have a difficult time believing what he now had to tell her.

"Who were you speaking with just now, Steven?" Aunt Celia asked. "No more secrets, young man. Do you understand?" She tapped her foot impatiently.

Steven knew there were still going to be some things he couldn't reveal to her, but he understood that if he didn't tell her a little, she would make his life impossible. "Aunt Celia, I was talking to Morag and Bastet. They're my friends."

"You can talk to a dragon and a cat?"

Steven nodded. "Yes. I know it sounds unbelievable, but for some reason, I don't fully understand, I'm capable of communicating my thoughts to them and hearing theirs. They always talk telepathically, through thought messages, and I can understand them."

"I never heard of such a thing." Aunt Celia scratched her head.

Steven glanced at the wall clock. "I'm getting ahead of myself. We have a lot to do. I'll tell you the rest later. Are you ready to go?"

Aunt Celia looked doubtful. "To Scotland? For real?"

"To Scotland," Steven replied, hoping not to have to answer any more questions until he had more time to think.

Aunt Celia crossed her arms in front of her chest. "You expect me to let you go to Scotland...to go with you to Scotland, without any other explanation?"

Steven realized time was passing quickly, and Morag's stomach was growling. "I'll explain it all later, but we have to go now. Please, Aunt Celia, you need to trust me. Think of your kitchen."

Aunt Celia let out a deep sigh, staring into Steven's eyes, and then looking at Bastet and the dragon. "Okay. Fine. We'll go to Scotland. Why? I have no idea, but I will phone and make our reservations and get our tickets. And by the way, have you thought how you are going to get a dragon on a plane? 'IT' is not your average passenger."

"That's not a problem," Steven replied, as he pressed the 'enter' button on the phone.

A blinding flash of light made Aunt Celia jump. Her eyes grew wide as a translucent sphere materialized in front of her. "Whoa!" Aunt Celia cried out at what looked like a whirling pool of light. She felt dizzy and rocked unsteadily on her heels. Celia stared at the strange sphere in the middle of the lab. Aunt Celia guessed it was about seven feet tall and equally wide. It was floating above the floor. Its center, a rapidly rotating disc of shimmering colors, reminded her of a kaleidoscope. The outer ring, much darker, was spinning in the opposite direction and was surrounded by a fine mist. She backed away. "What is this...this thing?"

Steven reached out to steady Aunt Celia. "Don't be afraid. This is our transportation. I call it the 'Portal.' It will take us wherever we want to go."

"This...this is our transportation?" Aunt Celia stood rigid, mesmerized by the rotating pool of multi-colored light. She stared in disbelief as Bastet, followed by Morag, stepped into the rotating circles, alive with strobe lights.

"You're next, Aunt." Steven pointed to the entryway in the center of the swirling light storm.

"Steven, I can't go in there," Aunt Celia sputtered.

Steven smiled. "Trust me, Aunt Celia, it doesn't hurt." Before she could protest another second, Steven grabbed her hand and pulled his hysterical aunt into the swirling circles of color.

"No," Aunt Celia screamed, but it was too late. Now that she knew about Morag and Bastet, she had to become part of the team, or Steven knew the Earth was doomed.

Chapter 4

S teven felt Aunt Celia's grip tighten on his hand as they whizzed through the entrance of the Portal, ablaze with flashing lights.

Aunt Celia was awash in the swirl of colored bands, still fighting to break away from Steven. Suddenly she was staring into a ceiling full of what looked like bright stars. They were so close she felt she could touch them. Her fear became a sense of awe, as the beauty of the strange night sky flowed through her, calming her.

Steven knew what Aunt Celia was experiencing as they were floating down into the bottomless void of time and space. He hoped she was no longer afraid. Steven remembered how frightened he felt the first time when testing the Portal. That first trip had been terrifying, but soon he got used to it, even enjoyed this fantastic way to travel.

As Aunt Celia was trying to make sense of what was happening to her, she found herself standing on a hard surface, fighting to maintain her balance. "Where am I?" she asked, her eyes struggling to focus in the dim light of what appeared to be a cave.

Steven released her hand. "You'll be safe here. It takes a few minutes to get your land legs again."

Aunt Celia leaned against the wall. She heard Steven's voice as if coming from a distance. "Is it safe?" It sounded as if he was asking someone.

Safe! Safe from what? Aunt Celia wondered dully as she was emerging out of her daze. *Who is Steven talking to?*

Yes, answered Bastet telepathically. *I don't sense any dangerous creatures nearby...other than you know who.*

Morag let out a low growl from deep in her throat. *Steven, I do not like it here. The scent of my mother's killer still lingers in these cavern walls.*

"He will pay soon enough," said Steven. "Be patient, my friend. Your time will come."

Morag let out an angry snort, thinking the boy is right, my time will come. And when it does, look out! Even Steven would not be able to stop her from getting her revenge.

Steven looked around the cavern again. Confirming they were alone, he tapped the 'APP' icon on his phone.

The Portal collapsed with a 'whoosh.' There wasn't any sign it had ever been there.

Steven hoped the transporter would reappear when he needed it. He was never quite sure. His aunt was coming out of her daze. He was glad she wasn't hurt but worried about how she was going to react when she became fully aware of what he had done to her. He knew his aunt could barely see and was still dizzy, two natural reactions from the trip in the Portal. He also understood, once she was fully recovered, the questions would fly. I can't wait, he thought.

"What was that we went through?" Aunt Celia asked shivering. "I'm drenched." She patted the front of her jacket, which felt as if she had been swimming in it.

Steven realized his aunt was almost back to her old self. "It's okay. I forgot to warn you. It's just a feeling you get from the Portal. I still get it each time I go back and forth. It will pass soon."

Aunt Celia shook her head as if trying to get water out of her ears. "I felt as if I was falling. White streaks of light flew by my eyes. Were they stars, Steven?"

"I'm not sure. There's still a lot I don't know. I guess you could think of them as stars."

"They were beautiful," Aunt Celia said. "Where are we?" No longer feeling dizzy, she turned toward Steven who was standing against the cave wall. She looked into his eyes as if trying to search his soul. "I'm sorry, Steven, I'm having a hard time with everything. Where, exactly are we?"

She turned to look around but almost banged into Morag's too-close face. "Yikes!" she cried, barely stopping herself from falling against the jagged rock wall. "I forgot about her." Finding herself nose to nose with Morag, she whispered, "Nice dragon." Feeling Morag's hot breath, she added, "She needs mouthwash. Dragon-breath."

Morag looked at Aunt Celia with an amused smile. *It was time to give this human a little scare.* She parted her lips. The dim light in the cave reflected off her massive white teeth.

Aunt Celia shivered at the sight. She had never seen anything like them and wished they weren't so close. She kept thinking she was having a strange nightmare, but her wrecked kitchen was all too real, as were these pointy teeth.

Steven rubbed his hand along Morag's massive neck. "Don't be afraid. She won't harm you. I promise."

"I just can't believe this whole thing." Aunt Celia forced herself to look directly into Morag's eyes. "Are you sure she doesn't bite?"

"Come here, Aunt Celia," Steven coaxed, still stroking the dragon.

Aunt Celia was not a coward, but facing a dragon was asking a lot of anyone. She walked very cautiously along the dragon's flank toward Steven. "I never realized how massive dragons were until now," she said.

"They're pretty big," Steven replied. "But she's gentle. You'll see." "Pretty sharp teeth," Aunt Celia said and backed away from Morag's head and those massive molars. "The books don't do her justice. No, indeed."

Bastet released an indignant meow. *I'm the god around here. She is just a dragon. Your aunt should be formally introduced to me first.*

"What was that strange noise?" Aunt Celia asked, gazing all around.

Steven laughed. "That's just Bastet. The great Egyptian goddess is jealous. She gets that way sometimes. Gods can be fussy."

Aunt Celia laughed uneasily. She was thinking, if I do not get over my fear now, I will never get over it. "May I touch the dragon?" She asked, forcing herself to be brave.

Oh, let your Aunt touch me? Morag said. I hate seeing a frightened old lady. Maybe she'll forgive me for the kitchen.

"Morag said you can touch her," Steven said. "She's more frightened of you than you should be of her," he added.

"I doubt that." Aunt Celia let her hand drop very slowly, very cautiously, onto Morag's back. She rubbed her hand lightly along Morag's bronze scales. "She's okay," Aunt Celia said, ready to lift her hand off quickly if the dragon's head turned toward her and she saw those terrifying teeth again.

"She likes that," Steven said. "You're very brave, Aunt."

Aunt Celia didn't feel brave but continued to stroke the dragon's back. Suddenly a thought popped into her head. "Do you ride her, Steven?"

"No. Morag has offered to let me fly on her, but I'm still scared of falling. To tell the truth, Aunt, I get a panic attack every time I even think about flying on her."

"I don't blame you," Aunt Celia said, feeling more confident as she continued stroking the dragon. "Steven, she seems very nice, but I would not like you flying on her. It's far too dangerous."

"Me neither," Steven said but knew that someday he might have no choice. One thing he'd learned from his few missions was that he could overcome fear if he made up his mind to do so.

"And now, my devious nephew, no more stalling. I want to know exactly why we are here and what all this is about? And most of all, I want to know if whatever you have gotten yourself into, is dangerous."

Steven knew there was a fear he might not be able to get over, the fear of telling his aunt the truth. He knew the greatest danger would be if she refused to let him continue with his mission. Dangerous as his adventures were, he was convinced he had little choice.

Chapter 5

S teven heard in his aunt's voice that she was not going to wait much longer for an explanation. A worried feeling grew inside him as he tried to figure out what to tell her. *Stick to the truth, at least part of it.* What to say and not to say; that was the dilemma.

Aunt Celia was looking very impatient.

It's now, or never, Steven thought, wishing he could stall a little longer. "Like I said before our trip, Aunt Celia, we are in Scotland, about five miles north of the town of Glencoe."

Aunt Celia stopped stroking the dragon. "Glencoe? How is that possible? One minute, we're here, and the next,, we're in Scotland?"

Steven nodded. "The Portal allows its passengers to go anywhere in the world almost instantly."

Morag, no longer being rubbed, walked toward a corner of the cave and sniffed the air. A low growl arose from her throat.

"Why did she growl like that?" asked Aunt Celia, alarmed again. "She was fine when I was stroking her."

Steven began to stroke Morag again. "Morag remembers being chained to the floor over there." He pointed to the spot where a steel leg iron lay.

"She was chained to that. The poor dear. Who would do such a terrible thing?" Aunt Celia asked, angry that anyone could do that to such a fantastic creature, even if she was still a little afraid of 'it'...her...even if 'it' had wrecked her kitchen, her beautiful kitchen. Later for that, she thought, awed by the size of the dragon and wondering how such a massive creature could ever have been chained up by anyone.

I will never be chained, beaten, or starved again; Morag bellowed.

Aunt Celia jumped at the thunderous sound.

"She was just expressing her joy at being free," said Steven, still afraid to tell his aunt the entire truth.

Aunt Celia rubbed her brow. "If that is what she sounds like when she's happy, I don't want to be around when she's angry," Aunt Celia said, still shaken by the ferocity of the roar.

Steven decided this was a great time to change the subject. "How does it feel to be in Scotland again, Aunt?"

Aunt Celia gazed out of the cave and saw the bright stars. "Steven, I'm still having a difficult time believing you are talking to a dragon, and a cat, not to mention that a moment ago, I was in Newport?"

Steven smiled. "I understand. It took me several trips before I believed the Portal had the power to take me anywhere in the world. Now that I think of it, except for jumping all over Aquidneck Island, this is the third time I used the Portal to travel outside Rhode Island. What a fantastic opportunity to learn about other places. Don't you think it's great? It's educational! What a great learning experience!" Steven hoped his aunt, a highly educated woman, would agree that the Portal was a great way to learn about other countries and cultures, so she'd forget about her questions. It was worth a try.

Aunt Celia shook her head. *Nice try, sonny,* she thought. Everything was happening too fast. *Steven's changed,* she mused, as she watched him walk toward Morag without any sign he feared the monstrous beast. Her mind was racing: *Is any of this safe? I am his guardian. I have responsibilities to take care of him. Shouldn't I be stopping this? A dragon?*

I am starving, Morag interrupted, shooting a telepathic complaint to Steven. *Can I go and feed now? The old lady is okay. I calmed her down.*

You did? Bastet yowled angrily. *Next, you'll tell me dragons are more potent than cat gods.*

"Morag," Steven said aloud, so his Aunt could hear him. "We must wait until it is a little darker. You will have plenty of time to fill your stomach tonight."

If the food is plentiful, Morag answered telepathically. *Okay. I will wait until it is darker. She moved* slowly back toward Aunt Celia. *But only if you tell her I liked the way she rubbed my back. Now, I want her to do my neck too.*

Steven sighed. Dragons are like spoiled kids, he thought. "Aunt Celia, Morag respectfully requests that you rub her neck? She liked how you did her back before."

Aunt Celia hesitated then held out her hand as Morag bowed her massive head. She touched lightly on the dragon's forehead and ran her fingers along the side of her muscular neck.

Morag stood still as Steven's aunt looked directly into her eyes. "Your eyes, Morag, reveal a soul of surprising warmth and compassion," Aunt Celia remarked as she stroked Morag's neck. "I must admit I am still a little frightened of you, but I sense goodness inside you, I did not expect from a dragon...based on all the legends and stories."

"You can't trust everything you read," Steven said. "A very wise lady taught me that." He stared kindly at his aunt.

"I know, You can't judge a book by its cover...or a dragon by the size of his teeth. Right, Steven?" Aunt Celia smiled and placed her hand on Steven's shoulder.

Steven pulled his body away.

Aunt Celia understood it was too soon for that, too shortly after his parents' death.

Steven, kindly express my regret for scaring your Aunt earlier today, Morag said, in between contented purrs, just loving the gentle stroking of her neck. *And for wrecking her kitchen. Although that was her fault.*

I've had enough of this 'mushy' talk, Bastet erupted. *Steven, we should leave this cave and look for a place to set-up camp if we are staying here all night. That dragon is not the only one hungry around here! Everyone always forgets about me! I'm the god around here, but does anyone care? No! It's the big clumsy creature that gets the attention, not the god!* She stamped her paw angrily.

Steven sighed. "You're right. I'm sorry. We're in Scotland, Bastet. What can you eat here?" He whispered to Aunt Celia, "I forgot her cat food." He realized the cat, the daughter of the great Egyptian God, Ra, wouldn't like that one bit.

16

Bastet grumbled. *Since someone around here forgot my food.* She glared at Steven. *I shall have to lower myself to hunting little furry critters, like some ordinary cat. How humiliating!*

"Sorry Bastet, I guess I was a bit preoccupied with my Aunt," Steven said.

Bastet scowled. *And with Morag. But never mind, I am sure the furry little rodents around here will make for a delicious meal. It has been a while since I have had the 'wonderful' opportunity to chase my four-legged friends without your interference. He's even worried about hurting rodents!* She glared at Steven again, angry at having been relegated to playing second-fiddle to a dragon.

Steven laughed, "You're right. Hunting like a real cat will do you good. You'll lose some weight. Besides, you deserve some time off. Go, have some fun."

Bastet growled, thinking the boy believed he was smart enough to fool an Egyptian god. *Very well, Steven, you keep neglecting me, and someday you'll see who is more powerful, that ancient dragon or your so-called, kitty cat.*

"I'm sorry, Bastet," Steven called as the cat stormed away.

As Aunt Celia watched Steven converse with Morag and Bastet, it dawned on her that the only explanation for all this had to be related to the scroll her brother had found in an Egyptian tomb, the final resting place of Seti I. She remembered something else her brother said. He spoke of a long lost manuscript that described how the ancient Egyptians were awaiting the arrival of a young boy and an Egyptian priest, to fulfill a great prophecy. *Oh, my goodness! Could that be what all this is about?* She looked at Steven and thought, I won't allow it! Absolutely not!

"I should have remembered Bastet's food," Steven said, wondering if Bastet was as angry as she sounded.

Aunt Celia appraised Steven. He said the cat's name was Bastet, the daughter of Ra. He was talking to a cat and a dragon. Could it be? What other explanation could there be to explain all this? She dug deep into her memories. She thought of the hours Steven spent in his parent's lab…he never let her in there and never offered any clue as to what he did inside that dirty laboratory. She also recalled the morning she found him dressed in hiking boots…he was covered with sand. Again, he offered no explanation. She was only now beginning to put everything together, she could be all wrong. All these unexplained events might be clues, or they could just be a coincidence. The cat was sitting on its haunches staring at her. Could Steven be the boy from the ancient Egyptian prophecy? Steven's voice warning Bastet to be careful brought Aunt Celia back to the present and her growing sense of urgency that she had to find out what her nephew was up to. "Steven, I want to talk to you about all this right now," she began.

Steven turned toward his aunt. "We have to go right now. It will soon be dark. We've got to find a place to set up camp. This cave isn't safe." He picked up his knapsack, hoping they were on time.

Aunt Celia got ready to leave but remembered something that had been gnawing at her, "Steven, you mentioned before the 'four of you' have used the Portal. But there are only three of you here: you, this cat, and that dragon, and you. I'm almost afraid to ask, who is the fourth?"

Steven was in a hurry to leave the cave before some creature decided to use it for shelter but saw his aunt wasn't moving, not until he satisfied her curiosity. "The Seeker," he mumbled and started to walk away.

"Seeker?" Aunt Celia grabbed Steven's arm. "What kind of name is The Seeker?" This is getting crazier and crazier, she thought.

Steven felt trapped. His aunt wasn't releasing his arm. "Okay. The Seeker is an Egyptian priest who has been guiding the rest of us to fulfill a prophecy that is—"

"Then, the prophecy is real?" Aunt Celia interrupted, terrified at what dangers this might mean for her nephew.

"You know about the prophecy?"

"Your father and mother told me about it when they returned from their first expedition to the pyramid of Seti I. They told me this prophecy spoke of a young boy and an Egyptian priest." She stared at Steven. "Oh, my word! Steven, do you really think you're that boy?"

Steven frowned. "Yes. I think the gods have selected me to fulfill the prophecy."

Aunt Celia shook her head hard. "No! I refuse to believe that! What do you mean the Gods selected you? That's not possible. It is much too dangerous!

You must be mistaken. It must be another boy. I won't allow it!"

Steven heard the fear in his aunt's voice. She was right about the danger. Steven faced many threats to his life already. He wished she was right, and the prophecy was about some other boy. But he knew better.

Aunt Celia wasn't letting up. "That prophecy was written over 2,000 years ago! How could you have been selected way back then? You weren't even alive. This whole thing doesn't make sense. You can't be the boy—"

"Please, calm down, Aunt Celia? Morag. You're going to scare her again."

Aunt Celia remembered about the dragon and realized her outbursts might upset the giant beast. She lowered her voice. "Steven, you are fooling yourself. No two-thousand-year-old prophecy could have chosen you. Be reasonable, and let's go home this instant? Yes, let's go home."

Steven sighed. "Aunt Celia, I wish you were right, and we could go home. I'd love to forget about all this."

"I am right," Aunt Celia said, a stubborn look on her face.

Steven shook his head. "I don't know why the gods picked me or how all this came to be. But I believe I am the boy in the prophecy."

"No, you are not." Aunt Celia wasn't backing down.

Steven wasn't either. "Believe me, I didn't choose this. One minute, I'm sitting at the computer, doing homework, and the next, I've got The Seeker telling me I've got to fight the Dark Ruler's evil servants—"

Aunt Celia interrupted, "The Dark Ruler? What Dark Ruler? Steven, this is some trick. This Seeker, if he is real, is playing tricks on you. Dangerous tricks."

Steven shook his head. "I wish. But Aunt Celia, wait until you hear the rest of the story? You'll see, I'm telling the truth."

Morag growled. *Steven, it grows dark. You must get to shelter. We know not what creatures may come in the night to this disgusting cave.*

Steven nodded. "Aunt Celia, we need to go before it is too late. I'll tell you what you want to know after we are safe. I promise."

Aunt Celia wondered what Steven meant by before it is too late but decided to hold the rest of her questions until after they set up camp. Whatever Steven was involved in; his safety had to come first. "Very well," she said, grabbing her backpack. "But you have a lot of explaining to do. Is that clear, Steven? Is that clear?"

Steven groaned. Where is The Seeker when I need him? "Yes, Aunt Celia. Now follow me. I know just the place to set up camp. You'll even be able to watch Morag hunt."

Bastet, chewing on a small rat, shook her head, grateful she was not a human with nagging relatives. She gazed at the darkening sky and wondered what dangers were lurking in their future. It was hard enough to put up with a dragon and a boy, but now, with this troublesome aunt too?

Chapter 6

Aunt Celia watched in amazement as Steven communicated with Morag and Bastet. It dawned on her the only explanation for all this had to be related to the scroll her brother had found in the tomb of Seti I in Egypt. She remembered her brother had said the ancient papyrus foretold the arrival of a young boy, and a priest, to fulfill a prophecy. *Could this be what all this secrecy was about?* Steven said the cat's name was Bastet. Egyptian legend had it that she was the daughter of Ra, the great god. Steven was talking to a cat and a dragon...could any of it be for real? She dug deep into her memories: the hours Steven spent in his parent's lab; the morning she had found him dressed in hiking boots and filthy with...sand? She began to put everything together. Were all these things clues she had failed to recognize? Could Steven really be the boy from the prophecy? Impossible! "I won't have it. Steven, I want to talk to you, now," she began yet again.

"Please, aunt. We've gotta go. It will soon be dark, and we gotta find a place to set up camp. This cave isn't safe."

"You're safety is my first concern." Aunt Celia picked up her backpack. "I'm ready, but I really don't know about this, Steven."

"Morag, get out of here," Steven said. "If he comes back, I don't want you seen."

Morag wished the opposite but quickly reverted to her smaller size. For now, she would obey the boy. She flew out of the cavern, surprising Aunt Celia by buzzing past her. She enjoyed startling the old lady. At least, I can have some fun, she thought, wishing she could remain in the cave.

As they hurried out, Aunt Celia repeated, "You said before there were four of you in the Portal. Who was the fourth person?'

"The Seeker," Steven said quickly and walked away.

"Steven, stop right now. I'm not budging until I get some answers." She planted her feet firmly on the ground.

Steven looked worriedly at the darkening sky. "Aunt Celia, we can stand here talking and hope Drooling Slayer does not return, or, better yet, get out of here fast."

"Drooling who?" Aunt Celia saw Steven was frightened. "Okay, but once we're safe, I want to know everything." She grabbed her pack and followed Steven as he hurried down to the bike trail. "Slow down. I'm an old lady." She was puffing in the thin air of the mountain trail.

"There is a plateau on the other side of that mountain where we can find shelter," Steven said.

"You can talk as we walk," Aunt Celia said, giving Steven a look that meant business. "Now, who is this Seeker?"

Steven sighed. "Can't this wait until we're safe?"

"No. It cannot. I want to know what my nephew has been up to." She stood stolidly, refusing to move.

Steven said. "Okay, let's walk. The Seeker is an Egyptian priest who has been guiding us to fulfill a prophecy that is—"

"Back to that prophecy again?"

"That's what it's all about. You said you knew about it." Steven glanced at the sky. He didn't want to be out here in the open after dark.

Aunt Celia was still rushing to keep up. "Your parents told me about it when they returned from their first expedition to Egypt. They said the prophecy spoke of a young boy and an Egyptian priest." She stopped to catch her breath. "Steven, do you really think you're that boy?"

"Yes. The Seeker says the Egyptian gods picked me."

"What do you mean the gods selected you? This whole thing is much too dangerous for a child. You must be mistaken."

Dangerous, she doesn't know the half of it, Steven thought. "Aunt Celia, I'm not a child. The Seeker says the boy picked to save the world is me. I don't like it, but that's what he says."

Aunt Celia frowned. "Boy. Boy? That prophecy was written 2,000 years ago! You weren't even born. The whole thing doesn't make sense. You can't be the boy. I won't allow it."

"Please, Aunt Celia, let's keep moving? I'll explain what I know once we are safe."

"Steven, this is nonsense," her breathing was labored from the climb.

Steven stopped and wiped his brow. "I wish it was nonsense. Aunt Celia, you'll see; unfortunately, I'm right."

"No. I'm right," Aunt Celia said, feeling she should put her foot down now on any more of these crazy ideas. "As your guardian, now that your dear parents are...gone." She choked at the words. "My answer is no."

Steven shook his head. "You can't stop it. Nobody can. I'm the boy in the prophecy."

"No, you are not."

Steven faced his aunt, furious she didn't understand. Then he calmed down because he didn't realize it all either. "Aunt Celia, I didn't choose this." He looked up the sky. He had no choice if he was going to get her to safety. "Okay, here's the deal. I was sitting at Dad's computer, doing my homework, and the next second, The Seeker arrives. I was going to scream, but he starts telling me I gotta fight the Dark Ruler's evil servants."

"The Dark Ruler? Who in heaven's name is the Dark Ruler? This Seeker, if he is real, and not a figment of your imagination, is just tricking you."

Steven shook his head again. "I wish it were a trick." *Where is that character when I need him?*

A cold blast of air and a loud noise in the distance startled Steven. "Aunt, we've got to get to shelter, or we could be in big trouble." He grabbed her hand and pulled her forward.

Aunt Celia was huffing and puffing, her feet aching and her eyes hurting from staring down at the pathway to make sure nothing was there to trip her.

Steven, holding her hand, forced her along, but all the while thinking if he didn't convince her that his story was right, he would be in more significant trouble than if a ravenous beast gobbled up his aunt. Well, maybe not.

Chapter 7

Aunt Celia was out of breath. Steven had dragged her for more than a mile, and they were now resting atop a small plateau jutting out over the mountain range above Glencoe. The air was brisk as the evening sky darkened. She watched in awe as the first quarter moon rose over Ben Nevis, Britain's highest peak.

"We can rest here," Steven said, freeing her hand. "Bastet is out again. I guess she's chasing down more rodents for dinner. I never should've forgotten her chow."

Aunt Celia was about to speak when she heard a loud squeaking noise from somewhere below.

"I guess it didn't take Bastet long to capture dinner," Steven said.

"Bastet is a wonderful catcher of mice," Aunt Celia said, never taking her eyes from the star-studded sky. "Where is your dragon?"

"We are lucky we only have a quarter moon tonight," Steven said. "Morag has to time her hunting to the cycles of the moon. She would be too visible on a moonlit night."

"Steven, we need to talk right now," Aunt Celia insisted, her eyes still taking in the chilly night which brought out all the stars.

"Very soon," Steven said, starting a fire in front of the cave made from scraps of wood and dead heather he found as they climbed the hill.

"You're quite a camper," Aunt Celia said, as she saw Steven igniting the small pile of debris.

The fire cast strands of flickering light on the stone floor of the plateau. An occasional snap and pop from the burning wood interrupted the quiet. The air was cooling quickly, and Steven could see a mist forming in the valley below.

Aunt Celia lowered her eyes from the stars and probed her nephew's face. "Ok, Steven, no more stalling. I demand you explain what you have gotten yourself into." She looked around. "What you've gotten me into as well."

Steven stared into the fire. "It's kind of complicated. I have no idea where to start."

Aunt Celia sighed. "Okay. Tell me about The Seeker. He seems to be behind all this."

Steven had been delaying this discussion, rehearsing in his mind what to tell Aunt Celia without divulging the whole scary story in one bombshell. "Okay. I'll try it." He stirred the fire with a long stick. "The day I met The Seeker, I saw a monstrous face with red piercing eyes in a cloud chasing me home from school."

Aunt Celia laughed, thinking he was telling her a lie, but she saw he was serious. "You saw a cloud with a face? Everyone sees things in clouds—"

"Yes. I know, but this was different." Steven shuddered when he thought of the menacing face and flashing red eyes that had appeared in the violent storm. "Do you remember that awful storm that day?"

Aunt Celia had a flashback. Steven had come home terrified of a storm that had appeared without warning. "Yes, I remember that crazy storm. I don't think I'd ever seen you looking that frightened before." Except when his parents died, she thought, hoping he didn't remember that awful day.

Steven nodded. "I really was terrified. I didn't want you to know I was afraid, so I ended up in my parents' lab after trying to hide in my room for a while. The thunder was awful. And that lightning!"

"Why did you hide in the lab of all places?" Aunt Celia asked, trying to get comfortable on the ground.

"What better place to hide from all that noise than in a sound-proof room, with no windows. I thought it would be a great place to wait out a storm?"

"I see." Aunt Celia wished Steven had confided his fear of the storm to her but understood that sometimes it is difficult to admit you are afraid, especially when it isn't to your own parents.

25

Steven continued, "As I waited for the storm to end, I loaded one of dad's CDs, "The Spirit of Time Travel," into the hard drive of his computer. Suddenly the lab went totally black."

"I remember our house was right in the middle of that awful storm. It was a doozie!"

"It really was. I hoped the CD would calm me."

"But why did you pick that particular CD?" Aunt Celia was trying to ease Steven's anxiety, which she noticed became extreme when he talked about thunder and lightning. She wished she had known how frightened he had been, but he had kept it hidden from her, like so many other things he apparently had not shared with her. Aunt Celia wondered if somehow she had contributed to his lack of trust. I hope not, she thought. She really cared about Steven, but sometimes found it challenging to deal with her responsibilities as his guardian. She knew she could never take the place of his parents, but now understood he needed her, even if he thought he could do everything himself. "You called it The Spirit of Time Travel. That's an unusual title."

Steven was impressed. His aunt had caught onto a significant clue to his entire mystery. "My parent's spoke about the CD after searching the tomb of Seti I, in Egypt. I thought I would start there for my summer project. If I only knew then, what I now know, I would have never touched that darn disk."

"Do you think the disk caused all this?" Aunt Celia asked, trying to understand.

"It sure seems that way." He shrugged. "The lights went out just as I was selecting the segment entitled, 'The Guardian of Seti I.' and—"

Aunt Celia interrupted, "That was the tomb your parents visited before their..." She stopped just in time. "But, Steven, isn't it more logical that the lights went out when a crash of thunder and lightning hit just outside our house? That's what most likely caused the blackout. We must be logical about these things."

"It's possible. I thought so too, but more strange things happened." Steven wondered if Aunt Celia would believe him, but decided he had to take the chance. "When I started for the door to run upstairs and find you, it got so dark I couldn't see. It was like I was blind."

"Blind? You must have been terrified, you poor boy." Aunt Celia felt awful; Steven had faced so much alone.

"I really was terrified."

"I can imagine."

"I was so relieved when the fluorescent lights started to flicker back on." He gulped. "I really wondered if I'd gone blind."

"So once the lights came back on you were alright?"

"Don't I wish? But there was more. As I tried to calm myself, I could have sworn the walls in the lab were crawling with all these thin blue tentacles."

"Blue tentacles? What do you mean?"

"I know it sounds crazy, but these wiry blue things were all over the walls."

"Were they caused by the electrical storm? It was a weird one."

"That would be one explanation," Steven admitted but wasn't sure he believed it. "Whatever they were, they raced on the power and computer cables, wrapping themselves around them like snakes. I yelled for you to come down, but who could hear me, calling from the lab? It is soundproof. Remember?"

"I never would have heard you anyway in that awful storm," Aunt Celia said.

"True. I felt trapped, not knowing what those things were up to. Suddenly, the blue tentacles began jumping from the cables onto my body."

"They attacked you?" Aunt Celia wondered if such a thing was possible. One thing was becoming evident, and that was that her nephew truly believed in every wild thing he was saying...and that meant he could be in real trouble.

Steven nodded. "I couldn't move. Those blue things started to wrap around my arms, legs, chest, neck, head, all over! My hair felt as if it was being ripped out by the roots. The chair I was sitting on was shaking violently. The whole room was shaking. I tried pushing away from the desk but found my feet were stuck like they were glued to the floor. I was yelling and screaming for help while pulling against the restraints holding me to the chair. My whole body tingled as if I'd hit my funny bone. You know how that hurts. I was exhausted from struggling to free myself. I was crying, and gulping as much air as I could, with these things squeezing on me."

"Steven, how did you escape?" Aunt Celia still wasn't sure what to believe but was increasingly alarmed for Steven's safety.

"That's also weird. Just as those things appeared out of nowhere, they suddenly vanished. I may have blacked out because when I finally could see again, I'm not sure how long that was, there was someone else in the room with me."

"Someone else?" This was getting to be a bit much, but after a cat god, dragon, and a trip through the Portal, Aunt Celia was almost ready to believe anything. Almost.

Steven smiled. "That was the first time I saw The Seeker. I think he made the monster tentacles disappear. I don't know how, but he was the only one there, so it had to be him."

"Steven, you must be more logical. I would be willing to bet they vanished when the electrical storm stopped," Aunt Celia said. "Steven, why didn't you tell me about all this before? You should have told me."

Steven saw the sad look on his aunt's face. "And what would you have done?"

"I would have tried to help. I remember you were quite shaken when you came into the kitchen. I thought you were frightened by the storm."

"Shaken? Terrified is more like it. I went to the lab to get away from the storm, but it appears I jumped right in the middle of it, inside our own home. And then it got even worse." Steven paused, thinking he saw Morag on the horizon. "Yes," he replied to the dragon's telepathic question.

"What is it, Steven?" asked Aunt Celia, trying to see what Steven was looking at.

"Morag was just over there." He pointed toward Ben Nevis. "Wait! There she is again. She is heading this way. I think I can make out something hanging from her talons. Yup, it looks like a deer. Great! I'm starving."

"A deer?" Aunt Celia gulped, realizing that Steven would barely make a mouthful for the dragon. Even she would be little more than a snack. Dragons do not have the best reputation, she thought, wondering if this one could be trusted.

Steven was grateful for the distraction, as they both watched Morag fly toward them.

Would you both like some venison for dinner? Morag asked.

"That'd be great," Steven replied.

Aunt Celia gave Steven a questioning look. "What did she ask you?"

"Morag offered to share her venison with us." Steven stood up and went back into the cave to retrieve his hunting knife.

Aunt Celia heard the whooshing sound from Morag's enormous wings as she approached.

In seconds, Morag's body filled the sky, causing Aunt Celia to jump back.

Without warning, Morag dropped the deer at the edge of the Plateau and then shot straight up out of view. The wind created from her wings caused the fire to flash up higher.

What a powerful creature, Aunt Celia thought, as she shielded her eyes from the wind. She is truly amazing. Such power and grace in one massive body.

Steven cut off just enough meat for the two of them to roast on the fire.

"Thanks, Morag," Steven called, as the dragon dropped again from above.

Morag lowered herself gently, scooping up the rest of the deer, and carrying it down into the gorge where she could eat without fear of being discovered, or being criticized for bad table manners, by Steven's aunt.

Aunt Celia settled back and looked up at the stars flickering in the sky, as the smell of the meat cooking, reached her nostrils. Who would have thought I'd be in Scotland tonight, dining on venison provided by a friendly dragon, she thought. "Steven come sit with me. Let's enjoy the starry night together. We'll talk some later. It is a lot to digest."

Steven breathed a sigh of relief. As he stared at the flames of the campfire, he thought of the flaming pit in one of his recent nightmares and remembered who had been standing behind the fiery abyss. Steven could almost see the towering body, and the flame-red eyes of the Dark Ruler staring directly into his face as if trying to reach for his soul. He decided that once Morag had finished feeding, it would be time to return home and get back to the serious work of the prophecy. What he still did not know, was how his Aunt would react, when he told her the rest of the story.

Chapter 8

Steven, Aunt Celia, and Bastet climbed to the top to view the range of mountains. The wind was cold, and the first snow of the season blanketed the side of the cliff and the valley below. As they stood in silence, a deer and two does cautiously step out into the field from the forest line.

Morag emitted a low growl.

Are you still hungry? Asked Steven.

Of course, she's hungry, Bastet said. *She's always hungry. Even a human should know that by now.*

Morag shot a puff of smoke at her, making Bastet cough. *No. But I think it is time. Is your saddle ready?*

Steven shivered. He had never ridden on Morag and wasn't sure he was going to like it. "Shouldn't we wait a while before we try this?"

"Try what?" Aunt Celia asked, wondering what her nephew was up to now.

"Morag wants me to go flying with her," Steven replied.

Aunt Celia jumped up and pointed her finger at the dragon. "Oh, no, you don't! If you think my nephew is doing something that crazy, then dragon or not, my answer is no!" She crossed her arms to make sure the creature understood.

Steven, you must explain to your difficult aunt that it is crucial for you to practice flying on me before you may need to do so in an emergency. It is perfectly safe. I think you will enjoy it.

Steven nodded. "Aunt Celia, Morag is right."

"Right about what?" Aunt Celia shook her head hard. "My answer is no.

No. No."

Steven wished he could accept that answer. He was still afraid of flying in the air with only a dragon to keep him from falling to his death, but he knew Morag was right. He couldn't take a chance that someday he'd need to fly on her back, but had never tried it before. "Aunt Celia, just think if I have to do it someday. Isn't it better than I did it before I need to?"

Aunt Celia sighed. "It isn't safe."

"Morag says she'll take care of me. She promises it is safe."

Morag nodded her head and gave Aunt Celia a pleading look with her eyes. *Tell her I'll treat you like my own baby.*

"I will not," Steven replied, angry that Morag had compared him to a baby.

"What did Morag say?" Aunt Celia asked.

"Nothing."

Morag shook her head. *Tell her. It will work. Go ahead.*

Steven glared at her, but said, "Morag says, it's really safe." Seeing his aunt wasn't convinced, he gritted his teeth and added, "She said she'll treat me like her own...baby." He gave Morag a disgusted look.

"She said that? Really?" Aunt Celia gave a giant sigh. "Okay."

"Okay?" Steven couldn't believe it.

Aunt Celia still wasn't crazy about the idea, but Morag had assured her she would be cautious with Steven, and this could save his life if he had to escape danger. *I would never let anything harm Steven,* she thought. "As long as she treats you like her own baby, I'll let you try it. But only this once."

Steven nodded. He knew the dense forest, and high mountains in this part of Scotland would be a perfect location. Morag would be less likely to be seen in this cold and barren region. But was he ready?

Aunt Celia saw her nephew was nervous. She saw the beads of perspiration on his forehead. He was shifting anxiously from foot to foot. He looked at her as if he wanted her to stop him. She thought about it but realized the dragon was right; it was better for Steven to learn how to fly now rather than being forced in an emergency. "It will be fine, Steven," she said, hoping she was doing the right thing.

Steven kept glancing at his watch. In one hour, it would be dark enough to climb on Morag's back and fly. He felt dizzy. He was terrified of hopping on the dragon's massive tail. *It's natural to fear this,* he told himself as Morag approached.

I am happy you want to fly with me tonight, Steven, Morag said, also sensing his nervousness.

"I can't wait." Steven smiled, but his chest tightened. He anxiously watched the long dark shadows creep out from beyond the trees. *It is almost time,* he thought, as he and Aunt Celia headed for the field.

I must scan the surroundings to determine if any humans are near. We wouldn't want anyone to report seeing a brave boy flying on a dragon. Would we? Morag said.

Steven liked being called brave. Even though frightened of flying on his friend's back, Steven tried to pretend he was as courageous as Morag thought.

Watch me, Steven. Morag leaped into the air and flew above the field. If seen from a distance, she would appear to others as a larger-sized bird.

"She flies beautifully, Steven," Aunt Celia said, "I almost wish I could fly her."

Steven wished she could too.

Returning to Earth, Morag reverted to her enormous adult size and dropped gently to her knees, so Steven and Aunt Celia could place the saddle on her back.

"It's a tight fit," Steven complained, cinching the saddle.

"Well, she is always eating," Aunt Celia said, thinking of how she too should go on a diet.

You see, Bastet yowled, *You're getting fat.* She paraded her sleek body before the dragon.

Are you ready, Steven? Morag asked, shooting an annoyed look at Bastet. *I'd like to see him hitch a ride on your lean back,* she shot at Bastet.

Steven looked up at Morag's face high above him and reluctantly climbed into the saddle. "Yes, I'm as ready as I'll ever be," Steven replied, swallowing hard, trying not to hurl up his supper.

Then we're off!

Chapter 9

Morag was racing with Steven pressed hard against the saddle, then thrown backward as Morag shot to the sky. He gripped the leather reins, squeezing his legs tighter against her sides as the dragon's great wings flapped hard against the air, lifting her massive body.

Aunt Celia watched in amazement as Morag climbed high into the sky and swiftly disappeared beyond the trees. "Radio check," she said, into a walkie-talkie she bought Steven a year earlier and insisted they use.

"I hear you," Steven said in a quivering voice. "I'm fine. Over and out. I'll see you when I return." If I return, he thought, holding on, surprised at the dragon's speed.

Steven and Aunt Celia had agreed to not contact each other after he was in the air. He and Morag would communicate telepathically during their flight. No longer rocketing skyward, Morag leveling off, as Steven adjusted himself in the saddle, legs still pressing hard against Morag's chest. This is not too bad, he thought, as he released his tight grip on the leather reins, feeling a little more confident. Steven was beginning to enjoy the sensations of flying, wondering why he'd made such a fuss. I should have trusted her, Steven thought, settling back and relaxing.

Are you alright? Morag asked, peering back at her passenger.

Yes! Steven said. *My heart was pounding, but I love it. I nearly fell off when you leaped into the air, but it's cool now.*

Good. We will head north into the mountains, said Morag, lowering her left wing and changing direction.

Steven grew more relaxed as Morag swayed back and forth in smooth rhythm and then glided effortlessly for long distances. He observed with awe how she raised and lowered her wings and finding air currents to let her massive body float. He was thankful he'd worn thermal clothing with a heavy parka and gloves. *It's cold up here,* Steven said, his teeth chattering.

The mountains of Scotland were topped with snow. *The Earth is beautiful from up here,* he said.

The dragon looked back and smiled.

Steven observed how Morag's head dipped as she scanned the ground below, assuming she was looking for heat sources, human or animal. He heard a low rumbling sound. *What was that?* Steven asked.

Just my stomach.

What else is new? Steven laughed, feeling Morag's stomach churning. He relaxed again, enjoying seeing the forest and fields pass far below. Steven decided to see what it would be like to be in command of Morag, the magnificent flying machine. *Bank to the left,* he commanded his powerful friend.

Morag, happy to see Steven was having fun, instantly dropped her left wing and lowered her head.

Steven was jerked to the left. Tightening his grip, he pressed his legs against the saddle and leaned into the turn.

Morag dipped to the right and made a tight circle followed by a rapid descent toward the treetops.

Steven rocked back and forth, as the cold wind tugged hard against his body. "Hey, warn me before you do that," he shouted, holding on tighter again on the reins.

I will try, although it might not be possible all the time, Morag said.

I was caught off guard by that last turn, Steven said telepathically.

You adjusted quickly for one who has never ridden a dragon before. Morag cast a smile back at Steven.

I wish I'd tried this ages ago. I love it. Steven released the reins and held his hands high in the air, like a boy releasing his grip from bicycle handlebars. "I wish my friends could see me now," he shouted. The smile on Steven's face quickly morphed to horror as a sudden wind caused Morag to veer hard to the left, and Steven, not holding the reins, tumbled out of the saddle, heading straight toward the ground.

Morag, not realizing Steven was no longer mounted in the saddle; suddenly heard terrified screams. She glanced back and realizing he was missing, folded her massive wings back against her body and sped down toward him.

Steven tried to flap his arms as he had seen Morag do with her mighty wings. He glanced down. The trees appeared to be growing more substantial and more defined as he plummeted to the Earth. *"Morag," hollered Steven "Please, please, hurry!"*

Morag was an arrow heading for her target, but could she get there on time?

Steven *closed his eyes, afraid to see as the cliffs racing up toward him. He could almost hear his body slamming against the rocks, feel his body explode with the crash. He was not sure what happened next because he passed out.*

Morag reached out with her talons, clamping them around him, unfurled her wings and pulled back with all her strength. They were still falling fast, but at ten yards from the jagged rocks, she flapped her wings hard and broke her fall, Steven tightly held. Once back in the air, she leveled off again, clutching the boy gently and praying he wasn't hurt.

Morag saw an open field ahead. She descended to the ground. Finding a soft patch of snow, she released Steven, unable to land in the small area surrounded by trees.

Steven fell face down, half-buried in the snow.

Morag circled above, and begin to shrink. She felt awful as she saw Steven not moving. Now the size of a large bird, she landed next to him.

Steven coughed hard, revived by the cold snow, but unable to move. He was freezing.

Steven, are you, all right? Morag bellowed, after trudging from her landing site several hundred feet away. She saw him waving his arm. *Oh, thank goodness.*

What happened? Steven asked, wiping the snow from his face with a frozen hand.

Morag pulled him gently out of the snow and sighed. *We got caught in a crosswind which caused me to flip over. I am sorry. You are so light I forgot you were on my back. I will be more careful.* She wondered if the boy would allow another offer to fly after this awful scare. She gently nudged him with her nose. *You must stand, or you will freeze to death.* She touched him again.

Steven, still dazed, picked himself up. He shivered, pulled his hood over his head, and gazed at Morag. *I was enjoying it until that happened.*

Shall we continue our flight, or would you like to walk back to the cabin? Morag gazed up at the dark sky. *I would understand.*

Steven shivered again and laughed. *Right, I'll walk. I only must walk about 40 miles, climb over mountains, and find a way across frozen rivers. It should just take me about three to four days to reach the cavern unless I freeze first!*

I get it. Morag said, feeling guilty. *I'm sorry,* she said.

Steven sighed and walked over to Morag. *"You saved my life. Thank you."* He threw his arms around the dragon's muscular neck.

Your aunt would never forgive me if something happened to you. She'd make my life hell, Morag replied, realizing she also loved the boy, something she never expected.

My aunt would never forgive you. Right, Steven said. *Like I believe that is the only reason?* He brushed the snow off his clothes and aimed his eyes at the saddle. He almost wished he could walk it, but said, *Aunt Celia, says when you fall off a horse, you must climb right back on.*

I'm not a horse, Morag said.

Well, you'll have to do, Steven replied, grabbing the reins and bracing himself again for Morag to launch herself into the air.

Morag, true to her word, flew back much more aware that she had an exceptional passenger on board. No more dips and rocket to the moon maneuvers, not after that close call. Every few miles, she glanced back and gave Steven a warm smile.

Steven almost wished Morag wasn't being so careful but knew she had felt terrified, and at nearly losing him.

Flying at a much-reduced speed, they returned to the cavern just as the dim light of dawn climbed up over the mountains.

Aunt Celia was dozing against the cave wall when Steven, carrying Morag, now a small version of herself, entered the cave.

"Aunt Celia," Steven whispered.

Aunt Celia jumped awake. "You're back. Thank goodness! How was the flight?"

"Great, but a little chilly," Steven replied, cuddling the now shrunken Morag, asleep in his arms. "Would you like to try it?"

"Maybe next time," replied Aunt Celia. "Not!"

Steven laughed. He was dying to tell Aunt Celia how fantastic flying had been and how silly he felt having been so frightened. "It really was amazing," Steven said, deciding not to tell her about everything that happened. The important thing was he was alright and had conquered his fear.

Aunt Celia yawned and said, "It is time to go home. We have a lot of work to do before you go back to school."

Steven had almost forgotten about school. And he was feeling so good that he also forgot that he and his friends had a new mission.

Chapter 10

"This must stop," Aunt Celia said, a look of determination on her face, as she stared at what was left of her kitchen.

Steven thought he'd changed her mind about letting him continue with his work with The Seeker, but realized he should have known better. One sight of her wrecked kitchen had been enough to bring back the old Aunt Celia. He remained quiet, knowing if he said the wrong words, he'd make things worse than they already were.

Aunt Celia was pacing around the wreckage. "I will no longer permit you to participate in this so-called prophecy. You are just a child and have your whole life ahead of you."

"That's the point. I don't. Not if I don't do what The Seeker says."

Aunt Celia picked up her busted coffee cup. "The Seeker again. I want to see this so-called Seeker. I'll give him a piece of my mind he won't soon forget."

"Did you call for me, Steven?"

Steven realized he must have called for The Seeker in his mind.

Aunt Celia jumped at the new arrival, a tall man in a robe with his beard hanging down almost to his rope belt. "Who...who are you?" She asked, backing away from the stranger.

Steven jumped in before The Seeker spoke. "Aunt Celia, this is The Seeker. Seeker, this is my Aunt Celia."

"This is The Seeker?" Aunt Celia rumbled. "I'm glad you're here. I have some things I want to say to you, Mr. Seeker, or whoever you are."

The Seeker looked amused.

Steven heard him mumbled several words, Steven did not understand.

"She's a fighter like you, my boy."

"Now, you listen here," not realizing she could hear him, "I refuse to let my nephew have anything more to do with you or your dangerous missions. I want him to have plenty of time to experience the joy that life has to offer."

Steven stood back as his aunt, face reddened, cast challenging eyes at The Seeker. He had never seen her look so livid. "Aunt Celia, it isn't The Seeker's fault—"

"Not now, Steven. I am speaking to your friend here, who is responsible for getting you into this mess and is going to get you out of it. Wait, I was able to hear you."

The Seeker let out an amused chuckle. "But you see, dear lady, I am not at fault in the selection of your nephew. We have been linked to each other by destiny. It is not my doing. Like your brave nephew, I must fulfill the prophecy. Neither of us can change what has been ordained. His fate has been so written, and therefore must be done. There can be no substitutions. I wish it were not so, but we must continue at all cost, or the consequences will be far worse than you can imagine."

"At all cost?" Aunt Celia screamed. "Steven is thirteen years old. And may I remind you that I am responsible for him. As his legal guardian, I have sworn to the courts, and my brother and sister-in-law, to keep him safe until such time when he no longer needs me." She smiled at Steven. "Which I hope will not be for many years to come."

"But, dear lady—"

"And don't you "dear lady" me—"

Steven sat down in his chair. *This will take a while, he thought, seeing neither was giving up.*

Just then, Steven saw something passing through the wall into his parents' laboratory. It looked like a small tornado. "Shu!" He shouted as a cloud of dust and wind made papers fly off the computer table.

Aunt Celia's eyes widened as the wind formed into the shape of a young man. "Now, what is happening?" She asked, backing behind a nearby computer.

"Aunt Celia, this is Shu! He's another of my team...friends."

"Not another one," Aunt Celia moaned.

Shu solidified into the form of a human. He was about 5 feet tall, although the ostrich feathers tucked in the gold band around his head made him appear much taller. He held a black ankh in the shape of a key in his right hand and a long wood staff in his left. His gold tunic covered him down to his knees. His wide eyes and pleasant smile gave him look totally opposite of the stern expression on The Seeker's bearded face.

Aunt Celia moved closer. She thought this new intruder looked quite handsome considering dust particles were floating all around him. "Shu, eh?" She frowned. "If I remember my college years studying Egyptian mythology, you are the god of light and air. You were also known for your desire to help humans?" She said once the dust had settled.

Shu bowed to Aunt Celia, then began speaking telepathically. *You are correct. I am here to help Steven. It was I who blew the Thunderhead that was after him far out to the Asian skies, where it is now trapped in a typhoon.* Shu laughed. *It should take several months for it to free itself from the grasp of the mighty storms,* Shu said with pride.

"Well done," The Seeker said.

As Steven's aunty you must be very proud of him, Shu said, moving closer to Aunt Celia, causing her hair to fly up and her dress to flutter.

Aunt Celia flattened her dress, a bit embarrassed. She saw his mouth moving but only felt the wind against her face.

"She's nervous about Steven's mission," The Seeker explained to the wind god. "This is all new to her, but she's quite intelligent. I am confident she'll get used to it."

Aunt Celia was finally able to sputter in protest, "I don't believe this! I am standing here speaking to what appears to be a ghostly spirit of some kind, and being blown around by an Egyptian wind god? This is all too much! I've had enough! Come, Steven, we're out of here!" She grabbed his arm and pulled him from the chair.

Shu flew to the door to block it. Your nephew is a courageous young man, he said.

Aunt Celia felt the wind building up against her. "Now what is happening?"

she asked, backing away from the wall of wind.

Steven translated, "Shu said, I am a courageous young man."

Aunt Celia faced Shu. "Ok, I know you're brave, tell him I have had quite enough. And, I demand to know what Shu, Bastet, and Morag are saying. No more secret languages! All I hear is wind. And furthermore, tell this friend of yours, I do not like my hair being tussled by some wind god either!"

Wow, she could be a thunder goddess, Shu said, raising his staff toward Aunt Celia. He waved it back and forth in front of her angry face.

"What is he doing?" Aunt Celia demanded, worried she may have gone too far, perhaps angering this god. Who knows how such weird creatures may react if you push the wrong buttons? She thought of apologizing but decided she had nothing for which to apologize. "Now, see here," she began.

Can you understand me now? Shu interrupted as a gentle gust of air blew from his lips.

Aunt Celia felt strange, the breeze was warm and calming. "Why, yes. Thank you."

Shu spoke softly in a kind voice. *I know this is a lot for you to understand, but please, Aunt Celia, give us a chance to explain? We mean Steven and you no harm. We are here to protect him.*

Aunt Celia sighed, enjoying the gentle warm breeze. "I do believe you mean him no harm...Okay, go ahead. Although I've heard many people who have been full of hot air before." She let out a nervous laugh at her joke.

Steven laughed too but realized The Seeker and Shu had no idea that Aunt Celia had made a joke. He'd explain it to them later. If there was a later?

Chapter 11

As I said, you have a very brave nephew, Shu said.

Steven shook his head. "I would not be so brave if you and The Seeker didn't protect me. They watch over me all the time, Aunt Celia."

"Thank you for protecting Steven," Aunt Celia said, beginning to understand that whatever these creatures were, they did seem to care about Steven, almost as much as she did.

We should be the ones to thank you for taking care of Steven. He has been a great help to us in freeing the spirits of the Guardians, Shu said.

"What are these Guardians?" Aunt Celia asked, feeling more comfortable with Shu than she had with the far more argumentative, The Seeker.

I'm glad you ask. The Guardians are the Dark Ruler's slaves. He turns the souls of dead humans into his mindless slaves and forces them to do his evil bidding, Shu said.

The Seeker interrupted. "Without Steven's help, the entire world would have been enslaved by the Dark Ruler and his army of Guardians by now. That is why we must continue this fight—"

Aunt Celia woke from her trance. "Have I not made myself clear? Steven will no longer participate in this dangerous war of yours. He will no longer help you. It is far too dangerous, and I must put my foot down for his benefit."

"You have made your wishes perfectly clear," The Seeker, struggling to contain his impatience. "But it is not as easy as you think. The Dark Ruler will not give up looking for Steven now that he believes the prophecy has started to come true. He will send his murderous slaves out in search of your nephew. As long as Steven lives, the prophecy is a threat to him. The Dark Ruler will hunt down 'the boy' with all of his might."

Aunt Celia gazed at Steven. "I must protect my nephew. Steven's involvement ends now." She smiled at Steven and said, "Dear, this is for your own good."

"But, Aunt Celia," Steven said.

The Seeker felt frustrated. "Aunt Celia, you don't understand—"

Aunt Celia interrupted. "Mr. Seeker, I am not your aunt!" She shot him an angry look and then turned with a smile to Shu. "It was nice to meet you, Shu."

Shu bowed. *The pleasure was mine.*

The Seeker glared at Shu. "Teacher's pet," he hissed.

Aunt Celia turned to Steven. "I will meet you upstairs when you are finished saying goodbye, for good, to your friends." She glanced at her watch. "Five minutes." She shot another angry look at The Seeker, turned and hurried out of the cellar before the others could try and change her mind. *It is for Steven's own good,* she thought, *and that is all that matters.*

The Seeker was fuming but kept it under control. "Steven, even though she is a stubborn, difficult, human being, I cannot go against your Aunt's wishes." He let out a deep sigh. "Without your help to prevent it, I am fearful your life is in great jeopardy, as are we all."

"I'm sorry," Steven said. "Maybe after a while, she'll change her mind." Knowing his aunt, he doubted it.

Shu said something in 'wind' which The Seeker translated since it was too fast for Steven. "Shu says he will keep the Thunderhead away from your home but does not know for how long. Thunderheads, like the wind, must be free to roam the earth, even if that means tragedy for the humans that encounter their might. Weather is a force of nature, and nature cannot be denied...not even by a wind god."

"I understand. Thanks." Steven smiled sadly. "What are you going to do now?" Steven asked, worried about his friends.

The Seeker returned Steven's sad smile. "We must continue our quest without you. Although I am not sure, we can release the Guardians' spirits without your help. It is in the prophecy."

Shu replied, *Steven, you must remain vigilant for the return of the Thunderhead, and any other slaves the Dark Ruler may launch against you. As I told your aunt, the hunt will continue until you are captured or killed. The Dark Ruler will not give up until he has destroyed the hope of the ancient prophecy, once and for always. I wish your aunt could understand that. Maybe she will eventually?*

"Not that stubborn woman," *The Seeker snorted,* regretting he hadn't used his magic to turn her into a frog, or a bat, or something much less painful and much quieter.

Steven replied, "I'll keep trying to get my Aunt to change her mind. But you see how stubborn she is."

The Seeker nodded. "Believe me, I know. Well, Shu and I must go. I will return when I can and check on you, and your stubborn aunt."

With that, The Seeker's form dissolved into a smoky mist.

Be well, Steven, Shu said and disappeared in a gust of wind that sent papers flying again all over the room.

Steven, Bastet, and Morag remained silent as the wind died down and then was gone.

Steven, what will you do? Asked Morag, flapping her wings, impatient to be flying again, with a secret mission of her own.

Steven sighed. "First, I have to clean up this mess again." He began to collect the papers.

I mean about the prophecy, Morag said.

Steven looked at the dragon. "I have no choice. I have to obey my aunt."

But you know how dangerous that is, Bastet said. *You heard what The Seeker warned. The Dark Ruler will still hunt you down, even if you are no longer a threat to him.*

Steven nodded. "You both also heard from my aunt."

She's one stubborn lady, Morag said.

Steven laughed "Yes, she is, but she also cares. Until I can change her mind, we will do what she wants. We'll keep a close eye out for the thunderhead and other threats." He rubbed his hand on the dragon's head. "I'm counting on you Morag, as you fly around the area, to let us know if you spot anything that could prove dangerous."

You know I will gladly do that, the dragon said.

What about me? Bastet asked, upset she had been ignored again. Ever since this dragon got here, I'm like nothing.

Steven smiled. "Yes, I know. I've been so focused on helping Morag get used to things, I've neglected you, my best friend. Of course, I need your help. I wouldn't be here now if you hadn't saved me so many times I've lost count."

Bastet appeared to grow taller, her head held high.

Steven sighed. "You both must be careful. I'm sure by now the Dark Ruler realizes you're helping me." He looked into the dragon's eyes. "You know, if you want, you can return home and live your life without all this? Bastet will always be here, but you have a choice."

Morag blew a puff of gray smoke. *We make a good team, my human friend. Come Bastet, you and I must work as a team. Together we will do whatever we can to protect our humans...even that stubborn lady upstairs.*

Steven watched Bastet and Morag head upstairs. He wondered if they really could be friends now that they had a joint mission to protect him. I guess I'm back to being an ordinary kid, he thought. Life and death struggles are a thing of the past. I hope.

As Steven rocked in his father's leather chair, he wondered why he felt sad now that he was no longer going off to face incredibly dangerous enemies. And the best of all, I get to sleep late. That will be nice for a change.

"Steven, are you coming up?" Aunt Celia called from the top of the stairs.

"Coming, Aunt," he called and switched off the lights in the lab, wondering if he'd ever see The Seeker and Shu again.

Chapter 12

C harlie was in his father's twenty-two-foot Boston Whaler, watching the morning sunrise above Aquidneck Island. He had motored out from Fisherman's Cove at 3:00 AM to fish along Rose Island's shoreline in the quiet before the other fishermen arrived.

Charlie had just turned fourteen and was a lineman on the school's football team. At one-hundred and fifty pounds, Charlie had a solid frame, broad shoulders and muscular arms and legs. He had grown up fishing on the bay with his father, who had taught him a love of the sea. He could handle the boat with great skill. It took a lot to frighten him.

A light haze covering the surface of the water was starting to disappear as the sun warmed the air. Rain squalls were predicted, later, for the afternoon; plenty of time for Charlie to reach his quota of saltwater blackfish.

Pouring a cup of coffee from his thermos, Charlie sat back in the white swivel deck chair and relaxed, waiting for another nibble on his hook. The sea had been calm, gently lulling him, almost dull.

Charlie felt the boat rock slightly. That's nothing to worry about, he thought, checking his line and settling back into the chair.

Suddenly Charlie felt the boat swing around hard, pulling back against the anchor line. "What was that?"

The boat was now facing south toward Castle Rock Lighthouse. Charlie saw what appeared to be a dark line stretching out across the horizon. Just morning clouds, he thought, turning his attention back to the fishing line in the water.

It took several minutes for Charlie to realize that the wind was increasing sharply and the water in the bay was becoming choppy. He checked the weather radio. A storm was not due until later in the afternoon, but the water felt rougher than it had been. He turned up the volume on the marine radio.

The announcer spoke in an almost mechanical drone: "Narragansett Bay and Providence area weather report: Light winds are from the south, with no predicted chance of rain until evening. The water temperature in the bay area is 55 degrees with calm seas...."

Charlie clicked off the radio and gazed at the horizon again. "This doesn't make sense. A storm appears to be building out there, but there's no mention of any turbulence on the radio?" He turned his eyes to the clouds forming to the south and watched with increasing curiosity as ominously dark clouds now stretched across the mouth of Narragansett Bay. "I don't get it," he said, seeing the line of white caps approaching. He still wasn't worried.

The Boston Whaler's bow shot up as a series of swells hit with surprising force. Saltwater sprayed up into Charlie's face. "Where'd that come from? I need to return to the boat ramp," Charlie said, placing the fishing pole onto the deck while trying to maintain his balance on the wave-tossed boat.

Grabbing the anchor line, Charlie pulled hard, trying to get the anchor to disengage. It must be stuck in the mud, he thought, struggling against the chain. I don't remember it being so shallow out here. He was fighting hard to free the anchor.

Charlie almost lost his balance again, the wind and waves now violently rocking the boat, as he struggled to pull the anchor free of whatever was holding it.

Finally, Charlie felt the anchor jump free from the mud. He hauled it up against the raging water and dropped it into the boat. "I'm getting out of here," he shouted and hurried to the console where he started the twin outboard engines.

The engines churning, Charlie again looked across the bay, then glanced back at the stern to check if salt water was being pushed out of the exhausts. All seemed well. He would soon be safe from this crazy storm that had appeared so unexpectedly on what had seemed a boringly calm sea.

Charlie turned the wheel hard to the right while pushing the throttle forward. The bow of the boat leaped up out of the water, as the twin outboard engines shoved the stern around, heading for home.

Charlie fixed his eyes on the coastline and raced toward Fisherman's Cove, a mile north of Rose Island, where he knew he would find safe harbor.

Another look backward and Charlie's chest tightened, surprised to see incredibly large dark storm clouds seemingly racing toward him. What the hell is going on, Charlie thought angrily. How could the marine weather forecaster not know about this storm? He reached for his handset, about to phone in a storm report.

A thunderous roar from behind the boat caused him to drop the handset, and leap into action. He pushed the throttles into the stops trying to gain as much distance as he could from the storm that appeared to be chasing him. "But that's crazy. Isn't it?" Charlie shouted into the wind.

Charlie gunned the boat through the waves. He glanced back to determine how close the storm was when he saw what he could have sworn were red eyes glaring at him from within the cloud at the head of the rain. He stared in disbelief at the piercing eyes and locked his hands on the wheel.

As the boat fought the waves, Charlie kept looking back at the pursuing violent storm and swore he could see the eyes within the heart of the black cloud becoming more distinct. They looked like real eyes!

Dark, large clouds were being driven up the bay by the increasingly powerful winds as if the raging eye-cloud was controlling them. A wall of water was rushing before them, forming what looked like wide-open hands reaching for the whaler.

The motors groaned as Charlie pushed the throttles again. He was panicking, trapped on the tossing waves with the tsunami wall closing in. He turned the wheel hard, and the boat surged forward, fighting the mounting swells.

Charlie was soaked to the skin. Saltwater spray blew against his face, burning his eyes, making it even more challenging to see the coastline. The hull pounded hard against the water, causing him to grip ever tighter on the steering wheel so he would not be thrown into the sea.

Charlie's feet lifted off the deck as the boat rose and fell against the waves with increasing ferocity. "I won't make it to the landing in time," he moaned, his heart racing, the rain pelting him like ice bullets. He scanned the coastline, desperately trying to find shelter in any cove near enough to reach.

"There!" Charlie shouted, his words lost in the sound of the thunder and pounding rain. He turned the boat with all his strength and raced for cover, praying he would make it.

The boat rocked back and forth, up and down, as the unending swells pounded against its sides. Weakening, soaked, and fighting for his life, Charlie struggled, but the bucking of the waves and pounding of the rain was draining his strength with each hammer blow. This was like no storm he had ever encountered, and he was terrified the boat would capsize and sink.

Charlie felt the air suddenly go ice cold and sensed the vast storm cloud was almost directly over him. He struggled to keep the boat upright as the mounting swells and wind pushed against its side. He was going to capsize but managed to change direction to compensate for the pitch. It was a constant, and the cove seemed as far away as ever.

Incredibly, the intensity of the wind continued to increase, and the size of the swells made them look like mountains about to crash down on him. Tears mixing with saltwater ran blurred his vision. "I am a survivor! I won't give up!" Charlie shouted, determined to get to shelter as the cove loomed just ahead.

A massive wave struck hard against his bow, sending him racing into the cove. Charlie pulled the throttles in reverse. "I'm here," he shouted, cutting the engines as the boat ran toward the rocky shore. Charlie threw the anchor overboard and felt it dig into the sand below. He flopped down, flattened, onto the deck, waiting for the storm to pass over him, praying it would soon be over.

It was over. As suddenly as it had whipped up in a fury, the storm disappeared.

Waiting to be sure it was over, Charlie remained in the bottom of the craft.

When no waves struck, and it appeared the rain had stopped, Charlie raised his head. Wiping his eyes, he breathed a sigh of relief. He was surprised to see the distinct line of the isolated storm appeared to be pushing north toward

Providence. "I don't believe it," Charlie groaned, falling exhausted back onto the deck, fearful the storm might return for a second shot at him.

Minutes later, Charlie, daring to hope the storm had passed, rose from the wet deck and fell into the pilot seat. "That was the weirdest storm I've ever heard of. It was almost as if it was aiming at me." He grabbed binoculars and saw the massive thunderhead, had separated from the rest of the clouds. It seemed to be moving north, over Narragansett Bay. Bolts of lightning churned up the water ahead of the column of clouds as the thunderhead headed away.

"Beat you that time," Charlie shouted at the retreating cloud.

The storm line stopped moving. It hovered still over the water.

"What? Impossible!" Charlie grabbed his binoculars. "This can't be right," he cried out, as he stared in horror as it appeared that the thunderhead was turning back in his direction.

Charlie watched in growing terror as lightning bolts striking the water around him warned of the returning thunderhead. "It doesn't make sense," he shouted. "Storms don't behave this way. It really is like it's targeting me!"

As the thunderhead moved closer, Charlie saw the same menacing face he had seen earlier, glaring at him from the center of the cloud. He could not understand the thunderous voice of the storm cloud as its eyes peered down at him.

"This must be the boy my master has been searching for," the storm cloud roared. "I shall be the one rewarded for finding him."

Charlie jumped, as lightning bolts flashed from each eye and hit the water just before his boat. "What is happening?" he screamed, ducking as another lightning bolt hit the surface of the water not ten yards from the bow of the Boston Whaler, causing it to buck high into the air and slam down into the sea.

Charlie could have sworn that the rain and hail were only pelting down on him, and not in any other part of the cove. It really is as if it is attacking me, and just me. I've got to get out of here, he thought, peering over the rail and realizing there was only one way out. But the thunderhead was blocking the entrance.

Continuing to be pounded with rain and hail again, Charlie threw himself onto the floor and pulled the white seat cushion down on top of himself. "Stop, please stop," he screamed over the howling wind and the pounding hailstones, now bouncing off the cushion. "What do you want from me?" He screamed, tears falling from his eyes. "Leave me alone!"

The Thunderhead was dismayed by the boy's fearful cries. He had been warned the boy of the prophecy was fearless and had immense powers. "This boy is the right age, has brown hair, but the boy is crying like a baby. Something isn't right. Can it be he is not the right one?"

As the Thunderhead hovered lower, he became less sure that the boy in the boat was the enemy he had been seeking. "Strange," he whined to the invisible Dark Lord, who he suspected was always watching. "Why has this boy not used his powers to stop my attack?" He howled even louder at the boy and saw the boy was trembling at the bottom of the boat, paralyzed with fear. "Is this the boy that has caused all this trouble for you, my lord? He is not brave and powerful as I was led to believe. Are you the boy of the prophecy?" he called to the boy.

The constant wind and rain made Charlie shiver with terror that at any second he was going to die. He kept mumbling prayers for someone to save him, tears falling from his face.

The Guardian's face, still visible in the storm cloud, shaking with rage. "The boy I seek would have understood my question. This pitiful mortal lies before me cowering like a dog and pleading for his miserable life. He cannot be the one I seek. I must continue the search elsewhere. Good-bye, you sniveling coward!" The cloud began to move off but paused. He gazed down at the boy in the boat, furious that he had wasted so much time and energy on such a worthless child, tempted to unleash his frustration on this ready target. "I could destroy you!" he screamed at the boy, but then, deciding such a being wasn't worth the effort, he backed away. Even for a powerful storm Guardian like him, it would take valuable time to lash this boat with enough power to drown this human rat. "No, he wasn't worth risking the wrath of the impatient Dark Lord."

Charlie remained under the cushion, not daring to move as the still angry thundercloud pulled away from the cove and returned to the army of clouds heading out into the bay. "I will find you and destroy you," the storm's winds howled as he renewed his search.

The war had begun. Steven was in great danger.

Chapter 13

The **Seeker** and Shu left Aquidneck Island attached to a stratocumulus cloud, traveling six-thousand feet above the ground. The black cloud was full of water. The Seeker watched deep in thought as Shu released droplets of rain from the water-soaked clouds.

"The prophecy requires two, me and the boy," said The Seeker. "Unless Steven rejoins the group, I am not sure I alone have the power to liberate the Guardians and face the Dark Ruler."

What will you do now that Steven has been ordered by his Aunt Celia not to work with you? Shu asked.

"What choice is there? I must somehow get him back into action. We cannot afford to lose our momentum now that we have finally succeeded to liberate a few of the Guardians." He thought hard. "With your help, my friend, we might be able to get Steven back and continue with our task to fulfill the prophecy."

You know I will do what I can, but what of Bastet and Morag? Should they not be here as well? Asked Shu.

"No. As much as I would value Bastet and Morag's assistance, both must protect Steven. It will be just a matter of time before the Dark Ruler finds where he resides," The Seeker replied.

You genuinely believe the boy is in danger?

"Yes. I have seen much over the past centuries while trapped in the transparent cube by the Dark Ruler. His sadistic pleasure at tormenting captured human souls and remolding them as his slaves made me sick every time I was compelled to watch. His attempt to turn my pure, unblemished soul to evil was the ultimate punishment he tried to inflict on me. I can only guess what horrors he has planned for Steven. We must destroy him," The Seeker said.

As they traveled north toward the Dark Ruler's lair, the sky was darkening.

Look, Shu gasped, pointing to a vast gray cloud forming below the peak of the Dark Ruler's mountain.

Shu and The Seeker settled down on the top of an adjacent mountaintop to observe what was happening across the valley.

Pouring out from the entrance of the Dark Ruler's lair were hordes of tiny black bats. The sky turned black as millions of vampire bats rose in a noisy throng. The valley, once bright with sun resonated with their high-pitched squeals as they spread out and flew across adjoining canyons.

Suddenly, a column of bats dove toward the ground.

Shu and The Seeker shivered with disgust as the bats attacked a herd of cattle grazing in the fields. The screams of the defenseless animals echoed in the canyons as they raced and bucked in agony, trying to shake off the clinging bats.

As night fell, Shu and The Seeker watched cow after cow drop to the ground, drained of their life's blood by the voracious vampires.

Can't we do something? Shu asked.

The Seeker sighed. "It is too late, my friend. The best thing we can do is prevent this same atrocity from being done to humans."

With dawn, the real horror of the previous night's attack became fully evident. The bodies of dead animals were rotting across the fields and valleys. Cruel-beaked vultures stood over the carcasses and ripped the flesh off the dead animals' bones.

"Look, Shu," The Seeker pointed to the sky. "The Bats. They're not returning to their caves."

Shu nodded. *They usually do after the sky turns bright. They fear sunlight.*

"There is something not usual about these creatures," The Seeker replied.

The Seeker and Shu watched the bats group together into distinct formations, and then fly off in different directions.

"I don't understand," muttered The Seeker. "Bats don't separate into columns like this, and they do not leave the safety of their caves in daylight." He was deep in thought. "I don't like this unusual behavior. We must follow the bat columns to determine what the Dark Ruler is up to. I am certain these vicious creatures are part of his evil plan."

Shu nodded. *Splitting up like this makes me think they are searching for someone.*

The Seeker bit his lip. "And I have a feeling I know who they are hunting."

The Seeker and Shu rose into the sky and followed a column of bats led by a giant bat with white wings. He appeared to be the leader.

"We must stay safely behind them," The Seeker said.

The bats flew in a straight column, The Seeker and Shu a short distance behind. Both were still trying to figure out why the bats were heading south as they crossed into Texas.

"I think I have it," The Seeker announced. "They are headed for Mexico."

Why there? Shu asked, dismayed by the bat's unusually disciplined flight.

"The pattern has been that the Dark Ruler has concealed his Guardians in tombs of famous rulers. I believe he has done this because who would look for them when it is the dead rulers that attract attention."

That is devious but logical, Shu admitted.

"Emperor Ahuizot's tomb is a perfect place to hide a Guardian. I think that is where they are headed." The Seeker said.

Later that day, Shu and The Seeker finally arrived in Mexico. The Seeker watched with interest as the swarm of vampire bats entered Emperor Ahuizot's tomb, confirming his intuition. He noted that several bats sat around the vents, peering out into the night sky.

"What are you up to?" asked The Seeker. "Why have you placed bats at this particular tomb?"

They're watching the entrance, Shu muttered, as he tried to peer into the cave. *Do you think they are on the look-out for us? Do you think the Dark Ruler knows we are releasing his slaves?*

The Seeker nodded. "I think he may know we might try and liberate the Guardian he placed here."

It could be just a coincidence, Shu replied.

"It could be, but I'm guessing that the Dark Ruler might be directing his slaves to guard these locations because he knows I observed him placing Guardians here during my captivity. I suspect he realizes I am the one causing his recent problems."

So, he would be most concerned about locations in which you observed him conceal his servants. Do you recall any others? Asked Shu.

The Seeker was trying to remember. "There is another Guardian in the Mammouth Cave in Kentucky, another likely site." He eyed the mouth of the cave. "I think we have hit on something. I suggest we travel there to determine if this is just a coincidence or something much more serious. If we are right, The Dark Ruler may already know our plans, placing Steven in even greater danger than we feared."

Shu agreed.

Without disturbing the bats, Shu and The Seeker left the tomb in Mexico and headed quickly for Kentucky. They hitched a ride along the outer ridge of a hurricane cell-sweeping through central Florida and up toward South Carolina. They checked behind them, to see if they were followed, by bat spies.

"We're here," The Seeker said, spotting the entrance to the Mammoth Cave.

It seems quiet, Shu said. *Perhaps it was a coincidence after all?*

The Seeker settled down behind a large boulder near the entrance of the cave and watched for any suspicious activity.

I'm tired, Shu complained. *I have been traveling across this country all day. I need a little cat-nap.*

The Seeker sighed. "Go, take your nap. I will wait right here. There is too much at stake for me to simply assume the bats all flying to that tomb in Mexico are just a normal migration, not in daylight."

The Seeker did not have to wait long. The fluttering of wings startled him as several vampire bats flew out of the cave and took posts along its ridge. Their red eyes were searching the night.

Shu jumped awake at the sound of the flapping wings and was now staring with hate at the bats. *They're here too?*

The Seeker nodded. "My friend, I'm afraid, as I suspected, this is not a coincidence. I believe the Dark Ruler has placed his vicious vampire bat slaves at every site where his Guardians are located."

But why? Why would he need these bats to guard his tombs? Shu asked.

The Seeker smiled. "I think it is to watch for us. That is the only thing that makes sense. We must assume he has guessed our plans."

Shu nodded. *There could be one more reason why the Dark Ruler is unleashing his flying spies. There were many columns headed in various directions.*

"I know," The Seeker said, "We must return to Steven's home and see if the bats are searching for him. His life could be in terrible danger if the bats find him." He had a horrifying flashback picture of the field of dead cows.

Chapter 14

Steven sat on a bench, surrounded by his friends in the school cafeteria. They were all munching on their sandwiches when Charlie said, "You gotta hear this crazy story."

Steven half-listened to Charlie's adventure, thinking his friend was just spinning another one of his 'big fish' tales. He was lost in thought, not happy with Aunt Celia's decision to stop him from working with The Seeker, trying to come up with a solution to get her to consent to him rejoining the quest. He jumped to attention when he heard Charlie mention a large thunderhead acting as if it was human. "Yeah, I was on my dad's boat when pow, this cloud comes along—"

Steven interrupted. "Did you say, 'Thunderhead'?"

"Yeah. This darn thing was not your typical dark gray cloud I've seen a thousand times before. It scared the dickens out of me!"

"You were scared of a cloud," Rusty burst in. "What a dweeb!"

Charlie scowled. "You can laugh if you want, but it was weird."

"What do you mean?" Steven asked, leaning closer.

"This cloud was changing directions all the time. At one point, it was moving away from me, with the wind, like it was supposed to do. Suddenly, it stopped, and I swear, it turned right around, racing toward me again."

"Clouds don't do that," Paul said.

"I know. It was like it was deliberately aiming for me. But that's impossible. Right?"

"What a dweeb!" Rusty burst into laughter.

"I never heard of a storm cloud doing that," Paul repeated.

"You know what else was weird," Charlie said, aiming his eyes at Steven. "This cloud had—and I know you'll think I'm crazy—but it had eyes in the middle of it."

Steven shivered. "I gotta go." He got up from the table and hurried away. I need time to think about this, he thought, as he saw the other boys laughing. They thought it was just a joke, another one of Charlie's fishing tall tales.

Steven's afternoon classes were a blur, his mind still working over Charlie's story. What did it mean that a storm had acted so strangely? Was it just Charlie's imagination? But then, how did he know about the eyes? He remembered those red eyes in the middle of the storm and how they had stared at him as if they hated him. He couldn't concentrate, eager to get home and report Charlie's story to The Seeker.

Dashing from Mrs. Smith's, van, Steven ran into the house, but kept looking over his shoulder. His anxiety had been building all afternoon. It gripped his body as he raced into the large house, calling for his aunt.

"In here," answered Aunt Celia, from the living room.

"I think it's back," Steven said.

"Who's back?" Aunt Celia asked, realizing from Steven's facial expression that what she was about to hear was not good news.

"The Thunderhead. I told you about it. My friend, Charlie, said a large storm cloud attacked him while he was out fishing Sunday."

"What are you talking about, Steven? Clouds don't attack—"

"This one does." As Steven related Charlie's story, he saw the smile on his aunt's face turn to a frown.

"Are you sure it is the same kind of storm that you say followed you home from school? This is hard to believe."

"Yes! Charlie's description was right on. He said he saw red eyes. That's what I saw too. I think we should contact The Seeker and let him know right away. I'm not sure what he can do, but he should know for his own safety," Steven urged.

"I don't know," Aunt Celia muttered, still afraid of the dangers of Steven getting involved again. "It doesn't seem possible. Why would this storm pick on Charlie?"

"Aunt Celia, don't you understand? Charlie looks a lot like me."

Aunt Celia gasped. "So, you think the cloud was attacking Charlie believing he, was you?"

"I think so. It makes sense. We're the same age."

Aunt Celia mulled this over. "I don't believe a storm can attack anyone like that. Charlie was just in the wrong place at the wrong time. That is a far more logical explanation."

Steven would have liked agreeing. "Yes, it could be, but what if Charlie is right and that cloud was aiming right at him? What if the Dark Ruler did send that cloud? It'll keep searching until it finds me. The Dark Ruler won't let me live, even if I try to stay out of this. Only The Seeker can help me. Please, Aunt Celia, you've got to see that we're all in terrible danger if we don't do anything and that storm was really searching for me?"

Aunt Celia saw Steven was serious and genuinely afraid. She hated the risks involved but was beginning to understand that not doing anything could prove far more dangerous than working with the others to protect Steven. What would his parents have done? She knew. They would have trusted their son. She let out a deep sigh. "I still don't like it, but yes, I agree. You need to find out if the attack was meant for you."

Steven jumped out of his chair.

"Hold it, Bud. I am allowing you to only follow up on only this one aspect. If you agree to abide by my rules, then hurry, before something else happens."

"Yes, yes, I agree. Oh, thank you, Aunt Celia. You'll see, I won't let you down."

Aunt Celia frowned. "Just be safe. I'll never forgive myself if something happens to you because I went against my better judgment."

"It's the right decision. You'll see." Steven turned and raced down the cellar stairs.

Morag and Bastet had been watching Steven from the kitchen counter. They saw Aunt Celia move toward the kitchen table, sit down on a chair slowly as if she was in pain.

She is very sad, Bastet said to Morag telepathically.

She is worried about Steven, Morag replied.

Aunt Celia wiped her eyes. "I was hoping this day would never come," she said softly.

It is not Steven's fault, Morag said.

Aunt Celia stared at the dragon. "I know. But it does not make it easier."

No, it does not, Morag agreed. *But we will protect him. You must believe that.*

Aunt Celia smiled slightly. "At least I have the comfort of knowing I have help from you, Morag, a dragon, and Bastet, an Egyptian Goddess. Thank you." Suddenly she had a thought, "Morag, how did that cloud get so close to us again? Could the cloud have followed you home after one of your feedings?"

The skies have been empty each time I left the house to search for food. I made sure I did not transform to my average size until I was a considerable distance away, Morag replied.

Aunt Celia nodded, thinking. "Then either the attack on Charlie was a weird coincidence, or the Dark Ruler has found out where we live, and Steven is in real danger. I wish I knew."

So, do we, Morag said. *We will do whatever we can to protect Steven.*

You can trust us, Bastet said.

Aunt Celia shook her head. "This is all too much for me. Please, for tonight, keep him out of trouble? I'm exhausted."

Morag and Bastet watched Aunt Celia get up as if a heavy weight had been placed on her shoulders. She was mumbling as she headed up the stairs. Closing her bedroom door, she let out a long sigh. The thought of Steven being hunted by the Dark Ruler was frightening. She didn't even bother to change her clothes. Almost instantly, she fell asleep.

Hours later, startled awake by a loud boom of thunder, Aunt Celia heard the rain lashing against the roof and windows. "It's just rain," she told herself, but her heart was beating fast. Seconds seemed like hours until the intense light of a bolt of lightning flooded her room.

"Ka-boom!"

"That was a big one," she muttered. "One one-thousand; two one-thousand; three...."

"Ka-boom!"

61

The house shook, and the windows rattled with a second lightning strike.

"No! It can't be! Steven must be wrong," Aunt Celia said, but knowing how terrified he had been of the last storm, headed for Steven's room. She knocked once on the door, and not waiting for a response, rushed in. "Are you alright?"

The bed was empty.

Aunt Celia hurried for the lab, praying Steven was there, seeking shelter from the storm.

When she opened the door, she was relieved to see Steven was inside. Why were his eyes glued to the computer monitor? "How long have you been down here, Steven?" she asked, realizing how worried she had been about him.

"I don't know. I couldn't sleep, so I thought I'd check the weather channel to see if they forecasted any more storms."

"The weather channel. Steven, are you deaf? We have one heck of a storm raging over us this minute. I was scared to death; you were out there!"

"Sorry, Aunt Celia. Is it bad?"

"Bad? Steven, I've never seen a storm like this."

"The lab is soundproof and has no windows," Steven reminded her.

Aunt Celia shook her head. "So, you wouldn't know there is a storm raging above us while you're down here."

"No. Mom and Dad wanted to make sure nothing disturbed their work. It's like a bomb shelter down here."

"They should have made sure nothing disturbed your poor old worried aunt," Aunt Celia said, with a deep sigh.

"I'm really sorry I worried you, but I like it down here in my parent's lab. It makes me feel close to them still."

Aunt Celia thought he looked sad. She thought of hugging him but held back. He wasn't ready for that, not from her. She decided to change the subject. "So, did you contact Shu and The Seeker?" She yawned, exhausted by all the stress.

"I can't find them," Steven said, a worried look on his face.

"I'm sure you don't have to worry about them," Aunt Celia said. "The most important thing is that you are not involved with this mess anymore. You are safe."

Steven wondered if that was true.

Chapter 15

Morag sensed Steven was afraid of something and wanted to help. *It is time for sleep, Steven,* she said softly. *You must be at your best if you are to help save the world.*

Aunt Celia realized the dragon seemed to really care for Steven. "Morag is right, Steven. Tomorrow is another day."

Steven sighed. "I am tired. This whole thing has exhausted me, especially having to try and convince my Aunt that I'm not crazy and we're in a battle against evil." He stood up and yawned. "Tomorrow is another day."

"I'm sorry I exhausted you, but you must admit it's a lot to swallow," Aunt Celia said. "Will you be alright now?"

He'll be fine, Morag said, *Bastet and I will be guarding him. You look exhausted as well.*

Aunt Celia nodded. "I'm an old woman, and all this is making me older fast." She rose painfully from the chair. "Goodnight, Steven. I'll see you tomorrow. Things will look better."

Steven yawned. "Thank you, Aunt Celia."

Aunt Celia nodded and shuffled away from the lab. She wondered if all this had been a dream, a nightmare. The storm was still raging outside. "It's just a storm." The powerful lightning striking so close made her wonder.

Morag saw Steven could barely keep his eyes open. *Come, boy, it is time for you to get some rest.*

Bastet rubbed her body against Steven's legs. *We will protect you, our friend,* she purred.

Steven pulled himself up from his father's chair, barely made it up to the stairs, and flopped down on his bed, fully dressed. "Are you going to stand guard here all night," he asked Morag.

Morag was on the windowsill, staring out into the stormy night. She didn't want to frighten the boy but knew Steven had to be alert to danger. *I honestly don't know if the storm is searching for you,* she said. *But Bastet and I will try and find out while you are safe.*

"You're not going out there!" Steven heard the wind lashing the rain against his bedroom window. Waves driven by the raging wind were pounding the cove below. As much as he tried to fight it, his eyes were closing.

We must go out into this storm if we are to learn the truth and protect you, Bastet said, wishing she did not hate water so much.

"Please be careful and watch out for that Thunderhead," Steven said, barely awake. "This isn't the best night even for a dragon to be out there..."

Don't worry, boy, Morag whispered, *A storm can't hurt a dragon and an Egyptian God. Not much,* she thought, as she spread her wings and leaped into the gale-force wind and rain.

Bastet leaped onto the thick tree limb outside Steven's window and disappeared down the trunk.

Steven watched Morag soar into the stormy night as if it was a dream. He was worried that she was no match for the ferocious storm. "Come back," he called, pulling himself up to the window.

The rain was pounding too hard to see anything. Reluctantly, Steven returned to his bed, praying he would see his friends again. I should never have let her do that, he thought.

A crash of thunder shook the house again.

Steven, nearly asleep, did not hear his door slowly open.

Someone was peering at him from behind the door.

"Ouch!"

Steven jumped to the floor, fists raised. "Who's here?"

Aunt Celia rubbed her knee where she had banged it against his bed. "Steven, it's me," Aunt Celia said, backing away from the boy about to attack her.

"Aunt Celia?" Steven lowered his fists. "I'm sorry, Aunt Celia. I guess I'm a bit jumpy."

"This storm can make anyone jumpy," Aunt Celia replied, still bent over, rubbing her knee. "Hey, where are your protectors, the dragon and Bastet?" She scanned the room. "They're supposed to be guarding you—"

"Morag and Bastet just left, into the storm, to find out if our house is being targeted by the storm. I hated seeing them go out in this."

"You're worried about them? They're supposed to be protecting you!" She saw the worry on his face. "Couldn't they have waited?" she asked.

Steven didn't want to worry her any more than she already was, so he didn't want to tell her that his friends were trying to find out if the storm was hunting for him. He thought quickly and came up with what he thought was a good story, "You know Morag. Well, she hasn't eaten for five days. Dragons must eat to maintain their strength. Remember, she is a growing girl."

"She went out to eat?" Aunt Celia thought of her kitchen, still a disaster area. "If that dragon grows anymore we might want to consider moving to the Scottish Highlands and buying a castle," Aunt Celia said, half joking, but picturing her wrecked kitchen again.

Steven took her seriously. "A castle could work. I think she'd love that. Great idea, Aunt Celia."

"Steven, I was joking." Aunt Celia was worried that if he thought she was serious, there was no telling what he might do next.

"No, really, Aunt Celia. Morag would be free to fly around the countryside and live a more natural life. It's a really great idea."

"I don't know, Steven. Scotland?"

"At least she wouldn't be out in a storm like this one," Steven said, wishing again he had not let them go out into the howling wind and rain.

"Don't worry, they'll be fine." Aunt Celia couldn't believe she was also worried about a dragon and cat goddess. "I think Morag can take care of herself." She gazed out the window at the pounding rain.

Steven watched her and said softly, "I've got another worry now."

"What's that?" Aunt Celia wanted to help.

Steven sighed. "I'm concerned for your safety now that you're involved." He gave her a smile. "I never should have told you."

"Hey, I'm my brother's sister! I can take care of myself," Aunt Celia replied but wondered if anyone could survive this nightmare Steven had become involved in. If it was real?

"Aunt Celia, you have no idea what The Dark Ruler is capable of."

"He has no idea of what we're capable of," Aunt Celia, said.

"I'm serious."

"So am I. Steven, if you are right, and this evil creature is sending this storm to search for you, well, he's got me to contend with now too." She raised her hands now tight fists. "Nobody messes with Steven's Aunt Celia!"

Steven would have laughed, but he didn't find anything funny about being a target again. He wondered if his aunt understood. "This won't just go away, Aunt Celia. I can't hide from him. He's not going to quit until he finds me and either kills me or make me his slave."

Aunt Celia gazed at the still raging storm. "I'm sadly beginning to agree." She let out a deep sigh, seeing lightning reflected in Steven's earnest eyes. "I see now that doing nothing will not stop this...will not protect you. I wish it would."

There was an uncomfortable silence between them. There were only the sounds of the wind, rain and the violent crashes of thunder as they both stared out the window, wondering if the storm was ever going to end.

Finally, Aunt Celia asked, "Where is The Seeker? He appears to be the key to this mess."

Steven turned toward her. "I haven't heard from him, or Shu. I'm beginning to worry. If The Seeker did go after another Guardian, alone, he might have been overpowered, and taken captive again." He turned back to the window. "I hope he shows up soon."

Aunt Celia saw the expression on Steven's face and wanted to make him feel less worried, even if she was concerned too. "It will all work out, Steven. Morag will return soon. And that Seeker fellow? I have a feeling he'll be back soon enough too. After all, he is a spirit, isn't he?" She pulled away from the window. "You should try to sleep. Go to bed now. Your friends are safe."

Steven fell back into the bed.

Goodnight, dear nephew," Aunt Celia said, as she started to close the door.

"Goodnight, Aunt Celia. Thank you."

Aunt Celia paused outside the door. I wonder if he would have let me kiss him good-night, she thought, realizing the boy had wormed his way into her heart. He is stubborn, doesn't always obey, can be very difficult, but he is also smart, caring, and brave, just like his parents. And that's what worries me. She shook her head sadly and then headed toward her own bedroom.

In her room, Aunt Celia stood in the dark, by the window, staring into the lashing storm. "Brother," she said, "Please help me? If, as The Seeker says, you knew of Steve's role in this so-called prophecy, help me learn how to keep him safe?"

As if in answer, a thunderclap made the house shake again.

Not receiving an answer, Aunt Celia finally settled into her bed, but could not sleep. It wasn't just the unrelenting storm. It was the voices arguing in her head, and the thought that no matter what she decided, her decision could cost Steven his life.

Chapter 16

After Aunt Celia left his room, Steven jumped out of bed. He had pretended to go to sleep, hoping she would go to her room and get a much-needed rest. Steven had enough to worry about without worrying about her health. He walked back to the window. The howling wind outside could be the thunderhead with the vicious eyes, and yet it had been a week since Charlie had seen the monster cloud. Could this be the same storm? It didn't seem possible, but his earlier adventures had proven that anything is possible. This can't be just a coincidence, Steven thought. They're searching for me, but how do they know where to look?

With so many unanswered questions, Steven returned to his bed. He wanted to sleep but tossed and turned all night. He kept having nightmares that Morag had been caught by the Dark Ruler and was strung across a lava pit, roasting and sizzling, much to the delight of the Dark Ruler's slaves who were circling the fire with teeth bared.

Jarred awake by his dreams, afraid to face another nightmare, Steven kept checking the window to see if Morag had returned, but there was no sign of her. It was an awful, endless, night. He was glad when he saw the sun's rays, indicating the storm had finally ended.

Steven heard a knock at his door. His entire body tensed. Then he heard another thump and smiled when he saw Aunt Celia enter the room. "Good morning," he began, "Am I glad to see you."

"Steven, we need to talk."

The phrase "we need to talk" caused the hairs on the back of Steven's neck to rise.

Aunt Celia picked up the chair on her way in and sat down in front of Steven, who was now sitting up, on the edge of his bed.

"I haven't slept all night. I've been thinking about you." Aunt Celia sighed. "After that horrid storm last night, I don't see any other way." She stared into his eyes. "Do you really want to work with The Seeker? Do you truly believe you must do this?"

Steven bit his lip. "Yes. Unfortunately, I have no real choice."

Aunt Celia nodded. "I believe you're right. As much as I hate it, I am coming to that conclusion." She smiled sadly. "Before I give you my permission, I need to know more. No secrets. I need to know exactly what you're doing. How dangerous is it?"

"Most of the time, we aren't doing anything dangerous—"

"Steven, I said I want the truth. I know when you aren't telling me the truth. Now if you want my permission, you will stop beating around the bush and tell me exactly what risks you are facing." She stood up and was glaring down at him, her arms crossed over her chest. "This is your last chance."

Steven realized he had no choice. "Okay. I'll tell you the truth. Mostly, we search for a Guardian, one of The Dark Ruler's slaves, whose souls we are sworn to free." He hoped he wouldn't have to tell her how that was accomplished.

"Isn't that very dangerous?"

"Not really." Steven caught Aunt Celia's frown and her tapping foot. "It can be...a little. But we have to do it. He's using these slaves to imperil the Earth, and every human and animal! He's a monster." He saw the unconvinced expression on her face and added, "But The Seeker helps me. He helps me a lot. We've become good friends, and he's taught me a lot. He helped me deal with my parents' death and get over my fear of the unknown. So, have you, Aunt Celia, but in another way. You really have."

Aunt Celia liked the compliment, but it made her even more concerned for his welfare. "Thank you, Steven." He is indeed becoming a young man, she thought, studying his face. If I allow him to continue this hunt for the Dark Ruler's slaves, am I sending him to his death? His parents trusted me to take care of him...so do the courts. How in God's name would I explain that my nephew was killed because I let him go on some incredible mission? How can I justify making him face all this danger to my conscience? I've got a headache.

Steven watched his aunt struggling. He knew she was weighing the pros and cons of letting him continue in this crazy business. He hoped the advantages would outweigh the disadvantages and he would be allowed to get back into the fight. The world depended on it.

"You understand why I've been so worried?" Aunt Celia asked, still unsure of what to do.

Steven gave her a half-smile. "I understand you care about me. I wish you could find another answer, a way to help me. I really wish it was possible. But I know I need to do this, or we're all doomed. That is my mission. I wish there were another way."

"And this all has to do with the death of your parents?" Aunt Celia let out a deep sigh. "They were really into all this supernatural stuff, weren't they?"

Steven got out of bed, unable to sit still any longer. The sadness of his face showed how painful it always was for him to think of the death of his parents. He felt anger rising inside him. "How can I do nothing? The Dark Ruler caused their death when he concealed a Guardian in the Tomb of Seti I."

"That Guardian killed them?" Aunt Celia had never heard of the Guardians until Steven had revealed their existence to her. She still found it difficult to accept such creatures existed.

Steven gritted his teeth. "That Guardian, under the orders of the Dark Ruler, killed them both."

"And you killed him?" Aunt Celia was afraid to ask but needed the truth.

Steven nodded. "The 'elimination' of that evil spirit was my first challenge." He did not tell her it felt good to get his revenge against that creature for the murder of his mother and father.

"Weren't you afraid of being captured or...killed?" Aunt Celia asked, startled at seeing Steven's strange smile as he spoke of freeing that spirit from its evil servitude. "I'm terrified for you."

"Of course, I was scared. I'm scared out of my skin each time I do this.

But I can't just sit here and wait for the Dark Ruler to find me. I can protect myself by freeing every slave of his that I find." Steven was unaware he was pounding his fist in the palm of his hand as he spoke. "A year ago, I'd have said this whole thing was impossible, crazy, but I know these things you call, 'paranormal phenomena,' are trying to kill me. I know they're real. I wish they weren't."

"I do too."

"The Seeker says I've been honored because the gods selected me. Honestly, Aunt Celia, I can't see how having to fight for my life is an honor." Steven realized he was opening up to her more than he wanted. "I often wonder what the gods would do if I refused to accept my role in this war. But it was impossible to not join this quest after finding out the Dark Ruler ordered my parents' murder and wants me dead too. It was a no-brainer. Maybe that is why my parents haven't given any sign to force me to stop. And yes, I believe they know and are protecting me."

Aunt Celia had always believed in ghosts. She also thought Steven's parents were watching over him, protecting him. But was her belief enough to let him continue? She jumped at a sudden noise at the window.

Bastet was scratching at the glass.

Steven hurried to open it.

Bastet leaped inside and shook her fur, sending water spraying in all directions.

"You're soaking my clean bedroom floor!" Aunt Celia moaned. "First my kitchen and now this?"

Bastet stopped shaking herself dry and stared at the puddle around her. *Sorry about that. She saw the scowl on Aunt Celia's face and decided to distract her. I must agree with Steven. His parents would have given him a sign if they did not want him to persist in this most critical quest. And, I might add, they would not have brought me here, to protect him, unless they believed all this was unavoidable.*

Aunt Celia was on her knees, mopping up the water with a towel. "I'd like to believe you are right," she replied, but still had her doubts about believing a cat.

"Where were you all this time?" Steven whispered to Bastet.

Morag sent me back. We both checked out this storm and believe you were correct. We think it is searching for you. I saw the eyes.

"That's it! We've got to hide you," Aunt Celia jumped up from the floor.

"Hold on Aunt Celia. I've got an idea. I'll ask Shu to push the storm away from us. After all, he is the god of the wind, and he did it before."

Bastet meowed. *Good idea, Steven. There's only one problem, we have no idea where Shu is.*

"Good," Aunt Celia said, thinking of all the times the wind god had blown papers around the lab. Really quite annoying.

"So, what should we do?" Steven asked, glancing at his Aunt.

Bastet stretched her lean body. *I think our best bet is to let the storm blow itself out. You should avoid going out when the Thunderhead with eyes is around. Learn to take naps like I do.* Bastet closed her eyes and was soon contentedly snoring.

"I don't believe it," Aunt Celia exclaimed, looking down at the end of the bed where Bastet was sleeping. "We're in serious trouble, and she just falls asleep? Some god!"

Steven smiled. "If you and I were in any danger, both Morag and Bastet would be standing right next to us." He walked over to the window. His eyes were gazing far into the distance, hoping to see Morag.

"You're still worried about your dragon?" Aunt Celia asked, joining Steven at the window. "Why don't I worry with you?"

Somehow, the way she said that, filled Steven with the hope that everything was going to be alright. But where was Morag? Where were The Seeker and Shu?

Chapter 17

The Seeker and Shu finally arrived at the Mammoth Cave in Kentucky. After a quick survey of the area, they settled near the entrance of the seemingly deserted cave.

Look, said Shu, pointing to the dark patch of sky in the distance. *Do you see all those crows?*

The Seeker nodded

The sound of cawing grew louder as more crows flew into the area. The Seeker watched with a growing sense of curiosity as the birds flew in widening circles over the rugged terrain. It became apparent that the crows were searching for something. But what?

After several minutes, dozens of the large black crows dropped down on nearby tree branches. The cawing as the crows communicated back and forth grew more raucous until the entire valley reverberated with their shrill cries.

The Seeker was surprised when five large crows dove toward the entrance of the cave.

What are they doing? Shu asked.

In seconds, a throng of bats came racing from the cave entrance.

"I think we have our answer," The Seeker replied. "The crows are after the bats."

The crows let out loud cries and smashed down in a furious attack on the bats. As more bats emerged to see what all the noise was about, dozens of hungry crows pounced on them with dozens more waiting their turn to catch a meal.

This is brutal, Shu hissed. *They're savage. They're killing every bat they can find.*

The Seeker smiled. "No, my friend, it is justice after the killing field these bats left up north. They would show no mercy for Steven, or us if they could trap us, as they did the afflicted cattle."

Are you saying these crows know what they are doing? Shu asked.

"Yes. I am guessing the crows have been following these vampire bats for some time. In nature, one never knows when the hunter will become the hunted," The Seeker said, thinking of the Dark Ruler and wondering, not for the first time, who was the hunter.

And Steven could be the hunted, Shu said.

"Yes. Unfortunately, so. We must leave," The Seeker said. "The Dark Ruler might think we are responsible for this attack on his bats."

Shu looked puzzled. *His bats?*

"I believe these bats are his slaves, sent here to watch for Steven and us."

You believe they are his spies? Shu asked. *Why?*

"Their behavior, my friend. These bats are like none I have ever seen. I am convinced The Dark Ruler has enlisted them as sentries. He will be furious when he learns of their demise. He will blame the boy for certain." The Seeker continued to observe the slaughter.

One of us should wait and see what happens here, said Shu. *If the Dark Ruler sends more bats to replace these, we can assume they are under his control.*

The Seeker weighed the choices. "My friend, can you enter this cave without being detected?" He finally asked.

Yes. I can attach myself to the evening wind and enter as the air is drawn into the cave's chambers. Shu replied.

"Then I think it is best you do so. See if we are correct and the Dark Ruler has concealed one of his Guardians within this cavern. I will head to the Emperor Ahuizotl's tomb in Mexico City to check that one out as well. We really must find out what is going on or Steven will be in great danger."

Be safe, my friend, Shu said.

The Seeker's human-like form became a smoky mist as he caught the breeze moving toward the East coast.

Shu waited until The Seeker was gone, and then searched for any vent in the ground which would allow him to enter the cave unseen. It turned out to be a painstaking process. He was deceived several times into believing that the leaves lifting into the air from the ground might reveal the location of an air vent through which he could enter the cave unseen. They were all dead ends.

Finding no possible entry vent, Shu was ready to give up and follow after The Seeker when sailing over the last ridge, he felt a stream of air emerging through a crevice below. Excited, he thrust his long thin body through the opening and caught onto the wind which carried him more than two hundred feet down into the cavern.

This will do nicely, Shu thought, as he plummeted deeper. He wondered if all the bats had been wiped out or if some might still be lurking in the depths of the cavern, performing their duty as sentries for the Guardian. He was grateful the wind would make it difficult for them to become alerted to his presence. Attached to the stream of air, Shu was carried through the twisting capillaries and veins of the cave. The search for the Guardian had begun, and he prayed he would be able to complete his mission without being discovered. He wondered if The Seeker would also be successful. One small mistake could destroy everything for which they had all sacrificed so much. One small mistake could mean the end for Steven.

Chapter 18

His throne was made of human bones. The Dark Ruler had just returned from the Roman Colosseum in the center of Rome. Located directly below the vast arena was a dark subterranean network of tunnels, shafts, and empty animal pens. In centuries past, he had felt anticipation watching the slaves of Emperor Titus building the labyrinth, knowing its evil purpose.

He knew because he implanted the idea in the emperor's brain. He knew that here he would find a new source for the horrors he found so entertaining. It was also here, he would conceal, deep within the maze of catacombs, one of his most significant prizes.

Trapped and executed by a mob on a Rome street, this man, forever known as the Butcher of Naples, was responsible for murdering and butchering twenty-eight women. The Dark Ruler made this murderer his newest slave.

"I will place you in Seti I to replace the Guardian releases by that menacing boy. They will not expect me to again place a guardian in the tomb."

What a fantastic prize, the Dark Ruler thought. Of the many humans he had killed, remolding their souls into becoming his mindless slaves, this murdering monster would be his masterpiece. His excitement caused the mountain hiding his lair to rumble violently as he laughed at the thought of unleashing the Butcher on humanity again. Soon. Soon, the entire world would be attacked by his army of mindless monsters.

The Dark Ruler remembered traveling through the Gate of Death, known in Latin as the Porta Libitinensis. The stench of blood, excrement, and death impregnated the tunnel walls even centuries later, lingering in his head. How he had enjoyed watching the slain gladiators being dragged by hooks in their heels from the arena, blood running into the sand. How he welcomed the eager stomping of ten thousand feet, the blood-thirsty screams of delighted crowds, as they hungered for the sight of man after man being cut to pieces, or better yet, being torn apart by lions and leopards. The screams of agony still echoed in his ears. The butchering of humans by each other, with swords, axes, spears, clubs, anything man devised to kill his fellow man, was evidence his influence was working. As days, weeks, months, and years rolled into centuries, he enjoyed this 'special' entertainment and loved spreading mayhem among humans. Whenever humans created their own horrors and wars, he was a very delighted spectator, eagerly witnessing the torture and violent death, and all leading to the inevitable arrival of more lost souls for him to harvest for his secret army.

Unfortunately, today was not a good day. The Dark Ruler had lost his good mood and was leaning on his throne armrest, staring balefully at the rocky walls. It had been a week and not a word from any of his vampire bats. He'd begun to question his decision to use the bats to guard the tombs where the Guardians were concealed when two of his spies flew into his chamber. "Where have you been? Report immediately," he roared.

"Crow atk," the bat nearest him squealed, shivering in fear.

"Crow Attack?" The Dark Ruler leaned forward. "What do you mean?"

"Cro Kil an eat sodrs."

"They killed and ate my soldiers? No!" The Dark Ruler flew from his throne, shocked at the news. "What about the boy? Did he do this? Did you see him? Answer!"

"No boyyy," squealed the second bat, nursing a wounded wing. "Mor sodrs need we!"

"Mor sodrs!" echoed the first.

"You want more soldiers?" hissed the Dark Ruler.

"Mor sodrs," the bats repeated, jumping around and squealing incoherently.

The Dark Ruler snarled, "What of the boy? You did not see the boy or his allies?"

78

The bats looked worriedly at each other. "No, boy," they squealed. "We run. No see the boy. Brds. Crows!"

"You let some unintelligent crows defeat you?" The Dark Ruler roared. "Not even the boy?"

The bats gave each other terrified looks but remained silent.

The Ruler was boiling but still needed his spies, so he tried to keep his cool. But it wasn't easy. "Crows eh? Very well. Go back and gather the others. I want that boy." The Dark Ruler waved his arm to dismiss them. "Well, what are you waiting for? Why are you not doing what I commanded?"

"We no eat." a bat said in a timid voice.

"We hurry here to you. We hungry," the other bat echoed.

Idiotic animals, the Dark Ruler thought but knew he still had to use them since he couldn't be everywhere the boy might attack. He swallowed his anger. "You have done well in reporting so promptly. Eat quickly now. Then return to the cave and continue your task. I want that boy!" He wondered how these bats had escaped what sounded like a massacre that had destroyed his other sentries. Cowardly creatures running from a bunch of crows. He was seriously thinking of throwing them into the lava pit, a fitting reward. Later, he would take care of that, he promised himself. "Go now and eat. You shall get your just reward after the boy is mine."

The bats, thinking only of their stomachs, needing no more encouragement, gave each other a sly glance and immediately jumped on the neck of the nearest Gargoyle, sinking their fangs into the leathery hide.

The gargoyle jumped and bucked, letting out agonized screams, begging for his master's help. His partner cowered in fear on the other side of the throne.

The Dark Ruler, surprised by the brutal attack on his pet, was nonetheless fascinated by the bats' sheer bloodthirstiness, their total surrender to hunger, daring to even attack his pets, in his presence. There was something enjoyable about such blind desire, he thought and decided to let the bloody feast continue under his watchful eyes.

The Gargoyle fearing his cruel master's punishment if he resisted the attack, allowed himself to be bled by the bats without protest.

The slurping sounds of the bats sipping blood echoed in the Dark Ruler's ears. He had to admit he was enjoying the gruesome sight and was thinking about how someday he would revel in doing the same, or even much worse, to the boy. *"You will soon be mine,"* he swore, *as he could almost taste flesh and blood of the mortal who dared to stand against him.*

After a short while, even the gorging of the bats grew tiresome. Another idea occurred to the Dark Ruler. He smiled at the bats and said, "Feast as you wish. I shall soon return."

Getting up from his throne, the Dark Ruler headed for the deepest part of his cavern. There was someone he had to see.

Chapter 19

The Ruler floated down the long winding tunnels that coursed through his lair. Rancid water ran down the walls from the cracks in the gray stone. He paid no attention. His mind was made up. It was time.

Stepping up to the thick steel bars that were bolted into the cave walls, he gazed with disgust at the beast, lying next to a half-eaten elk.

"Awake Gregor!" The Dark Ruler bellowed, as he unlocked the steel door and entered the monster's cell.

Gregor opened his eyes but didn't move. "What do you want?" he snapped. "This is the second time you have woken me from a sound sleep..."

"Hold your tongue!" the Ruler, roared. "Remember who you are speaking to, or I shall remind you."

Gregor did not dare to say more for fear that the Dark Ruler might punish him. He had been burned by the red hot flashes from the Dark Ruler's eyes before and saw the eyes pulsing orange already. Even his feeble brain knew better than to mess with the evil one's powers. "You woke me from a deep sleep," he said, a loud yawn releasing a horrid odor. "I do not know it is you, my Master."

The Dark Ruler addressed Gregor in a kinder tone, "That's better." He smiled slyly. "I have good news for you, my friend. I have decided to release you today." He saw the beast's puzzled face. "Yes, my friend, it is time for you to be free again."

"Free again?" Gregor could hardly believe his ears. He let out a hideous laugh.

The Dark Ruler laughed inwardly, the beast was reacting exactly as he hoped. "Yes, I have decided to reward your loyalty. My vampire bats will lead you to the Mammoth cave where you shall find shelter while you wait to do my bidding. Is that not wonderful?"

Gregor nodded. "I am loyal and will....what bidding?"

The Dark Ruler sighed. The beast had already forgotten their last conversation. "You will wait for the boy. Remember we spoke of him?"

Gregor only remembered about the dragon meat. "And the dragon?"

That he remembers, the Dark Ruler thought. All they think of is food. "Yes, you may do what you wish with the dragon, but only once you fulfill your duty to me. You will capture the boy and bring him back here alive. Is that understood?"

"What if there are other humans?"

"Do what you wish with them. I only want the boy."

The one-thousand-pound monster reached out to the stone wall for support and climbed up from his bed of rotting pelts. The thought of killing humans and feasting on dragon meat, free to roam the earth again, caused him to pound his chest with excitement. But then he spied the elk, half-uneaten. "I need more food before I travel such a long distance." Not thinking he needed permission, he waddled toward the pile of rotting meat.

"Food!" bellowed the Dark Ruler. "Look at you. You have grown fat and lazy in your years of captivity. You can hardly stand without leaning against the walls. Get out of here! Get out before I change my mind! You can feed on the dragon once you capture the boy!"

Gregor's mouth curled in anger, exposing his black teeth. But even he knew better than to argue with the all-powerful monster of monsters. "No matter," he said, backing down. "There will be plenty to eat once I leave this prison."

The Ruler stepped aside as Gregor lumbered toward the opening. "The sooner you capture the boy, the faster you will be able to roam the Earth, free to eat as many humans as you like. Remember, if you don't do what I ask; if you dare harm that boy, I will seek you out and destroy you in the most painful way possible. And you know I can do it."

Gregor grunted as he very cautiously passed in front of the Dark Ruler and headed up the tunnel. He was glad to be free of his cell again and feared the Dark Ruler might still change his mind. Once outside, he turned back to the cave, and thinking the Dark Ruler could not hear him, roared, "You captured me once! That will not happen again!"

The Dark Ruler laughed at the beast's insolence, staring at the disgusting mess on the floor of Gregor's cell. The sight of the elk, its body was torn in half, made him wonder if he had made a mistake in sending the brutish, brainless, Gregor for the boy. I want him alive, the Dark Ruler thought, heading back to his throne room. "He must be alive, so he can suffer every terrible torment I have saved for him. Won't that be wonderful?"

Chapter 20

The white light from her helmet's LED lamp pierced the darkness. Mary was tiring after crawling down through limestone crevices into the deep tunnel. As the tube became smaller, she felt claustrophobic. The PVC over-suit she was wearing was moist from the sulfa-smelling water dripping down from the ceiling. Even her undergarments were soaked with sweat. She stopped to catch her breath.

Mary Wright, an archeologist, working on her Ph.D., had been selected to accompany several other researchers to search for relics, such as spear points, that were made by the Paleo Indians who lived in the Carlsbad Caverns in New Mexico, ten thousand years earlier. She and her group had been exploring one of the longest caves in the world for the past four days. Excited at finally being able to live her dream, Mary had climbed down to the deepest part of the system, 1,604 feet below the surface of the earth. She hadn't realized how tired she was. Even her padded knees and elbows were sore from crawling over the jagged rocks on the tunnel floor.

"Mary," Judy called from above. "It's time to head back. We must rejoin our group. It's enough."

"Alright," Mary responded, preparing to push her way back out of the tight tunnel. She turned her head and saw a dark form moving along the wall. "Judy, I think...I see something."

"What is it?" Judy asked.

Something moved again.

"Is someone else here?" Mary peered into the dark.

"None of our group," Judy replied. "You're just tired. Come up."

"Get away," Mary screamed, pulling back from the shadowy arms stretching toward her. "Help!" Her blood-curdling screams echoed from the tunnel into the chamber above.

Judy, terrified by the screams, hauled back on the safety line, fastened around Mary's waist. "Hold on! I'm pulling you up!"

"Help me," Mary cried out again. "Please, help me!" She felt bony fingers press down on her neck, cutting off her air. She tried to kick free, but the tunnel was too tight.

Hearing Mary struggle, Judy pulled harder on the safety line. "Hold on Mary!" She yelled for help as she struggled to remove her from the tunnel.

Tom, the team leader, had been studying the engravings on the limestone wall a level above Judy. He hurried down the tunnel to see what was wrong.

"Something's happening!" Judy shouted, struggling with the rope.

Tom grabbed the end and pulled hard with Judy. "What the hell happened?" he demanded, as he tried to get a good foothold.

"I don't know," Judy cried, almost out of breath. "All I heard was screaming."

They both kept pulling, but the rope didn't budge.

"She's stuck on something," Judy shouted.

"Pull harder," Tom replied.

Pulling as hard as they could on the safety line, they felt Mary freed from the narrow tunnel.

Two more researchers, hearing the commotion, raced down the shaft. What they saw when Mary was finally pulled from the tunnel and turned on her back caused them to gasp in horror. Mary was alive, but her face was pale white as if all the blood had been drained from it. Her eyes were staring blankly toward the cave ceiling.

"Is she okay?" Mike asked.

Someone else asked, "Is she alive?"

"Mary? Mary!" Judy shook her. "Mary, are you okay?"

Tom was doing CPR. "I don't know," he shouted.

Judy stared into Mary's face. "Come on, Mary! Come on!"

Tom jumped when Mary burst into terrifying screams, "Keep away! Get away from me! Help me!" She clawed at her neck as if trying to pry something from around her throat.

"What is she doing?" Judy shouted. "Mary! Mary!"

Tom was trying to grab her arms.

"Make him stop," Mary screamed, shaking her head hard, back and forth, as if trying to throw off hands pressing down on her throat.

"Make who stop?" Judy asked. "What's wrong with her?"

Tom slapped Mary across the face.

Mary's eyes closed. Her hands dropped to her side. Her screams became a stream of low moans and incoherent words.

"I didn't want to hit her." Tom leaned closer and heard Mary mumble, "Ghost... ghost. Make him leave me alone. Help me! For god's sake, help me!"

"Mike, get me the ground cover," Tom shouted. "I think she's going into shock."

Judy was staring into Mary's face. "She's terrified. Look at her face."

Tom rolled out the large cover. "She's delirious. We've got to get her out of here. Help me get her on this thing?"

Judy gazed back down into the tunnel where Mary had been. She thought she'd heard something moving in the darkness.

"Lift," Tom ordered, as they picked Mary up and placed her on the ground cover. "Guys, let's get her back to the upper chamber, collect the others and head for the surface," he said, as they lifted Mary and started to carry her out of the deep cavern.

Judy walked alongside the makeshift stretcher, holding Mary's hand. "I'm here, Mary," she whispered. "You're safe."

Another ranger, reached the cave as the others rushed out.

"Jim," Tom said, struggling with the others to carry Mary, "Check the bottom tunnel. That's where we found her looking like this. Judy said she was screaming as if terrified of something."

"Is she badly hurt?" Jim asked.

"No visible wounds," Tom replied. "She does look scared to death, though. Be careful down there. Something happened."

"Gotcha," Jim said, thinking it had to have been a rookie's accident. Damn rookies always do something dumb. He entered the cavern, eyes probing the dark tunnel from which they had extracted Mary. What could have spooked her like that? His flashlight scanned the narrow walls below. "I don't see a damn thing," he said, and moved back, eager to catch up to the others and find out what really happened.

As experienced as he was, Jim failed to see the brown, leathery, figure hiding in the shadows, watching hungrily as his would-be victim was carried away. Lurking in the darkness, he would have attacked this intruder too, but the male appeared overpowering, and his flashlight's beam was blinding. The girl was a far more vulnerable target than this burly man and his bright light. With the humans now together, the shadowy figure that had attacked Mary, a short time ago, slithered along the walls hoping for a new opportunity to retrieve his prey and finish her off.

The entrance to the cave was a long way from the depths they were in. The twisting passages might provide him another chance.

Jim felt strange. He whirled around and caught what looked like a shadow moving along the far wall. Jim shot his flashlight at it, but it was gone. "Must be my imagination," he muttered but felt a chill. He headed toward the upper chambers, carefully scanning ahead.

The creature stalked them silently, watching for any opportunity where they might separate, or become so exhausted they'd leave the wretched girl behind.

Much to his disappointment, the four humans, though obviously tired from their exertion, were refusing to put their heavy cargo down. He thought of lunging himself down at them in a surprise attack, but then they would know about him...others might find out. There were too many for him to finish them all off. If even one escaped...

When the small group finally put Mary down, near the cave opening, hours later, the Dark Ruler's slave glared at them with fury. "I curse you all for robbing me of my prey!"

Jim had nearly caught up when he thought he heard something scrambling past him on the rough walls. "I've been down here too long," he muttered, his heart beating fast and sweat dripping down his face.

The Guardian paused. He peered back at the small group. The Guardian smelled their sweat and knew they were exhausted. He waited, one last hope the humans would leave the wounded female behind.

Tom, sweat blurring his vision, almost lost his hold on Mary when he thought he heard something scrambling along the walls. He stared back into the dark abyss, feeling a terror he'd never felt before in his many trips to the most bottomless pits of the earth. "Are you trying to scare the hell out of me?" He yelled as Jim, badly shaken, emerged from the tunnel behind them. "You look like you saw a ghost," he said, laughing at having been startled by Jim's sudden appearance.

Jim looked behind him. "Maybe I did," he replied.

Chapter 21

The Seeker was unaware of the events that were unfolding in Mammoth Cave as he rushed to Emperor Ahuizotl's tomb in Mexico City. He believed this tomb was a logical hiding place for one of the Dark Ruler's Guardians.

As he drifted over the mountainous ridges, The Seeker saw a small group of people surrounding an outcrop of rocks and boulders. To the right of the stones was a large hole in the ground into which they were staring. He sensed something strange was happening, so he dropped down from the clouds and settled on the closest tree to see what he might learn.

"Do you think Mary will be alright?" The Seeker overheard a man dressed in yellow coverall's ask, as he closed the flap of a tent. I must ask Steven what this strange outfit is, he thought, recognizing the concerned tone in the man's voice.

"I don't know," responded a young woman dressed in a similar outfit. "They say she's in shock."

The man removed his helmet. "I haven't heard what the Park Rangers said about what caused the accident."

The girl took off her helmet and wiped the perspiration from her face with a towel. "The whole thing is weird. They phoned, but it was hard to hear. It sounded like they said the girl kept mumbling something about a ghost. Another student, Judy, stated that the young woman was screaming that she saw a shadow just before the attack."

"In the cave?" The man sighed. "It was probably some prankster from the group."

"Everyone swears it wasn't them. This Judy said it was something supernatural." The woman laughed.

"There are lots of legends about these caves."

"There are, but as far as paranormal beings being seen by any cavers, I have not come across that in my research."

"There is always a first time." the man replied, reread his notes. "At least three people said they spotted something moving down there."

The Seeker decided he'd heard enough. He floated down to one side of the open hole until he saw a second opening in the floor. If the creature the humans mentioned was one of the Dark Ruler's slaves, he had to find him. This could be the perfect location for them to set a trap for the Dark Ruler.

The Seeker floated past the entrance to the cavern, which was surrounded by several men and a woman in yellow suits. They all had powerful lamps attached to their helmets. They appeared as if they were getting ready to enter the cave.

"If there's someone down there, we'll find him," one shouted as he tested the rope that would bind the team together.

Alarmed for the safety of the humans, The Seeker attached himself to a flow of air being sucked down into the open pit. He wished the trip down into the dark cave would go faster, knowing the humans would be easy prey for a Guardian, who he suspected was their sinister 'ghost.'

As he traveled through the tunnels, The Seeker heard more humans on their way out of the cave.

The Seeker steered away from the noisy humans, knowing he had to find the Guardian before the humans placed themselves in terrible danger. He scanned the cracks along the walls looking for byways that ran more in-depth into the cave.

Suddenly, The Seeker stopped moving. He felt a strange, tingling sensation as he searched the cave wall. Wedged in a crevice above the approaching search party, The Seeker saw the Guardian. He noted the creature's long, bony arms and legs tightly wrapped in a thin coating of milky white skin. Strands of dirty white hair hung from the monster's skull to his hips. The pale white color of his flesh was excellent camouflage against the cave wall where he was perched observing the humans who would soon be in striking distance.

The Seeker remained hidden, following the shadowy creature as it trod the walls stealthily, above four unsuspecting cavers. Remembering he too had once been human and young, he swore he would not let them be hurt, even if it meant his own destruction.

The Guardian slithered among the rocks above the young cavers, the shadows concealing him.

Why does he not make his move? The Seeker asked, each second bringing him closer to attacking the virulent stalker and risking his demise.

The Guardian stopped moving. He stared down at the woman on the stretcher. Hunger was in his eyes.

The Seeker sensed the Guardian's bloodlust, his intent to kill the injured woman. He knew she would be dead if it had not been for the other Cavers surrounding her. They were at risk too.

The Guardian glared at the humans, thinking, it has been a long time since I felt a person trying to fight me off as I tighten my hands around their throat. *Oh, if these blasted humans had not interrupted my fun earlier.* He wiped his lips with his blackened tongue, remembering the Dark Ruler's command that no human must learn about him. Seeing the humans were not leaving, he cursed them and swore *there would be other victims soon. Shrinking* away from the cavers' bright lights, he reluctantly headed back toward the lower depths of the cave, grumbling that he easily could have defeated four of these 'fleas,' but couldn't risk being exposed by them and then facing the wrath of his powerful ruler.

The Seeker was relieved to see the creature slink away. He had not had to defend the humans at least for now. Fighting the demon in front of them would have allowed them to see him and make things even more difficult for him and Steven. He decided to follow the Guardian through the ancient twisting capillaries. He would add this location to the growing list on Steven's computer, one more hidden lair for his evil army.

The Seeker stopped moving.

The Guardian was hanging on to a cave wall concealed by a crystal stalagmite, staring back into the cave.

The Seeker wondered if the creature knew he was being followed.

The cavern was deadly quiet except for the occasional sound of dripping water. It could almost lull one to sleep. The Seeker saw red eyes aimed in his direction. The creature was searching for something. Was it him?

The Guardian wasn't moving.

The Seeker concentrated his mental abilities and allowed his spirit form to dissolve and then reform as a thin sheet of moisture draped over a large boulder on the floor of the cave. Camouflaged, he waited.

The Guardian searched the area one last time and then slipped into the tunnel heading deeper underground.

The Seeker waited until he felt confident the creature wasn't returning. He then attached himself to a breeze in the cave, and let it carry him to where he now suspected the Guardian was heading. If we are to attack this monster, we must find his lair and gauge his defenses, he thought, as he followed the Guardian's trail.

Soon the narrow tunnel opened into a more massive cavern with a pool of water in its center. The Seeker halted, seeing the Guardian stop and gaze behind him.

The Seeker was tempted to finish-off this Guardian but knew such an attack could be precisely what the Dark Ruler wanted, the spring to a devious trap. *No, I will not take the bait. I will not let myself be captured again.* As difficult as it was to resist destroying another of his enemy's vicious slaves, The Seeker was resigned to just spy on the evil creature, and then report back to the others so they could mount a concerted attack that would assure success. But he almost hoped the monster would see him...that would be excuse enough.

When the Guardian was satisfied he was not being followed, he proceeded to wade across the pool.

As he continued to follow the Guardian, The Seeker twisted his form between the massive stalagmites dotting the surface of the pool. Clinging to a stalactite, he watched the Guardian squeeze through a crevice in the opposite wall. The desire to fight and free the Guardian was strong, but The Seeker knew that without Steven, it was impossible. The prophecy made it clear it would take both of them to succeed. To try to do so now would alert the Dark Ruler. *I must wait for Steven.*

Moving quickly toward the crack into which the Guardian had disappeared, The Seeker passed through the opening and into a small limestone vault hidden behind the wall. Peering around the small area, The Seeker realized the crack was the only entry. *Excellent, he thought*, this is where we can trap this evil creature. I must fetch Steven.

Leaving the vault, The Seeker stopped for a moment, still tempted to go back and destroy the Guardian, fearful he might escape before Steven could be brought. The deep blackness of the cave started to close in on him. Looking up, he saw what looked like tiny white stars pressed against the ceiling. The crystal flakes reminded him of the millions of people on Earth who would be destroyed if the Dark Ruler succeeded in his evil plans. Steven was the only hope for all of them.

Chapter 22

As dusk descended across the green pastures in the lower valley, just ten miles north of the Mammoth Cave in Kentucky, Shu was settling down on a thick cloud. Moving in a northerly direction, he observed a large hairy creature trudging along a stream. Detaching himself from the cloud, Shu descended toward the tops of the tall Aspen trees skirting the stream.

The hair-covered creature had just emerged from behind a vast gray boulder and was wading through the running water when Shu drifted across his path.

Gregor stopped when he felt the wind ruffle his fur. He sniffed the air. Satisfied nothing was following him, he continued toward the other side where Shu now sat waiting.

Where did this creature come from? Shu wondered. Could he be another one of the Dark Ruler's minions?

Suddenly three black bats appeared and circled above the creature's head.

Shu shot directly over the repulsive-looking creature, afraid the bats could be spies and might spot him.

A Red Hawk screamed and leaped up from her nest, disturbed by Shu's sudden blast of wind.

Shu settled on a tree limb to get a better look at this alien creature and the bats that were following him. Increasingly, he was convinced that the Dark Lord had to have his hand in this strange match-up of bats and this ferocious monster.

Gregor was still searching for the source of the wind that had brushed past him. When he saw the bats, he reasoned, in his feeble brain that they were the ones responsible. He knew the Dark Ruler had sent them but were they here to protect or spy on him?

Shu was fascinated by the bats still circling over Gregor. It was such odd behavior. He lifted himself into the air for another look.

A low growl rose from Gregor's throat when he felt another breeze ruffling his fur. He searched the sky but could not see anything that could be an enemy. I don't like it here, he thought, and still wary, lumbered away.

He appears to be heading toward Mammoth cave, Shu thought. The bats seem to be leading the way. He followed, keeping a safe distance.

Gregor stopped abruptly. He'd heard a long high pitch howl from some-where along the riverbank. He gripped the wooden club in his right hand.

Shu stopped moving.

Gregor sniffed the air. He couldn't identify the pungent scent. His sensitive hearing picked up the running water of a nearby river. He stood motionless, trying to determine if the smell was the unseen enemy he sensed was following him.

Shu heard something moving, but couldn't see what it was.

Gregor tensed at another howling cry. He remembered the sound from long ago. It was the keening wail of a wolf. His mouth watered. Wolves were extremely dangerous but delicious. Was this a lone wolf in the night or a scout for a hunting pack? A lone wolf might be very tasty, he thought, drool dripping off his chin.

The answer to Gregor's question came when another howl echoed the first eerie cry. Then there were more cries. They sounded closer.

Gregor thought of fleeing from what he now believed was a pack of wolves but knew he could not outrun them if they were close. Instinctively, he sought anything nearby he might use to protect himself. Gregor decided to face them on a narrow sandbar in the middle of the stream. He would stand his ground right here, ready with his club.

Another howl, followed by another, echoed in the night.

Gregor grunted, his eyes searching in the direction of the last howl. There, he thought, as a pair of yellow eyes appeared behind a thick tree. He growled a low warning at the wolf now walking toward the riverbank to what he thought would be easy prey.

Gregor, having confronted wolves in the past, knew he was staring at a large male, most likely the leader of the pack. He turned and saw four more wolves staring at him with hunger in their eyes. He held up the club.

Shu, watching from a nearby tree, felt confident the lone creature couldn't defeat a pack of voracious wolves. They would give the beast the ending he deserved if he was a servant of the Dark Lord.

Gregor aimed his eyes at the male closest to him. He was the largest of the four wolves, and his eyes were aimed at Gregor's face.

The remaining wolves lined up behind their leader. They were waiting for his signal to attack.

The leader gave a low rumbling growl.

The other wolves lowered their heads, teeth bared.

Gregor braced himself with his club held high above his head and let out a terrifying roar.

The lead wolf snarled at Gregor, exposing his white canines. He snapped viciously at the air as saliva dripped from his mouth.

The attack was swift, the lead wolf charging full speed at his vulnerable prey. One bite of his powerful teeth and this creature—he thought another puny human— would be wolf food.

Gregor guessed the wolf would leap into the air aiming at his throat. The timing was critical. He had to kill the male with the first blow or the attack by teeth and claws, would make him an easy target for the others. Not taking his eyes off the leader, Gregor aimed his club.

The wolf let out a fierce roar and charged through the water.

The water provided just enough time. Gregor swung the club in a wide arc.

The wolf leaped into the air.

Gregor's club came smashing down on the head of the charging animal with all his strength. He felt the skull break under the impact. The force of a second blow threw the wolf high into the air and into the water yards away.

Gregor turned quickly, unable to savor his victory, expecting the other wolves to charge. He let out a challenging roar and swung the club repeatedly around his head.

The other wolves were standing midstride in the water. They yapped impatiently, confused, as their leader floated past, but did not move. They knew he was dead or dying. They weighed the risk of another attack.

Gregor roared again, smashing his club hard on the ground as he stepped off the sandbar and advanced toward the remaining wolves. "I am Gregor, the wolf-killer!" he shouted and smashed the club down hard again. Water splashed up around him as he attempted to scare them off.

The wolves stood their ground, staring and snarling at Gregor with hate. But they weren't attacking.

What are they waiting for, thought Gregor not taking his eyes off the eyes and bared teeth of the predators?

A twig snapped behind him.

Gregor froze.

Another wolf, having snuck behind him, launched himself at Gregor's back.

The force of the surprise attack almost knocked Gregor down into the water where the others were waiting. He screamed in pain and shock, caught off-guard by the massive wolf's ferocious charge. The fangs cut deep into Gregor's right shoulder, causing him to almost lose his club. He gripped it tighter and braced for another, even more, deadly attack.

The wolf, tasting victory, prepared for another charge. He roared a warning for the others to stay back. He was now the leader. This victim was his. He let out another chilling roar and threw himself at Gregor's bloody chest. One more bite of his fangs and the prey was his.

Gregor waited until just the right moment and swung the club down on the wolf's head, but the wolf bit into his shoulder and held on.

With a terrible scream of pain, Gregor grabbed the wolf's head and ripped the fangs from his flesh. He screeched in pain from the wound, but with his bare hands held the wolf, now thrashing wildly, around its throat. Gregor tightened his fingers, strangling it. He felt the creature stop struggling. Gregor shook the dying wolf and realized it could no longer hurt him. He tossed the barely breathing attacker at the feet of the others.

The wolves were stunned, unsure of what to do.

Gregor was not taking chances. He let out another roar and ran toward the pack before they could attack him. He swung at the nearest, knocking him down into the water. He then brought the club around in time to hit the second wolf in the head, bringing it to its knees. Even though he was exhausted, he prepared for another attack, when he saw the remaining two wolves back away.

"I am Gregor, the wolf-killer," he shouted, pounding his club in the water.

The wolves, their leader dead, his successor dead, let out a mournful wail and ran back into the forest.

Gregor, let out a loud cry of victory, but his shoulder throbbed painfully. He feared another attack if they sensed his weakness. He picked up the dead wolf and draped its furry body around his shoulders. Afraid another pack of wolves might appear, he forded the slow-moving river to the far bank. Once there, he sank onto the sand, exhausted from the fight and in terrible pain.

Shu had witnessed the whole thing. He had prayed the wolves would destroy Gregor. For a while, he had felt hope, but now knew it would have taken a much larger pack, a more organized attack, to defeat the mighty creature. Watching Gregor climb up on the opposite shore, Shu saw the black fur on his chest was matted with blood. He also saw fresh blood dripping from the large gash in Gregor's shoulder. That should slow him down, Shu reasoned, amazed the beast could still stand after such a ferocious attack and with such severe wounds. He truly is a formidable fighter.

Gregor leaned into the river to wash his wounds, his club at his side. The pain was excruciating, but he couldn't give in to it.

Shu, despite his disgust at the beast's smell and appearance, was impressed by his brute strength and fighting ability. He searched his memory. I have seen this beast before, Shu though. *But where?*

The creature picked himself up from the river and gazed defiantly into the forest. Gregor then picked up the dead wolf and threw it quickly over his shoulders. Exhausted and in pain, he knew he could not remain here. The wolves might come back at any moment, and he felt too weak to risk another attack. He was in agony but began to trudge toward the caverns where he knew he would be better able to defend himself if attacked.

Shu continued to track Gregor through the night.

As dawn approached, Gregor entered the Mammoth Cave, still accompanied by the three bats.

Shu moved cautiously to the dark entrance of the cave. He hesitated. This could be a trap. If the creature had sensed he was being followed, the entryway would be a perfect spot for an ambush. He decided to go back into the forest and find the airshaft he had discovered earlier. It would lead him down to where Gregor might have his lair. Inside the narrow shaft, Shu found a downward draft on which to hitch a ride. Unfortunately, the air currents were not reliable, so it took him a long while to drift down to the lower levels of the cavern.

Shu was so focused on locating Gregor's lair, he did not notice the coffin in the corner of a hidden chamber in the lowest level of the cave. He didn't know it was empty. He did not see the evil creature huddled up against the chamber wall, staring out into the night, waiting for his next defenseless victim.

Shu floated over a small stream that meandered into a subterranean lake. He stopped when he heard a noise.

Gregor was kneeling, drinking water from his palms. The blood from the gash on his shoulder dripped into the lake, but he kept drinking. Suddenly he pulled himself up. Someone was near.

Floating up to the calcite drapery formations above the pool, Shu saw the creature squeeze through a small crevice in the limestone wall.

Sailing toward the crevice, Shu glanced cautiously into the opening. He saw Gregor, spread across the ground, his eyes closed, snoring loudly. Blood still oozed from the ugly wound on his shoulder. I can finish him off now, Shu thought but realized if he failed Steven's life would be in danger. The Dark Ruler would know they were on his trail.

Satisfied there was no other exit, Shu left the cave. He settled in the limbs of a nearby Aspen, directly in front of the entrance. He would remain here to see if Gregor emerged.

Shu heard loud screeching. He looked up just in time to see hundreds of bats swarm around the entrance of the cave. *Where did they come from?* He asked, hiding among the leaves.

The horde of bats circled the cave entrance.

Shu was astonished by their sudden appearance. He was even more dismayed when the colony of bats, as if by a secret signal, abruptly flew into the cave. He had only seen such coordination in bats once before, and that was when he and The Seeker saw the army of bats leaving the Dark Ruler's mountain.

Just as he was about to leave, Shu's attention was drawn to the cave again. He saw three bats had returned to the mouth of the cave and were perched by the entrance, staring out across the valley. Could they be protecting that horrible creature? If they were, then Shu realized the Dark Ruler must have a particular use for the brutal monster. A chill ran through his soul when he guessed what that purpose might be.

Chapter 23

The Seeker floated through Steven's living room window, closely followed by Shu.

Shu had just concluded filling in The Seeker about the hairy beast he had tracked into the Mammoth Cave. Snaking their way through the house, they found Steven working in his parents' laboratory with Morag and Bastet resting nearby.

"Good morning Steven," The Seeker said after materializing.

Steven's ears popped as Shu flew into the lab and took human form.

"Welcome back. I missed you guys," Steven said, turning to the computer monitor, "I've been doing a lot of research on caves where the Guardians could be hidden."

"Is that what you are doing on your computer thing?" The Seeker asked. "I've never understood that strange contraption."

"Yes. I figured we'd need as much information as I can collect on the caves so we can plan our next move."

"Very wise," The Seeker said, staring at the picture on the monitor.

Steven nodded. "This is the second cave system you mentioned. I've been exploring the Mammoth Cavern in Kentucky." Steven hit a button, and the screen changed. "See this photo?" He pointed to the picture on the left of the screen. "I've downloaded the video to view parts of the 400 miles of caverns, tunnels, and passageways. Based on what I've seen, I believe I've found a spot away from the cave visitors, where I can open the Portal without being observed, and putting them in danger. We have to think about that before we do anything."

"Shu and I have explored the cave system and can tell you the best location to place the Portal," The Seeker replied telepathically.

"I was hoping you'd do that, but I still had to see for myself."

The Seeker and Shu watched in amazement as the vastness of the cave was displayed on a virtual tour. They grunted when they saw the miles and miles of interwoven lava tubes, mirrored pools, and other features. "We didn't realize it was this extensive," The Seeker said.

You were wise to research this, Shu agreed.

Steven was leaning into the screen. "Look at those limestone walls covered with sheet-like deposits of flowstone. It must have taken centuries of calcite deposits to collect from the flowing water over the rocks and form these." Steven pointed with his finger. "Look, at the ceilings. They're more than 40 feet above the cave floors," Steven said.

"*Morag, you will have little trouble in navigating this part of the system, whereas other parts...I don't know. They may be too tight for you at your full natural size. That could make you vulnerable if attacked at these narrow points. I wish I knew for sure.*"

Morag, resting on her stomach, opened her eyes upon hearing her name and yawned.

"Did I wake you?" Steven asked.

It was a long night tracking game. Morag yawned again, then placed her head back down and closed her eyes.

She's as much help, as usual, Bastet yowled. *All she thinks about is her stomach.*

"Steven, Shu and I have a lot to tell you," The Seeker said.

"Good. Aunt Celia is upstairs, in the kitchen, preparing lunch. Bastet, please go get her?"

"Must we?" The Seeker looked anxious.

"Yes. I will not do anything behind my aunt's back from now on."

"Very well. I guess we have no choice." The Seeker hoped Aunt Celia would be more reasonable, but still had his doubts.

Jumping to the floor, Bastet raced out of the cellar and up the flight of stairs that led into the kitchen. Once past the door, she leaped onto the counter. The smell of raw fish brought her to a standstill. She eyed the tuna stacks hungrily. Her tail and whiskers quivered in anticipation of a meal. "Purr," she said, hoping her imitation of a housecat might net her a fish.

"I love your antics Bastet, but you must wait for dinner, like the rest of us," Aunt Celia said, giving her a warm smile.

The Seeker and Shu have arrived and are waiting for you in the lab, Bastet said, still eyeing the fish.

"Oh, dear," Aunt Celia said. Dropping the paring knife, she followed Bastet down into the lab. She tipped her head at The Seeker and Shu and walked over to the empty black leather chair. Aunt Celia sat down, and, like a queen, waited for them to speak, arms already crossed and face stern.

Steven smiled. "Aunt Celia, I told my friends that from now on you would be told everything."

Aunt Celia frowned.

"Good afternoon Aunt Celia," The Seeker said, feeling a little anxious. "How are you—"

"Let's skip the small talk and get to what you want," Aunt Celia said.

"Am I that predictable?" The Seeker sighed. *Trouble already?*

"Let's say, Mr. Seeker, you have a track record, and I know this is not a social visit. You have taken your sweet time getting back here for someone who is concerned for my nephew's safety." She leaned forward as if confiding a secret. "We could have been in serious trouble, and you were nowhere around."

The Seeker wished the others would help. *"Yes, of course. You are correct. I am sorry for the delay, but I knew that you were not in immediate danger."* Difficult woman, The Seeker thought.

"You knew that, did you? Very well, then let's get started, shall we?" Aunt Celia wanted to be all business, impatient to hear what The Seeker and Shu were doing to protect Steven.

The Seeker sighed. "Shu and I have information about a new threat," he began.

Aunt Celia shook her head. "Exactly what are we now facing?"

Chapter 24

The Seeker smiled uncertainly. "Shu, my friend, please fill Steven and his aunt in?"

Shu cleared his throat. Flying across the desert had kicked sand into his lungs. *Steven has been studying the Mammoth caves in Kentucky on his machine. I have just left that location after discovering a powerful creature roaming the area–*

"Another creature?" Aunt Celia asked. Will this never end, she thought.

"What kind of creature?" Steven asked, worried his aunt was going to shut down their operation again.

"Shu will explain in time," The Seeker said.

"Explain now," Aunt Celia demanded.

"Let me cut to the chase then," said The Seeker. "Our friend here likes to stretch things out a bit." He gave Shu a friendly smile. "After Shu and I left here, we decided to visit several well-known locations to determine which one would best serve our purpose to trap a Guardian and force the Dark Ruler to leave the safety of his lair to investigate. We have all agreed that he is more vulnerable if we can lure him away from his home."

"That makes sense," Aunt Celia said, but did not look any happier.

"At any rate, as we approached the Mammoth cave, we saw crows feeding on some bats at the entrance," The Seeker continued.

"What do the crows eating bats have to do with a Guardian?" Aunt Celia muttered, disgusted at the image.

The Seeker smiled. "That is an excellent question. Normally I would have dismissed this attack by crows, but the bats we saw are not indigenous to the area. In fact, they are vampire bats. So naturally, we wondered if the Dark Ruler had sent the bats to watch for our arrival."

Aunt Celia looked puzzled. "Why would he do that?"

"The Dark Ruler would send such scouts either before his own trip to the cave, or, more likely to check on a location before he sends a new Guardian into hiding."

So, the bats could be a signal that the Dark Ruler, or a Guardian, is present, Shu added.

The Seeker nodded. "Shu and I agreed it would be to our advantage for one of us to remain behind and watch what might happen. Shu stayed while I continued on to the next location, the tomb of Emperor Ahuizotl in Mexico–"

Steven interrupted. "Another great location for the Dark Ruler to hide one of his Guardians, Aunt Celia."

"Exactly," said The Seeker, giving Steven an approving smile. "As I crossed into New Mexico, however, I observed some people standing around a large hole in the ground. They appeared to be very disturbed. I sensed something was terribly wrong. I guessed it could be related to our mission."

"Can you point to the location on the earth map?" asked Steven, opening the Web site.

"Yes. I believe I can," The Seeker replied, moving toward the computer for a closer look.

"You said New Mexico, correct?" Steven typed New Mexican Caves in the search box and selected the magnifier icon. Lists of caves were displayed in the upper left-hand column. Not knowing which one to choose, he highlighted Lechuguilla Cave in Carlsbad Caverns National Park as the most likely location. Steven double clicked the icon and waited for the system to zoom in on that area.

"That's the spot," The Seeker announced.

"Did you ever find out what was causing the disturbance?" Aunt Celia asked, studying the screen through her thick lenses.

The Seeker looked nervously at Steven.

"Tell her the truth," Steven said, aiming stern eyes at his friend.

"I was going to. Yes. I overheard that a young woman was hurt while exploring the caves."

Cavers are always getting hurt and lost in those twisted caverns, Bastet remarked. *You should see how many clumsy tourists get hurt in the Egyptian tombs! Unbelievable! Humans are so awkward. Not like us, four-legged gods.* She caught an irritated look from Steven and Aunt Celia. *Sorry, but it is true.* She leaped up to the counter. *See?* She jumped down again and then back up. *I can do it a million times and not get hurt. You try it once and see what happens.*

Aunt Celia looked hawk-like at The Seeker. "Was this caver seriously hurt? The truth? Remember?"

The Seeker sighed and said, "She was almost killed." He caught Aunt Celia's disapproving look. "But she wasn't. She's fine now. At least she appeared to be when I last checked."

Aunt Celia sat back in her chair. "I don't like this. No, Steven, I do not like this one bit!"

Steven didn't either. "You checked out exactly what happened to her?"

"Yes," The Seeker replied. "Call it a hunch, I decided to investigate the cave. It did not take me long to sense a Guardian was lurking inside."

"You didn't know in advance the Dark Ruler had placed a Guardian in this cave before you entered?" Aunt Celia asked.

"No. We still do not know everything the Dark Ruler is up to," The Seeker admitted. "But, with Steven's help, we're learning."

"I don't like this," Aunt Celia repeated, rising from her chair. "What you don't know could hurt Steven. It could get him killed."

The Seeker understood her concern but knew he had to convince her that Steven would be in greater danger if he did nothing. "I understand how you feel, but Shu and I think this new discovery will work to our advantage."

"How?" Aunt Celia asked, not at all convinced.

The Seeker gave Aunt Celia a smile that he hoped to show confidence. "As Steven knows, I was captured and imprisoned by the Dark Ruler."

"So, you know how dangerous this all is," Aunt Celia charged in.

The Seeker nodded. "Yes. But let me finish. The Dark Ruler loved forcing me to witness him hiding his slaves until his armies are ready. He was gloating at how his armies could never be stopped."

"And this is supposed to make me feel better?" Aunt Celia asked.

"I think you better get to the point," Steven said, not feeling better either.

The Seeker nodded. "The Dark Ruler does not suspect that I know these new hiding places since he created several of these after I was free."

Aunt Celia nodded slowly. "So, you think because he doesn't know you are aware of these new hiding places, he has no reason to send guards to protect them. Is that right?"

The Seeker smiled. "If I am correct, we can use this to our advantage because he will not suspect our attack at this cave. He will leave it unprotected."

"Sounds good to me," Steven said, relieved at this news.

"Not so fast. Shu, what about this creature you mentioned before?" Aunt Celia asked. "The big hairy one?"

What creature? Morag asked, just waking up.

"From Shu's description, I believe his name is Gregor," The Seeker said. "I heard the Dark Ruler mentioned his name many times while I was in captivity. If it is him, we must avoid this monster. For centuries, he has been missing. I'm guessing he was captured by the Dark Ruler and is now in his service." He glanced at Steven. "I don't think we need to worry about him."

"Why, not?" Aunt Celia asked. "Aren't they all monsters?"

"Yes, but there is no reason to get Steven involved with this Gregor right now," The Seeker said. "There are monsters, and there are monsters."

"I don't understand," Aunt Celia said, worried again about what Steven had gotten involved in.

I believe Shu interjected, *we should take this Gregor seriously. He is a real threat to anyone who comes too close to him. He is currently nursing his wounds in the Mammoth Cave, but once healed, could quickly become a danger to any humans who venture near him.* Shu aimed his eyes at The Seeker. *It is time to tell them what you know about this creature.*

Aunt Celia braced herself for more worries. She had never realized just how brave her nephew was but now understood he, and his friends, had been facing terrible danger. How could she let him continue knowing his life was in danger?

Chapter 25

The Seeker took a moment to think before stepping closer to Steven and his aunt. "Aunt Celia, after I was imprisoned in that awful transparent cube, I was forced to travel the earth watching the Dark Ruler collect and prepare the scum of mankind to become his slaves. You can't imagine how horrible it was."

Aunt Celia frowned. "Oh yes, I can, after all, you have told me. All the more reason I don't want Steven to—"

The Seeker interrupted, "Wait, please? One day the Dark Ruler summoned me to see his latest acquisition. I was told his servants had found a unique beast. He sent his most trusted slave, Drooling Slayer, to obtain this creature. I had never seen anything like it before. The beast, even weakened as it was, was terrifying in its brute strength. The Dark Ruler ordered it imprisoned behind unbreakable bars."

"And this is the creature you want Steven to confront?" Aunt Celia was growing more alarmed with each detail.

"Please, Aunt, let him continue?" Steven said.

"Yes, no. Please allow me to finish?" The Seeker said. "Once this creature was safely behind bars, the Dark Ruler had me dragged down to his horrible-smelling cell. He forced me to stare into the monster's hairy face and announced that this beast was Gregor, the spawn of the underworld. He then hissed that he was saving his 'prize' for a special occasion."

"If the Dark Ruler was saving him for so long, why release him now?" Steven asked, hoping not to hear what he suspected.

The Seeker hesitated. "I believe, Steven, he may be reacting to our freeing of his two Guardians. From what Shu has told me, I believe Gregor has been unleashed to capture you, Steven."

"Or kill him," Aunt Celia muttered.

"You don't have to worry. I faced The Dark Ruler's slaves before," Steven said, trying to hide his fear. "I have my good friends to help me."

Morag stood on her hind legs and spread her wings. *If this beast thinks he can kill Steven, then he must go through me; first,* she roared. *Besides, I have a score to settle with this Gregor beast.*

A loud roar erupted next to the computer table.

Aunt Celia whirled around in fear.

Bastet had transformed into a lioness. *I am a God, lest you all forgot. I shall sink my claws and fangs into the flesh of this beast. I'll rip him to pieces. I'll annihilate him! He'll be cat food when I'm through with him.*

"The five of us make a formidable team," Steven said, smiling at Bastet. "And don't forget the Amulet. I still don't know all the power of my father's gift." He held up the amulet hanging from a chain around his neck.

"Very nice Morag and Bastet, nice charm too. But I need a lot more convincing," Aunt Celia said.

The Seeker sighed. "Stubborn woman." He shook his head. "Morag, tell Steven what you know about Gregor. It is time."

The dragon let out a puff of purple smoke.

"Morag, you know this creature?" Steven was surprised but remembered something the dragon had said earlier when he had noticed her showing an angry side he hadn't seen before. "You said, you have a score to settle." He saw the dragon staring at The Seeker, smoke building up in her nostrils. "What were you talking about?"

Morag let out a small puff of smoke laced with tiny flames. *Excuse me,* she said, gas, and continued, *After I was born, my mother taught me the ways of a dragon, how to defend myself against man and beast, lessons she learned from her parents–*

Aunt Celia sighed, her patience growing thin. "Please, get to the point?"

"Shhh," Steven hissed. "I haven't heard this before."

Morag scowled at Aunt Celia. *One day, I asked my Mom about the scars on her stomach. Morag's face darkened. She told me she got them in battle...a battle with the beast you call, Gorgor.*

Gregor, not Gorgor, Shu corrected.

Whatever? Morag shook her head angrily. *He's a beast.*

Your mother fought Gregor? Shu asked. *I thought The Seeker and I were the only ones who knew of this monster before today.*

Morag let out an angry puff of smoke. *My mother came across this beast over a thousand years ago. She'd just hunted a mammoth and was feeding on the carcass, not bothering anyone, when this beast stepped out from behind the trees.*

That could give you indigestion, said Shu.

"Stop interrupting you guys. We need to hear this." Steven signaled Morag to continue.

This Gregor snuck up on her like a coward and tried to grab the mammoth from her, but she refused to surrender any part of her food.

"Good for her," Aunt Celia said, and blushed when she realized she sounded like a cheerleader.

Agreed, Morag replied. *The problem was, how do you fight such a beast?*

Didn't your mother breath fire like you? Bastet asked.

She did, but Mother knew that engulfing him with fire was out of the question because she was only in her third year, not old enough to produce enough flame.

So, what did she do? Shu asked. *I've seen that monster, and he is not easy to kill. A pack of wolves failed.*

Morag sighed. *As they stood glaring at each other, she said that without any warning, Gregor charged, slamming into her with such force she was lifted off the ground and thrown down on her back. She tried to*

stand, but he, being a bad sport, lunged at her again and sliced a large gash in her abdomen with his sharp claws.

I saw his long nails when he fought the wolves, said Shu. *They could gut a lion.*

Oh, thank you so much, Bastet grumbled. *Why does everyone pick on us cats?*

Morag continued. *After finally kicking the beast off her, Mom whipped her massive tail around and knocked him across the ground, where he lay stunned. Unfortunately, that didn't last. Gregor jumped up and wrapped his massive arms around her neck, trying to bite into her flesh. Mother said she reared back and shook him off again, hitting him with her tail. She leaped on top of the beast and clamped down on his shoulder, ripping and tearing at his flesh.*

"He didn't give up?" asked Aunt Celia, not believing any creature could fight a dragon.

Hardly. Mother said the fight wavered back and forth, neither able to inflict the killing blow. Growing weak from her wounds, mother finally had no choice but to abandon the carcass and fly away. She said that she never came across this creature again. Once was enough.

The Seeker held up his hand. "Enough stories! We all now know Gregor is a threat to Steven, and to all humanity. So, the question is where and when do we confront the beast?"

Steven sighed. "The real question is, how do we defeat such a vicious monster if even Morag's mother failed?"

"We?" Aunt Celia asked, looking uncertainly at the small crew.

"We," Steven repeated. "You are one of us now. Somehow we all need to find a way to end this reign of terror."

"We?" Aunt Celia shook her head. "We?"

Steven nodded, "It will take all of us for us to succeed."

The Seeker stared at Aunt Celia. How could this big, stubborn woman be anything but another obstacle toward completing their mission? He hoped Steven knew what he was doing.

Chapter 26

S teven and Aunt Celia sat in the living room after The Seeker and Shu
left, with Morag and Bastet listening close by.

"I don't like you getting involved in all this," Steven said, breaking
a long period of silence.

Aunt Celia was rocking in her chair. "I don't see any alternative. Attacking
Gregor by surprise allows us to eliminate him before he arrives at the burial
site of the Guardian which The Seeker is targeting. If that happened I can see
it will make things much worse for you." She looked hard at Steven. "I just
don't know if I want to let you do this still."

This will take a good while, Bastet commented to Morag.

"I don't have a choice, but you do," Steven said. "There is nothing about
my aunt in the prophecy."

Aunt Celia shook her head. "I'm the only person who can shoot Gregor
from a long distance."

"I know. But we haven't decided exactly where to trap Gregor, so you might
not have to shoot him at all."

"I hope so, but we need to be prepared." Aunt Celia sighed. "So, where do
you think will be the best place to trap our friend?"

Steven frowned. "From what I saw of the landscape, I'd pick New Mexico.
If we allow the bats to see us near the cave, they'll report back to the Ruler,
and he will send Gregor thinking we don't know about him. That's when we
zap him."

"What if the Ruler decides to keep Gregor up north and arrives at the cave
himself?" Aunt Celia asked, trying to tie up all loose ends.

"If that happens, then The Seeker, Shu and I will have our hands full." Steven thought hard. "You and Morag should use the Portal to get to Gregor's location and wait for him to leave the cave to feed. Then finish him off. If he has already left, heading to New Mexico, the two of you will have to track him and decide where to get him before he arrives at our location and we have him, The Dark Ruler, and the Guardian to fight at the same time."

"I see you have given this a lot of thought. I just hope we've thought of everything that can go wrong." Aunt Celia sat back in her chair. "And you know something always goes wrong."

"You're right. We need to be able to communicate. Aunt Celia you'll need to get a smartphone, and we'll modify the software to control the Portal too."

"Yes, I agree. I also think we should add new Apps, one to keep track of each other's location and the second to notify us when the Portal is open."

"I'll take care of that," Steven said. He looked over at Bastet and Morag. Bastet's eyes were closed. Morag was snoring loudly. "It's late. Let's stop for the night."

"We still have a lot to do," Aunt Celia said.

Steven let out a yawn. "Tomorrow morning, I will download all the maps we need. As they say in the movies, we need to find a kill zone and an LZ."

"LZ?" Aunt Celia asked.

"Landing Zone, a place for you to land the Portal."

"You have been watching too many war movies," Aunt Celia said, smiling.

"I've been in a war movie," Steven said with a bitter laugh.

"With any luck, it will be over soon," Aunt Celia said, rising from the rocker.

"I wish," Steven muttered as he headed for his room, Bastet and Morag close behind, always his protectors.

Chapter 27

Steven and his aunt sat in front of his father's monitor and measured the distance between the Mammoth Caves in Kentucky and Carlsbad Caverns in New Mexico.

"It's about 1,100 miles as the crow flies," Steven reported after stretching a line between the two yellow place markers.

Morag and Bastet waited impatiently for breakfast.

"It will give us time to prepare for our ambush."

"Sounds like a western movie," Steven remarked.

"Morag, will you have trouble tracking him through this rough terrain?" Aunt Celia asked. "Lots of mountains too."

Tracking him should not be a problem. You and I will stay well behind him.

"I studied the travel route we believe he will take. Look at the rough terrain and the deep gullies he has to cross. It will take him several days to cross this region." Steven pointed to the end of the red line. *"Luckily, this area isn't too populated."* He increased the magnification. *"I think this looks like a good spot."*

Aunt Celia nodded. "Did you check the weather in the area? That could be an essential factor.

"Yes. Good point. Temperatures average from 15 to 20 degrees above zero." Steven scowled. *"Snow has yet to fall, but it is expected soon and may last a long time."*

Aunt Celia shivered. "Morag do you see a problem with this location?"

You said it is mostly deserted, which is good, but if the weather turns foul, then we should consider a warmer location. It is challenging to fly in snow.

"We can move farther south and eliminate the cold weather entirely," Steven

said.

"That would restrict us to one possible location suitable for an ambush," Aunt Celia said. "Move the map left, toward the Carlsbad Caverns."

Steven studied the map. "The gorges and valleys will offer plenty of hiding places. We need to draw him out."

"What do you mean, Steven," Aunt Celia asked.

"The way I see it, you and Morag could be flying all over the mountains chasing this animal. Why not set a trap? Morag, you said your mother was attacked when she was feeding?"

Yes.

"Then maybe we can place some bait in Gregor's path. He will attack you as he did your mother. Except for this time, Aunt Celia will shoot him with a tranquilizer gun as he feeds."

"I like your idea, Steven," Aunt Celia said. "I'm glad you found some way other than killing him to neutralize him."

We have another problem, Morag said.

"What problem?" Steven asked, convinced they had come up with a foolproof plan.

Bats!

"What about bats?" Aunt Celia asked.

Didn't Shu say they were protecting the beast? How do we get past them?

"How do we eliminate them is the better question?" Steven asked.

Morag sighed. I will act as bait for the bats. If they are near him, I will lure them to me, and when they think they've found a free meal, I'll turn them into toast.

"That's too dangerous, Steven said. "What if they overpower you? We don't know how many there are. There could be millions."

Aunt Celia laughed. "Tiny bats overpowering this great specimen of a dragon? I don't think so."

Morag let out a puff of smoke. *No bats can defeat me. Have you touched my body armor lately?*

Steven frowned. "Ok. I guess if it's an emergency, we can go with that. I'll contact The Seeker and let him know we are ready to proceed. I only hope we don't have to use you as bait."

* * *

At midnight the following Saturday, Aunt Celia and Steven were ready to test the two modified phones and the Portal.

"Bastet and I will transport next to Simmons Pond in Little Compton after you arrive at your destination," Steven said.

"Are you sure it's safe?" Aunt Celia asked.

Steven nodded but knew nothing was one hundred percent safe. "Okay. That should be far enough to test everything."

Steven handed her the other phone. "You and Morag will take the Portal to the Norman Bird Sanctuary and text me when you arrive."

Aunt Celia looked nervously at the phone.

"Call me if there is a problem," Steven said.

"There won't be." Still thinking she was crazy to do this, Aunt Celia opened the Portal and stepped through followed by Morag.

The Portal closed.

Steven stared at where it had just been, waiting anxiously.

"The view is superb," Aunt Celia texted. "You should hear the chorus of bullfrogs."

Steven texted back and informed his aunt he was porting to Simmons Pond. He pressed the Portal button on the phone, and the swirling lights appeared. "Here we go," he said and stepped inside.

Steven no longer minded the tossing and turning he felt in the Portal, but was relieved when it landed. He sent a note immediately upon his arrival. "I can also read your current location," he typed.

"As I yours," Aunt Celia responded and added, "You're a genius."

"Lock the Portal."

Aunt Celia waited for the flashing alert sign and the iPhone to vibrate. She selected the App to open the Portal and received a warning message. She texted a message informing Steven that the lockout worked flawlessly.

"Transport to my location," Aunt Celia typed.

Steven copied the coordinates, removed the Portal Lock, and pressed the enter button on the phone. Within seconds the Portal opened, and he and

Bastet stepped through. "Mission accomplished. Let's return to the lab and get to the real work ahead of us."

"Don't you think we should test this Portal thing again?" Aunt Celia said.

"You saw it worked perfectly," Steven replied, smiling at this aunt. "What can go wrong?"

Chapter 28

Gregor *has been in Mammoth cave for over two days. The only time he leaves is to forage for food,* Shu reported.

"That is good. We must keep the Ruler focused on this cave for the time being," The Seeker said, deep in thought. "Until we are ready to set the trap, the Ruler must think he has the upper hand. A report that a boy has visited the cave will keep him centered on this cave while we get ready to attack the other."

How can we do that without endangering Steven? Shu asked.

"You will check Gregor's precise location in the cavern before Steven's arrival. Once we know where the beast is, Steven can enter one of the other caverns with the Portal. The cave system is several hundred miles long. He'll be far away from danger."

Shu still wasn't sure. *If he's far away from Gregor, how will The Dark Ruler know Steven was there at all?*

"We will have Steven open the Portal away from Gregor's location to keep him safe. He will establish a campsite making it appear as if he is still there exploring the cave. He will leave candy wrappers, a hat, scraps of paper, and other items, as evidence he is returning to the site. He will then portal near the entrance and allow the bats to spot him–"

But the bats may attack him, Shu said.

"I don't believe they will. Once the bats see Steven, they'll race back to Gregor who will send a messenger to the Ruler. My hope is he will leave his den to search for Steven, who by that time, will be safe in his house."

It's a complicated plan, Shu said.

The Seeker nodded. "It's the best way to keep the Dark Ruler focused on this cave."

I hope you are right. I will track Gregor's movements and wait for you to return, Shu said.

"Excellent!" The Seeker said. "With any luck at all, Steven's problems should be over soon. Now let's return to Steven's home and hope his aunt is less obstinate. She's a charming lady, but..."

Chapter 29

"I hoped I wouldn't see you again," Aunt Celia said when The Seeker entered the lab.

The Seeker scowled. "I too wish this wasn't necessary." He directed his eyes at Steven. "Shu has confirmed that the Guardian and Gregor are resting in their cells, both in the Mammoth cave."

They're both there? Bastet said. *Double trouble.*

The Seeker nodded. "We have a plan. Steven, after you establish your campsite, you must portal to the entrance closest to the sleeping Guardian."

"That's your plan? I don't like it already," Aunt Celia grumbled.

"Patience, dear lady. Shu will help alert the bats of Steven's presence."

"You want the bats to know he's near?" Aunt Celia looked ready to attack.

"It will be fine. As soon as the bats spot him, he will portal home, to safety. We will take it from there." The Seeker looked at Aunt Celia for her approval.

Aunt Celia was frowning.

"I'm not going to be there for long," Steven said.

Aunt Celia sighed. "This better work. I want to know all the details before I agree to this."

Steven nodded. "I'll set up the Portal and we'll be ready to go."

"Maybe," Aunt Celia said, glaring at The Seeker.

Steven confirmed the correct coordinates were entered in his Phone before pressing the button. "Here, we go," he said. "Don't worry. I'll be fine."

"You'd better be." Aunt Celia watched glumly as Steven and Bastet entered the Portal.

As the Portal opened and Steven entered the cavern, he thought he heard water flowing from somewhere behind him. "Where's the water coming from?" he asked, suddenly standing knee-deep in water. .

Bastet screamed and reverted to human form. *Cats hate water,* she complained.

The water level was rising. Steven had to act quickly. He glanced at the phone to verify the coordinates.

Steven, where are you? Shu shouted, releasing a blast of wind which accidentally knocked Steven's phone into the water.

"No," Steven shouted, plunging his hand into the water and grabbing the phone. One look at the faceplate and Steven realized the phone was no longer working. Panic gripped him. "We've got to get out of here," he shouted to Bastet.

Aunt Celia, seated in the lab, heard the phone link go dead. "Steven's in trouble." She pushed her control button on the phone. "This better work." She pushed it again.

The Portal opened, and water rushed into the lab.

Aunt Celia, forgetting her own safety, charged through the Portal and into the cavern. Water sloshed all around her, as she pushed her way forward in the cavern trying to locate her nephew. "Steven?" She held the wall praying to find him. Water was pushing against her.

Suddenly, she saw Steven. He was slouched against the wall, arm wrapped around Bastet, now in the form of a lioness. His head was barely above water.

Fighting the rushing stream, Celia grabbed Steven's arm and pulled him up. "Come on!" she shouted over the roar. Almost lifeless, she pulled him back into the Portal.

Shu and Bastet followed Celia inside.

Once she saw they were all safe inside, Aunt Celia pushed the button on her phone to close the Portal. She then sagged to the floor, holding Steven against her. "Are you alright?" She shook him gently.

Steven opened his mouth, and a stream of water exploded from his lips. He nodded his head.

Bastet stood next to Aunt Celia and Steven in a foot of water. Once she saw Steven was all right, she jumped onto the computer table and shook the water off her fur.

"Hey, enough with the water. We don't need another shower," Aunt Celia said, shielding her face.

Did you all go for a swim, asked Morag covering her head with her wing.

Yes, it seemed like a good idea at the time, Shu replied blowing a stream of air at Bastet to help her dry off.

Hey watch it, Bastet screamed sliding across the table.

Steven was surprised to see Aunt Celia holding him. Pushing himself off the floor, he found himself standing in ankle deep water. He breathed a sigh of relief that he was okay but stared in disgust at his muddy boots. "Thank you," he said. "You saved my life."

Aunt Celia looked at the floor. "And you messed up my floor." She laughed. "But I don't care as long as you're okay."

Steven heard the slurping noise as the sub-pump running in the far corner of the lab was sucking out the water.

"Thank God your father installed the pump, or we would be carrying buckets of water upstairs and through my clean kitchen," Aunt Celia said. "Now, that would be an unholy mess."

"Do you know what happened?" Steven asked grabbing a towel from the hanger above the sink and wiping his face and hair.

Aunt Celia shrugged. "It just shows how well-laid plans can go south in a hurry. The Portal must have landed in a waterfall we didn't know existed in the cave."

Steven smiled. "If it wasn't for you and Bastet, I might have drowned. She helped me keep my head above the water."

"Remember that the next time you think I don't care about, or seem too worried, about you," Aunt Celia said and gave him a warm smile.

Steven knew she cared. The problem was he cared about her too. So how could he let her risk her life when she wasn't included in the prophecy?

Steven dry me off, Bastet said, reverting to her normal size. *I'm a Goddess, remember?*

Steven looked at Bastet and burst into laughter. He grabbed a towel from the rack and walked back to the computer table. Even though he was exhausted, he was glad he was still around to take care of his friend the way she had taken care of him. He hoped she would always be there if he got in trouble.

* * *

The Seeker and Shu saw a bat drop from a stalactite in the Mammoth Cave and head down the long narrow cavern. They followed at a safe distance.

The bat disappeared into a narrow shaft.

The Seeker waited to be sure he wouldn't be detected. He heard water cascading down the limestone walls. "Where did all this water come from?" he asked.

I am responsible, Shu said. *I unleashed a storm two days ago to nourish the arid land for the Native Americans that live here. It appears I dumped more water then I realized.*

"We nearly had a catastrophe. If Steven had entered minutes later, he might have drowned. As it turned out we were able to flush out a sentry posted deeper in the cave," The Seeker said.

Shu blew a sigh of relief.

"Silence, Shu. The bats will hear you."

The Seeker froze as a bat emerged from the narrow shaft.

A loud grunt and Gregor squeezed his body out of his hiding place. Picking himself up, he stretched his back, aching from being crunched in the passageway and then followed the bat.

"You flooding the cave may have forced the monster from his lair. Let's follow and see if we can discover his hiding place. That will be a big help to Steven,"

The Seeker and Shu followed a short distance behind as Gregor forced his way against the rising water in the flooded tunnels and subterranean caverns. He was becoming exhausted as he pushed his massive body against the torrent of water. He lashed out at stalactites hanging in his path as his temper flared.

The bat squealed angrily for him to follow and stop making so much noise.

Gregor felt like pounding the small spy's head with his club but pushed

123

against the surging water until he finally reached a dry ridge. Leaning on the cave wall, he took a deep breath. "Someone was here," he said seeing the camp site Steven left and the discarded paper wrappers and hat.

Gregor picked up the hat and sniffed the rim as if he was a giant dog. He searched the cavern. "His scent is strong," he grunted, and threw himself back into the water where he spotted an opening on the other side of the chamber.

The Seeker and Shu heard a savage roar thunder off the walls of the cavern.

"He has quite a temper," The Seeker said.

We might be able to use his temper to our advantage, Shu replied.

The Seeker was listening to the sound of wings and squeals coming from somewhere in the cavern. "More bats are entering the cavern," he said, a worried look on his face.

They are going to present more problems for Steven, Shu said. *These sly little lookouts have been placed throughout the system.*

The Seeker nodded. "We must search the caverns before Steven again enters to determine where sentinels have been posted. We can't risk him being spotted before he can escape."

What of the monster? Shu asked.

"You follow him while I check the sentinels."

Shu drifted along the tunnel and stopped when he heard a roar just ahead. It was Gregor.

Gregor was splashing up and down the cavern searching for the intruder. He pointed to the opening and commanded the bat, "Report back to me when you are satisfied that no human is within." He then headed into the thick darkness. If a human was near, he would make him sorry for entering his realm.

The Seeker and Shu watched the bats and Gregor disappear into the tunnels.

Once certain Gregor was out of range, The Seeker said, "You remain and notify me if the Ruler appears. I will return to the lab and tell Steven and his aunt that Gregor and the bats reacted the way we anticipated. This proves our plan will work." At least, it worked this time, he thought.

Chapter 30

Steven, wearing dry clothes, returned to the lab and saw Aunt Celia sitting next to the computer table. She looked worried and he didn't blame her one bit. "That was close," Steven exclaimed.

"I dare not think what would have happened if the Mammoth cave had been entirely flooded," Aunt Celia said.

"It was a fluke," Steven said. "An accident. It will never happen again."

Aunt Celia nodded. "But Steven, we must take measures to ensure nothing else goes wrong. We must be prepared–"

"Speaking of being prepared, I forgot to mention the other day to ask you to purchase red flares. I had to carry a flare gun to defend myself and ran out of them."

"You carried a gun on your last trip?"

Steven realized he shouldn't have mentioned guns, not even flare guns. "Flares would have given me light if I needed it and they would have been useful in fighting off the leopards."

"Leopards? Did you say leopards?"

Steven knew he'd done it again. "I was joking," he said and let out a laugh.

Aunt Celia frowned. "I'll bet." She bit her lip. "When I go out shopping again, I will pick up flares." She shook her head. "I guess I like the idea of you carrying a flare gun better than a real one. I'll also purchase extra battery packs for our helmet lights and smart phones. Leopard indeed."

"Good thinking," Steven said. "You're good at this. I think you're even beginning to enjoy being on our team."

Aunt Celia frowned again. "Don't fool yourself. I am still unhappy at the possibility of you getting hurt or killed but at the same time, energized at working with you and the others." She glanced at Bastet. "Anyone hungry?" As she headed for the lab door, she paused and said, "The only reason I am doing all this is to keep my promise to your parents. I swore I'd protect you and that is what I will do. Now, let's eat."

Race ya, Bastet shouted, leaping off the table and charging out of the room.

Morag unfurled her wings and sailed into the kitchen, landing on the countertop.

Steven closed the door to the laboratory and headed upstairs. "I wonder when The Seeker and Shu will return? I hope they're safe.

* * *

"Good morning Steven," The Seeker said, looking kindly at Steven lying in his bed.

Steven jumped up. "You startled me. How did you get into my room? Oh, I forgot, you can go through walls, windows, doors, whatever."

"I waited for you and Shu last night, but I had to turn in after the soaking I got yesterday in the Mammoth Cave."

The Seeker nodded.

Steven searched the room. "Where is Shu?"

"I left him at the Mammoth Cave to keep an eye on Gregor. Is your aunt up? I hope not." The Seeker looked nervously at the door. "She is charming, of course, but a bit difficult."

Yes, she is, meowed Bastet licking her paw and wiping her mouth.

"She's been doing a great job helping me," Steven replied, "Now that she realizes that it's more dangerous to do nothing than to try and stop the Dark Ruler before his army gets too strong."

The Seeker sighed. "Very well. Let's all go and have a word shall we?"

They found Aunt Celia in the kitchen already preparing breakfast.

"Good morning Steven...and Seeker," said Aunt Celia holding a spatula in her right hand.

Steven wondered if she planned on using the spatula as a weapon on The

Seeker.

"Would you like some coffee?" Aunt Celia asked The Seeker.

"I wish I could?" The Seeker said. "Unfortunately, I can no longer take pleasure in food and drink."

Celia nodded her head, sympathetically. "Please, sit down. We can talk over breakfast."

As they all sat around the table, Steven whispered, "when do we return to the Mammoth cave to free the Guardian?"

"Go back?" Aunt Celia muttered.

Steven shot The Seeker an apologetic look.

"We'll discuss that later." Aunt Celia served Steven his breakfast and then helped herself to a cup of coffee. She was deep in thought. "I reluctantly, very reluctantly accept that Steven has to help you free the Guardian but using him as bait is too dangerous. I just don't know if I can allow that."

The Seeker tried to remain calm. "I understand you care for Steven very much. We do as well. To assure his safety, Shu will continue to monitor Gregor's movements. We feel the Dark Ruler has become more aggressive in hunting for Steven, but we are overseeing all threats."

"But you still need Steven to free the Guardian? Is that right?"

"Sadly, yes. That is the prophecy."

"And does this prophecy of yours show he will not die?"

"I cannot lie. Sadly, no."

Aunt Celia sighed. "Well, at least you're honest."

"I am also honest when I say if he does nothing, he will be in even greater danger."

"I'm beginning to see that," Aunt Celia muttered.

Chapter 31

The Ruler hated terrible news. He listened to the report from his new servant, Beshena, the leader of the Kentucky bats, his anger growing with each butchered word.

"What did you say?" he demanded.

"Cro atack," Beshena squealed.

"Crows Attack? Where?"

"Ma-moth cave."

"Mammoth Cave?" The Dark Ruler leaned forward, a tic visible in his jaw.

Beshena nodded, ready to fly if things got out of hand.

The Ruler stood, startling the gargoyles, resting on their front paws on either side of his throne. They growled at being disturbed from their rest.

"Quiet," The Ruler roared.

The gargoyles looked frightened and dropped to the floor.

The Dark Ruler turned to the bat and smiled toothily. "Return to the cave and don't leave this time. I need you there to report to me any sighting of that troublesome boy."

As Beshena lifted off the floor, another Kentucky bat sailed into the den. "Boy seen," the bat cried shrilly.

The Dark Ruler groaned. "You too? When?"

"Lst nigh," the bat replied.

"You saw the boy last night?"

"Yth, Drkness," the bat said.

The Dark Ruler let out a terrible roar. "Must I do everything myself? Wings of Fire, rise up!" he shouted, raising his arms toward the ceiling.

A large orange ball of flame rose slowly from the lava pit in front of his throne.

"I'll take care of this boy myself," The Ruler shouted and stepped into the ball of lava.

* * *

An explosion from the molten lava ball landing in a pool of water rocked the cave and sent Gregor searching for cover. Scalding steam raced through the passageways.

As the steam vaporized, Gregor emerged from where he'd hidden, pushing his obese torso through the opening of the chamber. He stared at the giant ball.

"Where is the boy?" the Ruler bellowed, leaping from the lava ball.

Surprised to see his cruel master, Gregor cowered against the cave wall. "Boy not found. Water fills the cave. Bats not find boy."

The Ruler's anger boiled. "Are you telling me, you do not have the boy as your prisoner?"

"No," growled the beast.

The Dark Ruler shook his head hard. "Wait! No, you are not telling me, or, no, you do not have the boy?"

Gregor was confused. "Yes, I no have boy."

"But he was here?" The Dark Ruler was fighting to keep a smile on his face when his fury was building to an explosion.

Gregor shrugged. "No."

"You said, no?"

Gregor smiled. "No, boy."

The Dark Ruler's smile now looked ugly. "Then what am I doing here?" he asked, letting his long claws show. "Why did you send for me when the boy is not in your grasp?"

Gregor shrugged again.

That was all the Ruler needed. The roar and explosion from his eyes made Gregor run back into the crevasse in which he had hidden earlier.

After ten minutes of this temper tantrum, the Ruler calmed down. "Get back here," he said to Gregor, who immediately obeyed. "You will remain here until that boy is caught or I grant you permission to leave. Is that clear, you big, ugly lump of hair?"

Gregor was furious but knew he had to obey. He nodded.

Turning to the bat hanging from the ceiling, to remain out of the Ruler's reach, The Ruler gritted his teeth and commanded, "You will post new, better, sentries throughout the cave. I want the entire system searched again to make sure that the boy is not hiding in one of the tunnels. Gregor, come and show me where he was discovered."

Grudgingly Gregor trudged down the tunnel, followed by the Ruler. Neither one uttered a word as they searched the tunnels and caverns on their way to the location where Steven had been seen.

Shu followed the two at a safe distance.

Gregor stopped walking upon arriving at the spot where the bats had seen Steven. "The boy camped here. Leave hat and papers."

The Ruler floated around the scene, examining the evidence. He inhaled deeply.

"No scent now," Gregor growled.

The Ruler glanced at him and then resumed searching around the stalagmites. As he moved around, he saw several footprints. "Here! He stood here," he said, pointing down to the footprints. "The water has removed all other prints," the Ruler mumbled. "He will return. I know that boy and he will be back." He eyed Gregor sternly. "Go back to your den and wait for the bats to alert you when the boy returns. This time, I want no mistakes, no excuses."

Gregor nodded.

The Dark Ruler raised his arm, and the pool bubbled violently as a massive ball of fire erupted from its depths. Steam from the boiling groundwater filled the cavern, sending bats flying away before they were consumed by flame.

Gregor tried backing away, but his fur was charred by the hot flames.

The Ruler laughed at the beast's clumsiness and then was consumed by the red burning ball.

Gregor screamed from the scalding water on his skin, the blame even burning through the leather tunic on his chest. He glared at the spot where the Ruler had just stood. "Someday, I'll show him who the boss is," he roared, and still in pain, trudged back into his cave.

Shu noting where the sentries were hidden left the cave and headed north. The sight of the Dark Ruler had unnerved her. She wondered if they really could defeat such a powerful monster.

Chapter 32

The predawn air was cold as Morag skimmed above the trees. The patches of ground fog covering the field made it difficult to locate the buck she had spotted earlier. She reverted to her smaller size and dove into the forest in search of another meal. As she headed north, she saw thick clouds building on the horizon. *I'll move into the foul weather where it is less likely that humans will see me.*

Morag's physical powers were becoming stronger each day, allowing her to travel longer distances from her new home. She had spent long hours in the sky foraging the northern country in Canada. Her dark-colored scales protected her from the bitter cold and winter winds in the north.

There, Morag thought, veering to the left.

Just ahead, in an open field, stood a deer scraping the snow in search of grass.

Morag circled the area, alert for heat sources from humans. *No sign of them,* she thought and reverted to her larger size. Once fully enlarged, she dove for the prey. Talons extended, she swooped down, grabbed the deer, and lifted it into the sky. Effortlessly, she headed for a ravine. Dropping to the ground, Morag soon consumed her meal.

Her hunger satisfied; Morag looked up the valley. The smell of rain filled her nostrils. She decided to search for a cave to rest during the approaching storm. Leaping into the black night sky, she turned west and flew toward the mountain range. She knew this might be the last hunt for her, but was willing to sacrifice herself to repay Steven's kindness.

Hours later, Morag landed behind Steven's back porch. *I have returned!* She announced telepathically.

"Good morning Morag," Aunt Celia said, opening the back door and standing aside to let the miniaturized dragon enter the kitchen. She remembered too well how the dragon had wrecked it earlier, but with everything replaced, she no longer felt angry. In fact, she was growing fond of the house wrecker. "Was your hunt successful?" Aunt Celia asked.

The north is full of food although the winter storms are building and soon I will be unable to travel there to feed. Morag didn't want to let Aunt Celia know that she was afraid this might be her last hunt. *The old lady has enough to worry about,* she thought.

"We will find a new source of food for you when the winter shuts down your feeding grounds," Aunt Celia said. "Why don't you go wake Steven and Bastet. Tell them breakfast is ready."

Morag leaped off the floor and flew up to Steven's room. She landed with a thump on his bed. *Breakfast is being served,* she announced. Launching off the bed, she returned to the kitchen.

"You're not getting all my food." Bastet raced after her.

"Morning Aunt Celia," Steven said as he walked over to the kitchen table.

Bastet sat next to Morag chewing on a sliver of ham while watching Morag with a wary eye.

As Aunt Celia settled in her chair, Steven felt a slight breeze across his face. "Shu, are you back?"

The pages of the morning paper fluttered on the table.

"Not again." Aunt Celia grabbed the papers before they were blown all over the room.

Has The Seeker arrived? Shu asked, giving Aunt Celia an apologetic look.

"We haven't seen him," Steven said, biting off a slice of crispy bacon.

"Hold your napkin down," Aunt Celia warned, giving Shu an annoyed look.

I will wait in the lab where I am less likely to rearrange the room, Shu said and flew down the stairs.

"Well, she does make a mess," Aunt Celia said.

Finishing their breakfast, the team headed for the laboratory. Steven saw The Seeker had arrived and was engaged in a conversation with Shu.

"Come in, Steven. Welcome, Aunt Celia," The Seeker said.

Steven and Aunt Celia walked over and sat down on the leather chairs by the computer table while Bastet and Morag jumped up on the table.

Steven asked, "What's up?"

The Seeker replied, "The sky." He looked confused.

Aunt Celia stepped in. "He means what is going on?"

The Seeker chuckled but seeing the serious expression on Celia's face got serious too. "As we expected, the Ruler arrived at the Mammoth cave after the bats spotted Steven. His minions found your camp site and the article's you left. He also found your footprints."

I heard The Ruler command the bats to disperse throughout the cave and wait for your return, Shu said, letting out a puff of air.

The Seeker paced the floor. "We have to speed things up. The Dark Ruler suspects too much already. We must get Gregor out of the cave so we can free the Guardian without risk to Steven."

Aunt Celia smiled, leaning forward in her seat. "I have an idea. If the bats see me shoot Gregor, they will report that a hunter trapped his servant, not a boy. Steven will appear not to be involved."

"Yes," The Seeker said. "We can make it look as if the hunters got him."

Steven sat back in his leather seat. "I think this could work," he said.

"Morag, I want you to go with Shu and watch Gregor when he hunts. Search for the best place Aunt Celia can hide along his trail," The Seeker said. "Watch out for the bats."

"Things are looking up," Steven said, glancing at his aunt.

"If nothing goes wrong," she muttered.

Chapter 33

S teven opened Google Earth and selected Mammoth Cave. "I measure about one mile between the dense forest and the mouth of the cave and approximately six miles to the nearest populated area. The cave entrance, parking lot and buildings sit in the center of the park grounds. There is also a winding river to the west."

"Surely the monster does not leave the cave during the day?" Aunt Celia said.

"It would make our job easier if he did. We will open the Portal here once we determine Gregor's hunting pattern. That will place you about five miles from the cave entrance." Steven turned to Morag. "Morag, in addition to watching Gregor, keep a lookout for park rangers. I don't see any campsites in the area, so you should not have to worry about campers. Remain as small as much as possible."

Bastet hissed, *The forest should be loaded with animals to even satisfy your appetite.*

I will do just fine, Morag replied.

Steven looked at Bastet. "Bastet, stay in the forest and get ready to help Morag in case there is trouble," he said, hoping he hadn't left anything out.

We will be alright, Bastet said. You humans worry too much. But she was worried also.

Steven turned to his aunt. "I will place you here. If you need to return home just open the Portal. Have I forgotten anything, Aunt Celia?"

"Not that I can think of," Aunt Celia replied, still wondering if this whole thing was a huge mistake.

* * *

At noon the following day, The Seeker watched as Aunt Celia, Bastet, Morag, and Steven entered the Portal. Steven had entered the agreed location, a wooded area north of the cavern entrance.

"Just as you planned it," Aunt Celia said, stepping from the Portal.

Steven inhaled. The smell of wet leaves and decay hung in the still air. The forest was oddly quiet.

"There is an outcrop of rocks just beyond the trees to our left," Steven said. "A mile beyond is the winding river I mentioned earlier. From what I observed on the map, there is a small island at the northern end of the river. The water appears to be shallower there. I believe this is where Gregor crosses when he searches for food."

Aunt Celia felt the wind pick up and peered warily at the forest.

"Here comes Shu," Steven said.

Aunt Celia was relieved. She hated breezes that came from nowhere. "Anything to report, Shu?" Aunt Celia asked.

Gregor will most likely hunt tonight. Each time he leaves the cave he heads west, across the river and then north on a trail that he is familiar with.

"Since you can't be sure of where he will go, I, *Bastet and Morag, will wait here until you contact us and provide us his location,"* Aunt Celia said.

"Does he usually return to the cave before morning?" Steven asked.

Always, Shu replied.

"Good. I will return to the lab for now and check out a few things. Let me know if Gregor does go out tonight," Steven said. "I don't want to take any chances."

"We will be fine. You don't need to worry about us," Aunt Celia said, but was still very afraid of what was about to happen.

Steven pulled his smart phone from his pocket and pressed the lab App. "Good hunting," said Steven as he entered the Portal. The forest fell quiet as a whooshing sound was emitted when the Portal collapsed.

Aunt Celia picked up her backpack and moved deeper into the forest in search of a place to set up a temporary campsite. Bastet and Morag followed.

All waited for Shu to return before starting their search.

Steven wished he had kissed his aunt goodbye. Maybe soon, he thought as the Portal speeded him toward his next battle.

Chapter 34

Morag took to the sky in search of any humans that might enter the danger zone.

Bastet explored the surrounding area seeking a place for shelter. Coming upon the group of rocks Steven had mentioned, she circled around the perimeter to verify it was safe to cross over the open ground. *If anyone did notice her, she was just a small cat searching for rodents.* She discovered two deep tunnels between several outcrops of rocks. One was large enough to allow a human to remain out of sight. Moving deeper down into the tunnel, she discovered that the cave made a sharp incline. Following the incline, Bastet saw that the ground opened beside a boulder far back, concealed by the tree line. *The hole is covered by underbrush, several hundred feet from the Portal site,* she announced.

As dawn broke, the team moved back into the forest to rest. If Shu was correct, Gregor should leave the cave tonight and hunt.

Shu arrived after dark and informed them she had seen Gregor leave the cave and head north.

Morag leaped into the night sky. She spotted Gregor as he emerged from the forest into a small field. His heat trail was unmistakable in the chilly night. She also detected three bats hovering over his shoulders. She remained well above and behind, circling with the air currents.

Around midnight, Morag spotted a wild boar rooting along the ground just ahead of Gregor.

The bats also spotted the boar, but Gregor moved in before they could attack.

Morag watched helplessly as Gregor savagely struck and killed the boar. Throwing the bloodied carcass over his shoulders, he headed back toward the cave.

Unknown to Gregor, two men were sitting across from each other in tree stands nearby. Today was the first day of hunting season. Catching the noise created by Gregor's movement, one of the men trained his gun toward the ground and fired when he saw the wild boar.

Kaboooom! The 12 gauge shotgun roared.

"Got him," Sam shouted, looking down the trail.

Gregor was knocked back when the buckshot ripped into the flesh of the boar he carried across his shoulders. Momentarily stunned from the impact, Gregor dropped the carcass and looked toward the source of the blast. Infuriated, he charged toward Sam.

Sam was standing up on the tree stand's ladder. His shotgun was strapped across his back. He heard a noise. It sounded as if something large was pounding its way toward him. He grabbed his high-powered light and aimed it at the shadow below. "What?" he shouted at the top of his lungs. He stared in disbelief and then jerked his leg up the ladder, just pulling away from the outstretched hand.

Gregor's sharp claws just missed his foot.

"Big Foot," Sam shouted. "I shot Big Foot!"

John West, sitting across the trail heard Sam screaming. He turned his flashlight down and watched incredulously as the beast grabbed the aluminum ladder, trying to pull it away from the tree. He spotted Sam climbing higher as this dark creature shook the ladder, screaming at the terrified hunter.

"No!" John shouted, firing his shotgun several times, but in the dark, hitting the ground near Gregor's feet.

Gregor jumped back. He looked up to where John was reloading his rifle and screamed in rage, shaking his huge fist. Turning from the stand, he grabbed the boar and ran down the trail, growling as he went.

As the sound of his feet faded, Sam and John remained in their stands, afraid to come down. Neither could believe what they had seen. They kept looking down the trail, afraid the beast would return.

Morag, sitting on a tree limb, had observed the fight. When the shooting and roaring stopped and the beast appeared to have escaped into the forest, she leaped off the tree and followed Gregor as he fled from the two men and their shotguns.

That morning, Sam and John were at the local breakfast shop.

"What happened to you?" The owner asked, "You two look like you seen a ghost."

The two men looked at each other and blurted out to everyone in the store that they were attacked by Big Foot.

At first, no one believed them, but when John showed the scratch marks on his boots, marks that could only be made by something larger than the small bears that hung around the forests, some of the patrons wondered.

A few went home and spread the news, perhaps thinking it was ridiculous and funny.

The news of a possible Big Foot sighting quickly spread through the town. Most still laughed at the story, but the local paper decided to print it and the park service, learning of the report, came to question the two 'heroes' who had 'out-gunned' Big Foot. True story or not, the news of the incident became viral.

Having returned to the house the day after the alleged Big Foot incident, Aunt Celia was listening to the nightly news. She was astonished to hear about yet another Big Foot sighting. She almost dropped her coffee cup on the kitchen floor when she caught the location. She rewound the short announcement:

'Big Foot was last seen in the dense forest several miles from the Mammoth Cave in Kentucky National Park. Two hunters reported being attacked by him after they had fired at what appeared to be a large buck. This is believed to be the first sighting of Big Foot in the Kentucky Mountains. Last year he was reported being seen near the Neches River in South Texas. Local hunters have started to search the area in the hope of capturing this elusive creature. We will keep you posted as we hear more from the local authorities.'

The reporter was obviously trying to stifle a laugh. Aunt Celia wasn't laughing. Not anymore. halta

* * *

"Steven," shouted Aunt Celia from the hallway stairs leading up to his room.

Hearing his aunt's urgent call. Steven opened his bedroom door.

"I think we have found a solution to our problem with Gregor. Come down, and I will tell you."

Steven hurried down the stairs and into the kitchen.

"What's up?"

"Gregor has been seen outside the Mammoth Cave. It was just reported on the news. Two hunters claim they fired at Big Foot, but we know differently."

"Yes," Steven shouted. "I love it when a plan comes together."

Aunt Celia stood and stared at her nephew. "What Plan?"

Steven frowned. His aunt was right. Did they really have a plan that could stop a Big Foot?

Chapter 35

D
ozing in his chair of bones, the Ruler dreamt of capturing the boy and returning The Seeker to imprisonment. His mouth watered as he visualized Gregor returning, swaggering across the dirt floor, carrying his leather hunting bag. He saw the squirming bag. How delightful. He saw his hand reaching down and untying the knot and then dumping the wriggling content on the gray floor. "Boy, it is you, at last," he said. He saw the fear in the boy's face just before he vanished.

"What! Not here?" The Dark Ruler thundered, his voice echoing through the lava tubes and caverns. Furious that he had only been dreaming, he jumped from his chair and stormed into the preparation room.

Standing on the rock ledge, he glared at the two Grool Hogs crouching next to the body of a human victim. "What have you done?" he demanded, eyes pulsating fiery red.

Crouching, even lower the lead hog, his brown leather tunic smeared with blood from the body, replied anxiously, "Us leach."

The Ruler saw the fat black leeches squirming along the stone floor and on the preparation table. "Get out," he screamed, pointing to the tunnel in front of him.

The hogs, terrified of his rage, raced to the tunnel, squealing all the way.

The Dark Ruler stared at the shriveled body on the table. "Don't they know I need my bodies whole?" he screamed after them. A sound above his head caught his attention.

Two bats were fluttering below the craggy ceiling.

"What are you doing here? Did I not leave you to see that Gregor remained where I place him? Did he leave again?"

"Grgor sen," a bat squealed.

"Seen? What do you mean?" The Ruler asked, staring up at the flapping bats and wondering how bat meat might taste well-done.

"Hums hunt Grgor," the closest bat squealed.

"When?" The Dark Ruler asked, venom rising in his mouth.

"Two night go," a bat said, staying as far away as possible.

"Two nights and you tell me this now?" The Ruler turned and went back into his throne room with the bats following a short distance behind. Standing next to the lava pit, he called up his ball of fire.

The bats, feeling the intense heat, fearing they were about to be thrown into the fire, flew toward the ceiling.

"I'll take care of you two later," The Dark Ruler hissed. Within seconds he disappeared into the hot ball of flame.

It didn't take long before steam filled the cavern as the 2,200-degree molten lava ball vaporized the water in the pool. Floating toward the entrance to Gregor's cave, the Ruler entered and approached the sleeping beast.

Startled by the sudden appearance, Gregor lunged at the Ruler.

"Hold," shouted the Ruler placing a transparent shield between himself and Gregor.

Shaking sleep from his head, Gregor realized the supposed attacker was the Ruler. He quickly dropped his fists to his sides. "I did not know it was you, your highness," he said, noting the rage in his master's eyes.

"You fool. What use are you to me now that you have been discovered by the humans? Did I not warn you?" the Ruler bellowed

Gregor cowered, fearful of the Ruler's fury. "It not matter. Humans get tired of waiting. They leave soon. You see."

"You better be right. Meanwhile, stay away from them," the Ruler, hissed. "Or I will return you to your cell in my care."

Gregor trembled. "I obey," he stammered.

The Ruler shot him another warning look and walked back into the fiery ball.

Gregor raised his fists and let out a loud roar.

Shu had heard every word as she clung to the rafter above the chamber's entrance. After the Ruler left, she drifted out of the cave and into the night air. The stars were shining as she headed back to Rhode Island to warn Steven that the Dark Ruler knew he had been in the cave. She hoped The Seeker would rethink the idea of using the boy as bait.

Chapter 36

A breath of sea air ruffled the curtains as Shu entered through the kitchen window which Celia had left open while cooking.

"Shu?" Aunt Celia asked, setting down the tea kettle and wiping her hands on a towel.

Bastet having her morning snack, looked annoyed at Shu's arrival.

"Bastet would you please tell Steven, Shu has arrived?" Aunt Celia said.

"Why can I never have a peaceful meal?" Shu grumbled, Jumping from the counter. She raced down the cellar stairs into the lab. *Shu's here*, she announced.

"Cool! Please ask her to......" Steven began, but Shu rushed into the lab whipping papers up into a funnel of air.

"Not again," Aunt Celia groaned, entering the lab in time to see the papers float to the floor.

Sorry, dear lady, Shu said.

Aunt Celia and Steven began collecting the papers.

"Did The Seeker return with you?" Steven asked.

I have not seen our leader since he left the Mammoth cave two days ago.

"You must have something to tell us, or you would not be here, correct?" Steven said.

"She better after making this mess," Aunt Celia mumbled, her back aching from picking up the pages.

Just then, The Seeker materialized next to Steven's monitor, waking up from her nap next to Steven's father's computer.

"Well rested, are we, dragon?" The Seeker asked, glancing at Morag.

"Staying out all hours of the night seems to be cutting into her beauty sleep," Steven kidded.

Morag whiffed an indignant puff of smoke from her nostrils.

"Heartburn?" Steven teased.

It must have been the wild goat, Morag said.

After everyone laughed, The Seeker turned to Shu. "You were supposed to keep watch over the beast. Why have you returned, my friend?"

Shu settled to the floor. I thought you would want to know what I observed. As you predicted, The Dark Ruler must have placed the bats in the cave because he came to the cave shortly after they flew out. From what I heard, The Ruler was furious after the bats reported Gregor had been seen by humans.

Humans saw Gregor? The Seeker asked.

Yes. The Dark Ruler was screaming his anger in the monster's face that he had let humans know about him.

That's good. Any hostility between those two demons may help us.

He was hostile alright. But so was Gregor. In fact, for a second, I thought Gregor was going to attack the Ruler.

"That would be too much to hope for," Aunt Celia said.

"I would love to see that happen," Steven said.

No such luck, Shu said. I stood there and watched for several minutes as they hissed and growled at each other. But nothing more.

"So he didn't remove Gregor from the cave?" Steven asked.

No. In fact, he ordered Gregor to remain in the Mammoth cave. He also warned him to wait for the humans to leave the area before he hunts again. The beast didn't like that one bit.

"Kentucky hunting season has just started," Aunt Celia said. "This month the hunters are allowed guns, next month only bows and arrows. The woods will be crawling with hunters for the next two months."

"Can this creature remain in the cave without feeding for two months," Steven asked.

Not possible, Morag replied. I couldn't do it.

You're telling me, Bastet grumbled.

Steven studied the map around Mammoth Cave. "It's only a matter of time before he gets seen again," he said. "Maybe the hunters will catch him."

The Seeker sighed. "He has eluded hunters for centuries."

"But in the early centuries man was limited in the tools he had to use. In this century, humans concerned for the welfare of their families will use unlimited resources to find and kill him, if anyone spots him," Aunt Celia said.

That could help us, Steven thought. Let the hunters eliminate our problem.

The Seeker read Steven's mind. "Let's hope they can. As I said, it may not be as easy as you think."

"What about us helping the hunters find Gregor," Steven suggested. "Is there some way we could pinpoint his location and give it to a hunting party."

"That's a good idea, Steven," Aunt Celia said. "But we can't just walk up to any hunter and tell him where Gregor is located. They'll think we're crazy."

I can lead the hunters to him, Bastet said.

"That might work," Aunt Celia said, "although I don't like you being bait. A lion running around the forest during hunting season? Not a great idea."

"I would suggest that I follow Gregor instead of Morag," interrupted The Seeker. "There is a full moon tonight and tomorrow. There is a good chance I will be able to track him through the forest."

"I agree," Aunt Celia said. "Nothing can hurt The Seeker."

Let her believe what she wishes, The Seeker thought, remembering the agony he'd felt as a prisoner of the Dark Ruler.

The Seeker nodded. "Then I recommend we head to New Mexico after Gregor is taken care of and release the Guardian in the Carlsbad Cavern. This will take the Ruler by surprise. He does not suspect that I know he had placed a guardian there. Steven, you have plenty of time to prepare while Shu and I map out the cave system," The Seeker said.

Chapter 37

Shu and The Seeker hurried to the Carlsbad Cavern. They knew Gregor was contained somewhere in these caverns that ran under Kentucky. As they passed the entrance, The Seeker saw hundreds of bats hanging from the limestone ceiling.

Shu, trying not to disturb the bats, moved slowly, carefully.

The seeker said, "Shu, you will search for Gregor in the back half of the cave while I head down the left. We will meet here once we have explored the entire cave."

After an exhaustive search of the underground cave system, The Seeker and Shu met at the rendezvous point.

"What is wrong, my friend?" The Seeker asked Shu who looked upset.

I found no bats, but saw something strange.

Something strange?

Shu looked worried. "I discovered some particularly large rodents wedged in deep holes in the cave walls.

"We did not see those before," The Seeker said.

Shu nodded. "I know. My discovery came after I caused the air pressure in the cavern to change. The rodents must have sensed it and moved to the opening to investigate."

It is fortunate that you found them.

I would not have seen them if it had not been for their annoying squeaking noises. They're quite chatty. Lucky for us.

The Seeker stared at the Cave wall. You said they are large, so how did we not notice them before? This adds a new wrinkle Aunt Celia won't like. I don't like it.

They are very large, but they blend into the walls.

Perhaps they are native to the caves and not placed here by the Ruler?

I think not. I watched as one emerged from its hiding place and scurried into the Guardian's tomb.

Perhaps he was seeking food?

Not likely. A few seconds later, a second rodent raced out of another tunnel and scrambled into the same opening.

That could be a coincidence.

I hoped so too, until I saw two rat-like heads popping out from this very same entrance. Seconds later, the Guardian and the two rodents emerged. Do you still believe this is a coincidence?

The Seeker shook his head. "It appears that these rodents may be more sentries for the Guardian. Okay, how bad are these new opponents?"

They are the size of a large cat, answered Shu. *They have long curved incisor teeth extending from both jaws. The are difficult to spot in the caves and quite agile.*

"None of this is good news. How far from the Guardian are they located?"

Of the ones I saw, one is at the entrance of the subterranean cavern and the second entered from another tunnel.

"And the Guardian. You said he was with them?"

Shu nodded. "*He seemed frail. Are you sure he's such a threat?*"

"He may appear weak, but we have seen how deadly they are. We must never underestimate them. They are the souls stolen by the Evil One and under his control they have supernatural powers and are not able to be killed easily. We must do everything we can to keep these evil beings separated from each other."

"Why can't I and you, with all our powers, fight them without Steven?" Shu asked, worried about the boy he had grown fond of.

I wish we could, The Seeker replied. *Unfortunately, the ancient prophecy, much of which has already come true, makes it clear that unless the boy is with us, we cannot defeat this evil force.*

But you said, he could die?

The prophecy does not reveal that answer. So, yes, our friend could die. We must do what we can to keep him safe, but if we must sacrifice one boy to save millions, then so it must be.

He is not one boy. He is Steven, Shu said.

"And that is why he knows," The Seeker replied.

Chapter 38

Gregor sat in a pool of water, leaning against a stalagmite. His fur was matted and soaked. Six days had passed since his last hunt. The loud rumbling in his stomach indicated it was time.

Standing up, he stumbled and fell over a stalagmite just barely sticking up out of the water. A fierce roar erupted from his mouth as he pounded his fists against his chest. Pulling himself up, he plowed through the pool not caring about the noise he was making. *Let the stupid humans find me, he thought. I will destroy them as I have done to all others.*

It took hours to climb, wade, crawl, and swim for Gregor to get to the entrance of the cavern. As he neared the opening, he moved slowly and stayed within the shadows, listening for any type of sound. He waited as darkness settled over the land before he ventured out. Slouching down close to the ground, he silently moved across the open field, staying in the shadows of the buildings and trees. Finally reaching the tree line, he plunged into the forest and safety. Or, so he hoped.

The Seeker was not far behind while Bastet ran through the trees adjacent to the deer trail.

An hour later, as the full moon cast long shadows along the floor of the forest, Gregor stopped. He sniffed the air. Satisfied he hadn't detected the human stench, he moved deeper into the forest. Having hunted in this area before, he headed toward a rock formation he had noticed before and slid between two flat boulders. There he would wait for an unsuspecting animal to pass. Resting his head against the cool boulder, he dozed off. The dampness of the forest filled his senses. Memories of days past flashed before his eyes.

The large and savage predators, some that had hunted his kind, were long gone. They had been replaced by weak humans. He could easily defeat them in a fair fight, but they had the sticks that barked thunder. He wanted no part of those sticks. He remembered the explosive noises as the bullets had rained down him only a few short days ago. If a human spotted him, he would gut that poor soul before he could fire his thunder sticks and Dark Ruler's orders or not, he would feed.

* * *

Gregor has stopped and is hiding behind a group of rocks, reported The Seeker telepathically as he settled on a large oak limb.

Bastet arrived minutes later and climbed the boulder directly above Gregor. Her mouth curled in a snarl as she looked down at the beast. *I am ready to attack,* Bastet announced.

"Not yet! There are no hunters near. I think we should wait. You might get lucky and not have to risk yourself," The Seeker said.

Move away from him for now. I will let you know if he moves, Morag said telepathically.

Bastet reluctantly pulled in her claws.

* * *

Traveling along the darkened highway in his pickup, Fred quickly pulled off the road onto a small fire trail cut deep into the woods. "We need to get well off the road. I don't want the Rangers to get the site of the truck or our blind," he said. "Deer shining carries a stiff fine if we're caught."

"We ain't never been lucky during the day. Nighttime poaching seems the only solution," Fred replied.

"If our luck holds, we should get our first deer of the season tonight." Carl smiled, admiring his shotgun. "Yessir, tonight will be something special."

Fred suggested their best chance at bagging a deer was to split up and cover the east and west deer trails they had found during the summer. Each had their cell phones and agreed not to make contact unless it was an emergency.

* * *

Dreaming of days gone by, Gregor did not hear the five deer moving slowly up the trail. It was not until the third deer passed that he was startled awake when the hoof stepped on a stick.

'Crack!'The twig broke.

The deer abruptly stopped, eyes turning toward the faint sound to her left. She stood still as a stone; head high in the air waiting for the night to release a warning of danger. She moved her head slowly back and forth as she sniffed the air, ears searching for the slightest noise.

Gregor rose to his full height as he prepared to attack. Clutching his long steel blade tightly in his right hand, he waited for the last deer to advance down the trail.

The deer cautiously started to move along the path.

Faster than a blink of an eye, Gregor launched himself from between the boulders upon the panic-stricken deer. Death was swift as Gregor's sharp fangs sliced deep along her throat but not before a loud shrill cry broke through the silence of the forest.

The other deer, stunned by the sudden attack, watched their companion fall under the weight of the monster before scattering in the woods.

All fell quiet as the sound of pounding hooves moved away from the forest's edge.

Gregor knelt beside the fallen deer and smiled at the sight of blood dripping from the wound in her broken neck.

* * *

Fred jerked his head in the direction of the sudden noise. He waited. *Nothing!* Pulling out his cell phone, he called Carl. "Did you hear a scream? Not too far off." Fred whispered into the mouthpiece.

"Yes! What was it?"

"I don't know. It was horrible."

"Stay where you are. If you hear it again call me."

Fred lowered the rifle toward the trail and waited.

* * *

Gregor not sensing any movement or sound, picked up the dead deer and tossed it over his shoulders. He headed down the trail directly toward Fred.

Still tense, Fred listened for any movement.

Gregor's pounding feet soon alerted him that something big was heading his way. Aiming the rifle with his flashlight taped on the barrel, he waited.

The deer was twenty yards in front of him. "Come to Papa," Fred whispered and switched on the light.

The high powered light struck directly into Gregor's eyes, momentarily blinding him. An alarmed scream rose from his throat as he dropped the deer and raised his arms.

Fred saw something large standing below the tree, pounding his chest. Fear spread across his face as he looked down at what? This thing, whatever it was, was screaming. He peered at the circle of his flashlight. This thing was covered in hair; head as big as a basketball.

Gregor let out a hellish scream.

Fred, shocked by the sound, recoiled, his rifle falling from his hand, grabbing it by the barrel just in time. The high powered light hit his eyes, blinding him for a terrifying second. He screamed as fear of this raging thing raced through him. He tried to shout out Carl's name, but no sound passed between his lips.

Gregor, no longer blinded by the flashlight, was shaking the metal ladder attached to the tree, just inches away from Fred's boots.

"Carl," Fred screamed as Gregor reached for his boot.

Stretching his long massive arm, Gregor clawed at the boot, just missing with each thrust.

Shouting hysterically, Fred climbed to the next limb. Facing death, Fred tried to point the rifle at the beast from the high branch. The shotgun quivered in his hand as he fired.

The bullet racing past Gregor's startled face struck the ground below. Gregor glared at the human, let out threatening roar but dropped down to the earth. Staring up at the man hanging onto the limb above, he growled again and then ran toward the deer. Grabbing it by the legs, he threw the carcass over his shoulder and raced into the darkness.

Hearing the shotgun blast, Carl had grabbed his phone. "Fred! Fred!" He shouted into the mouthpiece.

There was no answer.

Carl dropped from his blind and moved cautiously toward Fred's location. He was surprised to hear whimpering sounds coming from the tree. "Fred? Is that you?"

"Bigfoot," Fred stammered, huddled in a corner of the blind, rifle clutched in his shaking hands.

"Don't shoot. It's me," Carl said.

"Bigfoot...tried to kill me," Fred said, eyes scouring the forest.

"Bigfoot? There's no such thing as Bigfoot," Carl replied. "Put your rifle down. It's only me."

Fred looked down at Carl, eyes red from crying, a manic expression on his face. "It was him. I know what I saw with my own two eyes."

Carl, rifle held at the ready, looked down the trail. He then moved his flashlight along the ground. He knelt down on his knees. "What the hell?"

Large footprints, far larger than a man's bare feet, were embedded in the soft soil around the tree.

Carl stared at a trail of blood drops that led off into the woods and then back at the over-sized footprints. "We better get back to the truck and wait till morning. I don't fancy standing face to face with that creature no matter what it is."

"It was Bigfoot," Fred repeated, refusing to climb off the tree stand.

"You're alright now," Carl said, reaching up to his friend.

"If my gun hadn't gone off, he woulda' got me."

Carl had never seen Fred so frightened. He'd also never seen such large footprints before.

Chapter 39

Gregor trudged through the thick woods heading away from the humans he'd encountered in the trees. Climbing up a ravine, he searched for a place to hide and eat the deer still stretched across his shoulders. Exhausted, Gregor stumbled as he picked his way around the rocks jutting up from the ground. Stopping for a breather, he peered out over the mountain range and down into the valley.

The valley was covered in a blanket of mist, hiding from view what lay below. Were humans following him?

Gregor shielded his eyes as the sun rose above the eastern mountains.

He had to keep moving. He could not be seen in daylight. Balancing along the high ridge, he found what he was looking for between two large gray boulders, concealed by towering Evergreens. It was the entrance to a cave. Squeezing through the tight opening, he moved down into the black hole. The cave twisted and turned as he descended between the rocks until it opened into a large cavern. Moving deeper, he waded through knee-deep water until he reached a flat limestone shelf. The smell of sulfur drifted off the pool as he splashed through the water.

Reaching the far wall, Gregor dropped the deer and leaned back against the rough rock, exhausted. His head dropped onto the carcass, as if it was a pillow, and he fell asleep.

In his panic to escape the humans, Gregor did not notice two pairs of eyes had followed his every movement. Seeing he was asleep, the pair of bats headed back to the Dark Ruler's lair.

Gregor awoke several hours later and dragged himself toward the pool of water to drink. He then returned to the carcass. Sitting against the wall of the cave, Gregor ripped large chunks of raw meat from a leg. Tossing the bone into the pool, he feasted until only the skeleton lay bare, scattered across the pool and limestone floor. Satisfied at last, he dropped off into a deep sleep, forgetting about his close call with the humans.

* * *

The Ruler listened attentively to the squealing bats in front of him. His cherry-red eyes grew more fiery as his anger mounted. "Enough," he shouted, scattering the bats. Furious, he summoned the 'Wings of Fire' and disappeared into the abyss.

Still asleep from his huge meal, Gregor didn't hear the arrival of the giant lava ball. A sudden flash of light, followed by intense heat and scalding steam sucked the air from the cavern and he awoke gasping for air.

"Again, you defy me?" A voice thundered.

Gregor, still half-asleep rubbed his eyes.

"How dare you defy me?" The Ruler bellowed. His high pitched, shrieking voice resonating off the cavern walls.

Gregor, still dazed, pushed himself up to his full height and locked eyes with the Ruler. A menacing growl erupted from his throat. "I do not have to answer to you or anyone," he growled.

The ruler let out a hair-raising roar. "I am your ruler. I warned you of what I would do if you were seen by humans again."

Fully awake now, Gregor realized he was facing the most powerful creature on the planet. "Master, I did not know it was you," he stammered, bowing his head. "I was asleep."

"You disobeyed me and the humans saw you," The Dark Ruler bellowed.

"How was I to know there were hunters in the woods? Master, they were not looking for me. They were hunting deer." Gregor did not dare look up, knowing the Ruler's eyes were like blazing fireballs. "I would not disobey you. No sir. Not I."

The Ruler stared at Gregor. I need this beast or I would boil him as he stands.

Gregor didn't move. He knew he was in big trouble. Should he take a chance and attack. Could the element of surprise help him against his powerful foe? He felt the heat from the other and decided this was not the right time nor place for such a risky attempt. "Master, I am your slave. I only obey you."

The Dark Ruler wondered if the bats had told him the truth. Perhaps they hated the beast as much as he did. He felt his temper dissipating, his eyes losing their fire. "If I find out you disobey me," he began.

"Oh, no, Master. I stay here until you command. Humans no spot me. I stay here."

"You'll stay right here," the Ruler said, steam still rising from his flesh, but calming gradually. "Staying here places you between the Guardian in the north and the one in the south. That is why I need you right here."

Gregor nodded his head, but didn't understand much of what the Ruler was saying. He only knew that someday soon he would find a way to destroy this monster that thought he could control the most ferocious beast that had ever roamed the Earth. And someday, not much further in the future, he would be free to hunt the humans who now believed they were the masters of the world.

Chapter 40

Steven was staring at the pictures of the Lechuguilla Cave, in the Carlsbad Caverns National Park, in New Mexico, on his computer, when The Seeker hurried in.

The Seeker listened silently as Steven and his Aunt discussed the layout of the caverns. He knew it was crucial for them to become familiar with what lay ahead in the winding tunnels. He remained invisible in the shadows as they discussed their preparations.

"Did you notice the length of the cave?" Steven asked his aunt.

"It's much longer and deeper than the Mammoth Cave," Aunt Celia said, sounding worried. "That could make it difficult to find our target."

Steven nodded. "From the entry point, the twisting tunnels, caverns, and subterranean pools cover over 120 miles. The deepest cavern is over 1,600 feet below the surface of the desert sands." He looked up. "How will we ever find the Guardian in this maze?"

"Do you think Shu can locate where the Guardian is concealed?" Aunt Celia asked.

"That's a good idea." Steven frowned. "What we also need to know is where the sentries are located. The Dark Ruler placed them in the cave to alert the Guardian."

"All this seems like a lot, even for a wind god to do." Aunt Celia shook her head. "I better check if we have sufficient supplies." She got up from the computer chair and walked over to the table. Worried about her first exploration into a cave, she had gone to the local sporting goods store and purchased everything she could find to match a list of equipment Cavers had posted on social media.

"All this?" The Seeker exclaimed, surprised at the tables overflowing with supplies.

Aunt Celia jumped at The Seeker's sudden appearance. "I wish you wouldn't sneak up on me like that. My nerves are as tight as springs."

"Aunt Celia has done some shopping for our trip," Steven said with an amused expression his his face. "She bought out the store."

"I did not. I only want to be fully prepared. As you can see, we have a rifle, cartridges, flare gun, six flares, six battery packs, four for the helmets and two for the smartphones, six bottles of water, extra socks, and enough ready-to-eat meals to feed an army."

"Stop exaggerating, Steven," Aunt Celia said, seeing his amused face and glad for once he wasn't being so serious.

"She also bought new boots, hiking shorts, knee and elbow pads. Very fashionable," He joked.

"I also bought pen lights, two hunting knives, backpacks, a compass, and 50 feet of nylon line."

"We'll need a truck for all this stuff!" Steven let out a laugh.

"I want to be prepared," Aunt Celia repeated, only slightly annoyed that Steven was making fun of her.

"But seriously, who is going to carry all this?" The Seeker asked, not understanding Steven's amusement.

"Steven and I," Aunt Celia responded.

"I was afraid we were going to need to hire some camels," The Seeker said.

Aunt Celia glared at him. "I think we should be prepared for any possibility. What are you doing here anyway?"

Difficult woman, The Seeker thought. "Shu and I have completed our sweep through the Lechuguilla Caves and discovered there are no bats inside." The Seeker shook his head again at the sight of all the supplies on the table. He whispered to Steven, "I'm surprised she didn't also buy baseball bats...to hit the bats with."

Steven laughed, but catching his aunt's disapproving look quickly said, "Awesome! We should be able to take out the Guardian without the Dark

Ruler being alerted. No bats is good news."

"And the bad news?" Aunt Celia asked, suspecting there was more.

"You are a wise lady," The Seeker said, wishing she wasn't quite so wise. "It will not be as easy as you think, Steven. While we didn't see any bat sentries, there are large rodents in the cave, possibly to alert the Guardian of nay intrusion. It does not take much to arouse them from their hiding places. Shu's presence alone created a change in the atmospheric pressure was enough to alert them."

"Rodents?" Aunt Celia looked worried.

"They are like an alarm system planted by the Dark Ruler, much like the bats in the other caves, but much larger." The Seeker held his hands as wide as his shoulders and then even wider.

"That will make a surprise attack difficult," Steven said, staring at the outstretched hands.

Bastet said. *I can take care of a bunch of rodents.* She showed her sharp claws.

"Not these monsters," The Seeker replied. "I have no idea what they are."

"What do they look like?" Aunt Celia asked. "Perhaps we can figure out what they are if you describe them. Are they 'normal' rodents or some monstrous ones created by the Dark Ruler?"

"Normal rodents?" Steven sighed. "There is nothing normal about anything having to do with the Dark Ruler or (yuck) rodents."

"I did not see them myself, Shu said, they had long snouts and long sharp incisors extending from their upper and lower jaws? He said they are covered in bushy, brownish, hair and have long legs. They are much bigger than Bastet," The Seeker said.

I can still handle them if they are rodents, Bastet yowled.

"We can't take a chance," The Seeker replied. "If you miss even one it will alert the Guardian. Far too risky."

Steven shook his head. "I think I saw something similar to what you just described on the Prehistory Channel." Steven started typing on the keyboard. "Here. Is that it?" Steven moved the mouse on the screen. "Do they look like this?"

"I can't be certain since it was Shu who described them, but yes, I believe these do fit his description," The Seeker answered.

Steven looked again. "It's a prehistoric squirrel. How much trouble can a squirrel cause?" He laughed, relieved it was just a squirrel they had to deal with.

"Let me have a look," Aunt Celia said, moving next to Steven. "Hmmm? I've also seen this creature. Several years ago, Dr. Sam Adams, a friend of your parents, discovered the skeleton remains of such an animal in the New Mexico desert. He told me the animal, thankfully, now extinct, roamed the earth 2,000,000 years ago. They were much larger than our modern domestic cats. They were horribly vicious hunters."

The Seeker studied the computer image. "Shu said he witnessed these savage beasts attacking a wolf at least five times their size. He said they attacked as a group and ripped it to shreds."

"I find it hard to believe such creatures are alive now," Steven said, staring at the photograph of the supposedly extinct prehistoric squirrel.

"I guess that the Dark Ruler has resurrected them specifically to protect this Guardian. More trouble for us," The Seeker said.

Steven nodded. "A rat protected by rats. What else is new?"

Morag who had been listening in silence spoke up. *If these creatures are alive, then they must feed....*

Steven smiled. "Leave it to Morag to always think of her stomach at a time like this."

"No Steven, Morag is right." The Seeker gave Morag an approving nod. "She has given me an idea. If they leave the cave to feed, we can attack them in the open, where they are away from the Guardian and most vulnerable. From far away, they can't alarm the Guardian to our presence."

Morag beamed. *That was my plan exactly.*

"Yeah, right," Bastet muttered.

Without warning the papers in the lab started to whirl into the air, followed by Shu appearing next to The Seeker.

"What is it, Shu?" The Seeker asked. "Why are you here when you are supposed to be back at the cave?"

As you suggested, I followed several rodents through the cave, hoping they would go in search of food. What I saw was not what I expected.

"What do you mean?" Aunt Celia was beginning to hate surprises.

The four I found guarding the Guardian joined a mob of other rodents, perhaps thirty or more, in the desert, at another opening, near the back of the cave.

"There's another entryway?" The Seeker asked. "That means we may have to divide our forces to guard both escape routes. That is bad news."

"There's more bad news. Observing these rodents, it appeared that the four from the cave are the leaders of an army of these beasts. Once they were all gathered ihn one area; these four from the cave positioned themselves on a high rock staring out at the crowd. The others quickly became silent–"

"There's nothing in the report here that talks about armies of these squirrels. Are you saying they are organized?" Steven asked, a worried look on his face.

Shu replied, *There is still more. The leaders let out loud cries, and the others were turned toward them. They appeared to be listening. I could not understand, but I think the leaders were issuing commands.*

"Commands?" The Seeker asked.

"I've never heard of squirrels being this organized," Aunt Celia said, glancing at Steven's face.

I believe it was a signal to start the hunt, because immediately afterward, the other rodents split into four groups, each following one of the leaders, Shu said.

"They were that organized?" Steven found this hard to believe in prehistoric squirrels, in any squirrels.

Yes. The amazing thing was how the rodents attacked. Shu said, shivering at the memory.

"What do you mean?" Aunt Celia's hands were twisting nervously in her lap.

I thought once they split up, we could easily overcome each group. Bastet said, realizing these were not like mice, she could easily cut to shreds.

We could each take one group and make mincemeat out of them, Morag said.

It's not that easy, Shu replied, shaking his head. *The desert was silent as the rodents stalked their prey, but all hell broke loose around midnight.*

"I wish you would stop being so dramatic," The Seeker scolded Shu. "Just get on with it!"

Shu nodded. *The rats were hunting in four different directions as if the search was pre-planned when a large deer entered the clearing. In seconds, as if from nowhere, the four groups of rats converged into one attacking army.*

"What happened, although I can guess," Steven said.

Once they surrounded the buck, he lowered his head and tried to fight them off with his massive antlers. The attack was from all sides, vicious and I believe, coordinated, Shu said.

Aunt Celia looked stunned. "They really were that organized?"

Shu shivered again at his memory of the horrible sight. *The stillness of the night was replaced with ear-shattering screams from the deer and the battle cries of the much smaller rodents, who attacked in waves, a few at a time. One after the other, the same groups, like small teams, assaulted from all sides of the deer. Finally, sensing their victim was unable to fight, all the rodents converged on him as one, and drove him to the ground.*

"Shu, you're saying they teamed up against the deer as if they had a strategy? That is not good." The Seeker frowned.

"Did they look like this?" Steven pointed to the monitor.

Shu looked at the computer. *Yes, that looks like them. Ugly creatures and greedy too. Once the deer was down, the rodents fought each other to get at the flesh of their victim. It was an amazingly ugly sight.*

"Wait! So, once the deer was no longer a problem, the rodents turned against each other?" The Seeker asked, visualizing the attack.

Shu nodded. *They are genuinely savage, beasts. Even before the deer meat disappeared, the rodents turned on each other as if forgetting they had recently been a team.*

"Right," Steven said with a nervous laugh. "I guess these really are not your average 'normal' squirrels."

Nothing ordinary about them, Shu replied. *Disgusting creatures!*

"Shu, did all the rodents get to feed on the deer?" Aunt Celia asked.

Why are you asking that? The Seeker cast a puzzled look at Aunt Celia.

"I'm looking for anything we can use to fight these monsters."

Shu replied, *Some did not eat. Several rodents were also attacked as they struggled to get at the carcass. These weaker rodents were killed and eaten by the larger and stronger of the group. It was horrible.*

"So, they're cannibals," The Seeker said, deep in thought. "We may be able to use that against them."

"Until these rodents are eliminated, Steven will not step foot in that cave," Aunt Celia said, crossing her arms. "That is non-negotiable."

"Absolutely," The Seeker said, but he was still thinking how this new information could help them defeat the army of prehistoric rodents.

Steven wondered how many more obstacles the Dark Ruler would throw at them.

Chapter 41

Aunt Celia, after giving her ultimatum, felt she had nothing more to say, so she left the team to prepare dinner. How they resolved the threat of the ravenous prehistoric squirrels was a matter for them to work out, but she had no intention of letting them risk Steven's life. *Even if they beg, I will not put him in that kind of danger. Prehistoric squirrels? What next?*

"Suggestions anyone?" The Seeker asked. "Your aunt is a tough lady."

"She's right, though. Fighting more than thirty vicious rodents without them alerting the Guardian and Dark Ruler presents a problem," Steven said, and walked over to his father's leather chair and sat down.

I should be able to exterminate most, if not all of them with my dragonfire, Morag said. *One puff from me and they're squirrel fricassee!*

"And you don't think they'll scream while they stew," Bastet asked.

Maybe a little, Morag said, disappointed at not being able to roast the rodents.

"One little squeal would be all that is needed to alarm the Guardian." The Seeker shrugged his shoulders.

"Shu, you mentioned the horde of rodents broke up into groups to hunt?" Steven was thinking aloud.

Yes, they did, Shu responded.

"That means we would have to follow four different groups," Steven said. "We'd have to split up. Not good."

"What if we could lure them to a distant location, one that will result in their total destruction all at one time?" The Seeker said.

Lure them with food, Morag suggested.

Food? You're always thinking of your stomach, Bastet meowed.

Yes, but it will work. Once they start feeding far from the cave, they will think of nothing else. I can swoop down and roast them. No more rodents! Morag growled a puff of smoke drifting from her nostrils.

And just what will you use to lure a hungry horde of prehistoric squirrels? Bastet asked.

Morag smiled right at Bastet.

Oh, no, no, no! Bastet jumped to her paws. *I am not going to be bait for anyone, especially not giant prehistoric rodents!*

Don't worry, oh great cat god, I will cook every last one of those things before they can repay you for all the rodents you have devoured over the centuries. Morag smiled.

"While that might work, Bastet could get hurt," The Seeker said.

I'll protect my little buddy, Morag replied with a snort.

Hey, I can take care of myself, Bastet mewed. *Besides, we can't take a chance that even one of these little rats will escape.*

"No, we can't," The Seeker agreed.

"Well, my aunt won't let any of us do anything as long as these killer squirrels are around," Steven muttered. "Hmmm? Morag could be right."

I am? Morag looked surprised.

"Yes. We need some kind of bait to lure the rodents away from the cave, something they can't resist," Steven said.

"Steven is right." The Seeker was staring at Morag. "Morag, you are a great hunter. Do you think you can capture some animal and bring it back alive to lure the prehistoric squirrels away from the cave?"

If I have to fly every night, I will bring meat to the party, Morag replied, flapping her wings. *I guess that is a better idea than using Bastet.*

A much better idea, Bastet grumbled.

Steven was still thinking hard. "I have another idea. We can place video monitors outside the entrances to the cave. That will eliminate the need for us to be there, especially at night, thus keeping us safe. That should make my aunt happy."

"Excellent idea," The Seeker said. "What are vid...vio monsters?" He asked.

"No. Video monitors. Never mind. I'll take care of it myself," Steven replied, realizing that his friend had no way of knowing what video cameras were. "Morag, we want those squirrels as far away from the cave as possible, so they can't alarm the Guardian inside. Can you manage that?"

Don't worry. I get it, Morag replied, impatient to get going.

"Don't take any chances," Steven said, worried about his friend.

Morag placed his leathery wing on Steven's arm. *You do not need to worry about me, Steven, but thank you.*

I think we are ready to talk to your aunt, Steven, Shu said.

"I wonder," The Seeker remarked, a worried frown on his face.

* * *

While The Seeker, Bastet, and Morag were listening intently, Steven patiently filled in his Aunt on their plan to eliminate the prehistoric squirrels, of course, with no danger to Steven. "So, what do you think, Aunt Celia?" he asked, confident he had won her over.

The Seeker wasn't so sure. *She's one stubborn lady,* he thought, seeing the worried look had not faded from her face.

"Prehistoric squirrels? I don't know. It would be a lot easier if we could find prehistoric nuts," Aunt Celia said, laughing at her own joke, although she didn't find any of this funny.

Steven shot up in his chair. "What? Aunt Celia? I don't believe you said that! Where in the dickens would we find prehistoric nuts?" He burst into laughter.

Everyone laughed at the idea of trying to locate prehistoric nuts to lure ancient squirrels away from the Guardian. But The Seeker was deep in thought. "That's not a bad idea," he said, giving Aunt Celia a smile.

You're joking, Shu said, still laughing at the idea of using some kind of ancient nuts as bait for ancient squirrels.

The Seeker's face showed he was dead serious. "Squirrels eat nuts, right? Therefore, why wouldn't prehistoric squirrels eat prehistoric nuts?"

Steven stopped laughing. "If scientists can clone a Wooly Mammoth, why not prehistoric nuts?"

They all became silent. Finally, Aunt Celia said, "I was only joking, but it would make me feel much better."

"I wonder," Steven said, as he raced over to the computer and searched for any references related to prehistoric nuts. "I don't believe this," he exclaimed, looking up from the monitor. "There actually is a scientist that is developing prehistoric nuts to feed to the mammoth elephant being cloned by a laboratory at Harvard University."

"My suggestion wasn't so bad after all," Aunt Celia smiled, knowing she had meant it only as a joke.

"There," Steven said, pointing to a tall shape on the screen. "The nuts are stored in this silo." He looked at the others.

"Now that I've found the location of the nuts, how do we get them?"

No one answered.

"Got it," Aunt Celia said. "Shu, could you create a wind funnel and suck the nuts from the silo?"

Yes! I'm sure I can do that, Shu said.

"Then we are in business," Aunt Celia said. "Another great idea from your aunt." She extended a fist toward Steven.

Steven tapped his closed fist against hers and said, "Right on!" He had to admit she impressed him now that she seemed to be growing used to the idea of becoming part of the team.

Morag sighed. *So, I get to fry those rats?*

"I suppose that is the only way," The Seeker said. "But we don't want to become vicious killers like the Dark Ruler."

No, I guess not, Morag replied. Hunting for food to survive is one thing, but I'll leave it to the Dark Ruler and his minions to kill just for fun.

"Ok, so be merciful. let's get this done quickly," Aunt Celia said.

"Shu, you get the nuts. I will purchase the cameras, power supplies, and program the computers to monitor the videos. Each camera will have a motion sensor to alert us when the rodents leave the cave. The second camera will be placed on the rock formation facing out into the desert to verify that no rodent returns to the cave once we lure them away."

"I just thought of one other problem," Steven said. "We don't want him showing up to the 'party' uninvited when he smells the nuts and the barbequed squirrels."

The Seeker gave Steven a frown. "Good thinking, Steven. Shu and I saw him. We believe he is still holed up in the Mammoth cave and should not be a problem."

"Are you sure Gregor is still there?" asked Aunt Celia not wanting to be blindsided by the beast.

"Not positive, but there is no reason he would head down to the Carlsbad Caverns. We have not tipped off our hand that we know the Dark Ruler has placed a Guardian in Carlsbad," The Seeker said.

"That sounds reasonable," Steven replied. "But after we throw the squirrels a roasted nut party, I think we should take care of that monster, before he hurts any humans. There have already been some incidents."

The Seeker frowned, "Steven, we must focus our energies on one of the Dark Ruler's evil creations at a time, but you are right, Gregor is a threat that we may have to deal with."

I wonder if we can, Steven thought.

Aunt Celia was thinking the same thing. *Prehistoric nuts? Why didn't I keep my big mouth shut?*

Chapter 42

Steven was sitting at his father's computer when the speaker sounded the alarm that the sensor on the camera he set by the cave detected movement. He had the night shift but was falling asleep when the beeps sounded. Switching on the monitor, he watched, fascinated, as the prehistoric squirrels came scurrying out from a hole, almost hidden from view by a large boulder.

"Yeah, Baby! Don't you just love it when a plan comes together?" He was about to call the others, but something was wrong. "Why are they just milling around the hole?"

Steven leaned closer, watching as four of the larger squirrels were screeching at the group of animals standing in front of them. That's interesting, he thought as, if on command, the mob of squirrels separated and formed into lines behind each of the four squirrels. "I'll be damned," he exclaimed. "They're grouping up like a real army! Shu was right!"

Bastet, on hearing the alarm, had jumped from the counter, where she had been dozing. She now ran upstairs to wake Aunt Celia.

Morag yawned, stretching her wings in anticipation of the hunt.

Steven was still observing the rodents running out into the desert when Aunt Celia hurried into the Lab. "What's happening? Bastet came racing up the stairs and woke me. Are you okay?"

"They've started their hunt," Steven announced, as Aunt Celia walked over to the computer table. "I'm worried. They act like they know exactly what they are doing."

"Morag, are you ready to search for more prey if they don't all go for the prehistoric nuts?" Aunt Celia asked. "Although why prehistoric squirrels would not like prehistoric nuts is beyond me," she said, thinking how crazy this would all sound if she told anyone about it.

More than ready, growled Morag. *I just hope it won't be necessary. I hate hurting other animals, except to eat, of course. We all need to eat, don't we?*

Some of us more than others, Bastet shot at her.

"Morag's always ready for a hunt," Steven said, opening the Portal. "Good hunting!"

Steven and Aunt Celia watched silently as Morag entered the waterfall within the portal and disappeared.

"She's gone," Aunt Celia said.

"You can see her exit on the monitor," Steven said, looking at the monitor to watch Morag exit the Portal upon reaching her destination.

"Nothing we can do but wait," Steven said. "I guess we placed the old nuts just in time. Did you smell those disgusting things? Shu dumped a bunch of them on the floor here earlier this morning after he left a load more in the desert. I almost hurled when the smell hit me."

"Is that what smells in here? I thought it was dragon BO." Aunt Celia sighed. "Whoever thought I'd have to worry about stinky prehistoric nuts or dragon body odor?"

Steven wriggled his nose. "Yeah. It still stinks even though I threw them in the yard as fast as I could."

"Great! They'll probably attract every stray cat in the neighborhood," Aunt Celia muttered. "Wreck my kitchen, wreck my yard."

Steven laughed. "I don't see Morag anymore. I just hope she doesn't stop to feed herself."

"As usual," Bastet grumbled.

"Speaking of food. Are you Hungry?" Aunt Celia asked.

"Starving."

"I'll go fix us an early breakfast," Aunt Celia said.

"Two eggs, four pieces of crisp bacon, plus home fries, please aunt?"

"Anything else your majesty?"

"Yes, no prehistoric nuts. Please?"

* * *

Morag stood on the sand, eager to fly. The dry night air warmed her protective scales. Being in the fresh air was a welcome change from the cold temperatures of the air-conditioned lab.

When she had reached full size, Morag jumped into the sky and spread her wings, hurling sand into the air. Within seconds she was several hundred feet above the ground and climbing, searching the floor below. She soon spotted the horde of prehistoric squirrels running across the sand dunes, occasionally stopping to gobble up the small piles of nuts that Shu had dropped, a trail leading away from the cave.

Pushing harder against the night air with her wings, Morag opened the distance from the rodents to where she hoped to start her search for fresh bait. Her infrared eyes would help her identify a heat source that would indicate any animal foraging far below.

As she scanned the desert floor, Morag saw several small red spots. Moving higher into the sky, she searched for the updraft that would allow her to glide above the desert sands without flapping her wings and alarming her target.

If only my mother were here riding the air currents with me, she thought, remembering when her mother taught her to hunt.

Morag often wondered if there were more of her species, somewhere in the world. She wished she had a time when the Dark Ruler was not causing trouble to go searching for a mate, with whom to share the joy of flying in the night sky. *Steven's safety has to come; first,* she reminded herself, refocusing on the mission.

Dipping her wings to circle the area again, Morag's eyes picked up a faint heat source to the left of an outcropping of rock. She tightened the circle as she observed several wolves gorging on a deer.

Morag launched herself down toward the pack. *Are those wolves in for a surprise!*

Morag tucked her wings against her body and dove toward the unsuspecting predators. Extending her talons, she swooped down and snatched the deer from the jaws of the wolves who didn't know what had hit them.

With the deer trapped in her claws, she climbed back into the sky. She laughed when she heard the distant howls of the frustrated wolves. Now, that was fun, she thought, wondering if the wolves had any idea that they were 'robbed' of their feast by a dragon.

Morag headed back to the trail and saw the large pile of prehistoric nuts left as bait by Shu. She gently dropped the deer carcass into the center of the pile of nuts, and then soared back into the night sky, eager to wait for the rodents to arrive for the party.

* * *

The first group of prehistoric squirrels were eagerly following the scent of the nuts and the blood of the deer.

The leader sniffed the air. "Follow me," he squealed, dashing toward the inviting smell.

Morag saw the squirrels race across the sand toward the bait. Out of the corner of her eye, she saw the three remaining groups change direction too. Their speed increased as the scent of blood, and prehistoric nuts grew stronger.

Morag allowed the gas to build in her stomach in anticipation of launching a massive plume of fire at the rodents. She circled overhead, waiting for the horde to become fully absorbed in tearing at the carcass and scrambling for the nuts.

She noticed that some had already been driven away from the deer. She worried that they would escape the trap, but was relieved when she saw them return and start to fight with the others for the treasure.

They won't be paying attention to me now that the feeding frenzy has begun, she thought.

The squirrels were making some racket, chomping down on the deer, gorging on the nuts, and squabbling with each other.

"Now!" Morag shot down toward the massive army of prehistoric squirrels, all fighting and clawing at the bait and each other.

Leveling off, Morag opened her mouth and blasted fire over the entire mess of rodents and prehistoric nuts.

The screaming of the squirrels and the smell of the nuts reached far into the night sky.

Circling around again, Morag sprayed the area a second time to make sure all the rodents had been burned to a crisp. This time, she heard no screams. All she heard were her wings as she surveyed the charred area, flames still burning below.

All the prehistoric squirrels had been eliminated. Satisfied, Morag leaped high into the sky and headed back toward the cave entrance. *You were meant to die millions of years ago,* she shouted but realized she was too. Perhaps soon, she thought, reminded again of her loneliness.

Back in the lab, after a hearty breakfast, Steven could not take his eyes off the monitor, hoping nothing had gone wrong. He waited and waited, and finally, breathed a sigh of relief when he saw Morag drop to the ground.

"Open the Portal, Aunt Celia," Steven asked, wondering why Morag didn't look happy.

"Is it safe?" Aunt Celia asked. "None of those squirrels could follow Morag here?"

"It's never safe," Steven replied, knowing this was only one battle won in a dangerous war. And this one had been only against prehistoric squirrels.

Chapter 43

The surf crashed against the jagged rocks drowning out all the sounds of night. Calm filled the void as the waves receded only to be followed by the second, then the third wave, all crashing against the shoreline. The night was moonless, making it challenging to see your hand in front of your face, let alone the human you were stalking. The ground covering the field was wet from a brief shower during the day.

The water from her coat dropped silently onto the wet leaves that covered the ground. Pupils dilated, she cautiously lifted her head above the shrubs, hoping to locate the target. She jerked backward scraping her arm against the beach roses, startled by a sudden noise.

It was a rabbit hopping in the brush below her.

Aunt Celia's heart raced as she remained frozen. She did not move as she tried to filter out the pounding surf from the sounds around her.

There was a scratching sound to her left.

Aunt Celia turned her head in the direction of the faint noise. Nothing! She listened for more sounds: scraping, twigs snapping, startled wildlife fleeing.

"Gotcha," Steven shouted as he pulled the trigger on his gun. The blue splat of paint on Aunt Celia's backpack showed his shot was good.

"No," Aunt Celia moaned as she jumped up from the ground. "I can't believe you got me again." She swung the backpack off her shoulders and stared at the blue blotch of paint dripping from the pack. "How did you find me?"

"At first I wasn't sure where you were. I knew you were in this area, but I wasn't sure until I heard the scratching sound."

"A darn rabbit startled me."

Steven, you know what you said was not true, Bastet said, sitting next to Aunt Celia's boot.

Steven looked down at Bastet, then up at his aunt. "I must confess, I found you because I sent Morag to locate you."

"Traitor!" Aunt Celia shouted, looking up at Morag flying overhead.

Thanks for the rabbit, Morag called back. *I've been playing cat and mouse trying to catch it.*

Mouse? Bastet said, *looking around hungrily for the mouse.*

Aunt Celia cradled her gun. "We've been out here practicing every night for the past week. I think we're as ready as we'll ever be."

"I agree, Aunt Celia." Steven said, wiping the blue paint off his aunt's backpack. "I'll contact The Seeker tomorrow," he said, as they walked to the car park area.

Aunt Celia wanted to take her nephew's hand, but held back. She wondered if he'd ever be ready to accept her. As courageous as he was, he seemed to be afraid of being loved and cared for. She knew that was to be expected when parents are killed in such a terrible way. She only hoped she'd be able to protect him from a similar fate.

* * *

"How were the War Games? "The Seeker asked.

"I beat my aunt bad," Steven boasted.

His success is questionable, Morag reported.

The Seeker looked at Steven then back at Morag.

"Explain," The Seeker asked.

On the last night, I was directed to search the battlefield and report to Steven where his aunt was hiding, Morag responded. *That, I would think, is cheating.*

Steven sat in the leather chair, looking very sheepish. "A win is a win. I chose to use all the tools I had available."

"You cheated," Aunt Celia said. "You'd better watch your back, mister."

Steven laughed and made his fingers look like a gun. "Pow," he said softly.

The Seeker frowned. "Now that we have sharpened our skills with your games, it is time to take out the Ruler."

"Bring him and his uglies on," Steven said.

The room exploded into a torrent of wind. Shu swirled into the lab and landed next to The Seeker.

"Why do you always do that?" Aunt Celia groaned, staring at the piles of papers whipped into the air. "I'm not cleaning it up this time." She folded her arms across her chest.

Shu was busting with news. *Gregor is no longer in the Mammoth Cave. I lost him. I have no idea where he is.*

"You gotta be kidding me," Steven exclaimed. "When did you last see him?"

The Seeker glared at Shu. "How did you lose him?"

He did not return from a hunt two nights ago, Shu replied. "I don't know how I lost sight of him, but I did. I'm sorry."

"Have you searched the area carefully?" Steven asked.

Yes, and there is no sign of him

"We must assume the worst," The Seeker said, shaking his head.

"Do you think he is heading to New Mexico?" Aunt Celia asked.

"I doubt it," The Seeker responded. "He has no way to know that we have discovered the cave in New Mexico."

"Steven has there been any more sightings of Bigfoot?" Aunt Celia asked.

"I haven't looked for any for the past few days." Moving quickly to the computer, Steven clicked on the Louisville News icon and started searching for Big Foot updates from Kentucky. 'Bigfoot Sighted Again,' read the headline in the back of a local edition. "Listen to this," he said, "A hunter reported being attacked by Bigfoot in the early morning hours as he was setting up his blind. He claimed he suffered severe lacerations on his arms and legs as the beast, which he alleges is Big Foot, tried to rip him down from the tree."

Aunt Celia looked puzzled. "Do you think the creature we are tracking is Big Foot?"

Steven didn't answer, but continued reading, "The hunter stated that when the beast saw him on the trail, he started to growl fiercely shaking his fists at him. Mr. Silverman claimed he was able to escape by climbing higher up the tree. He said the beast then ran toward the ladder and started to yank it back and forth, almost knocking Mr. Silverman out of the blind."

"This can't be the creature we're hunting," Aunt Celia said.

Steven glanced at her and continued reading the article aloud. "He claimed that he fired his gun at the creature. He went on to say that after the gun went off, the beast jumped from the ladder, picked up what looked like the carcass of a dead deer and charged into the woods."

"When was this story released?" Aunt Celia asked.

Steven searched for the front page. "Tuesday the 14th."

"That's close to when we saw Gregor in that area," The Seeker said.

"Do you think he'd stay there once humans spot him?" Steven asked.

"We must assume he is either holding up in another cave nearby, or was ordered to move closer to another Guardian," The Seeker said.

"The closest one is in Carlsbad," Aunt Celia said, studying the map on the computer screen.

"Then we have no more time," Steven said. "We must release the Guardian now, before Gregor gets there."

"Shu, return to the area and continue to search for Gregor," The Seeker commended. "A creature so vile cannot be hidden from us too long."

Shu hurried from the room, throwing papers into the wind.

Aunt Celia sighed, for once not about the papers everywhere, but about the look on Steven's face when he said that he had to act fast or Gregor would be able to join the Guardian before they could free the cursed soul. Was it the look of fear?

Chapter 44

Blackness filled the cavern. Was it day or night? Gregor could not tell. He sat by the pool, his back against the limestone wall, listening to the water dripping nearby. He had been confined to this underground cave for a week waiting for the Dark Ruler to return. He had devoured the deer days ago. Only the gnawed and broken bones remained strewn across the blood-stained cave floor. As hunger pains again gripped his stomach, his frustration mounted at not being able to leave in search of fresh meat. He shattered the bones to suck out the marrow. The Master had no right to treat a loyal servant this way. Servant? Someday, I shall be the Master.

Gregor's body tensed as he felt something brush lightly against his foot. He drew in his breath. Could it be food?

There it was again!

He felt it rub against his toe. A rat! he thought, now fully alert.

The rat sniffed and then nibbled at Gregor's filthy heel.

Saliva dripping from his cracked lips, Gregor anticipated a mouth full of warm, delightfully- bloody rat meat.

Gregor felt the rodent climb up his leg. Picturing each step of the rat's movement, he waited until the rodent neared his open hand. In the center of his palm was the last dab of marrow. Not daring to breathe, knowing if he even let out a tiny breath, the rodent might escape, he waited for the rat to find the marrow.

The rat paused.

"Take the food," Gregor silently begged.

The rat was in Gregor's hand, sniffing at the bone marrow.

The air exploded from Gregor's lungs as he clenched his iron fingers around the rat, squeezing the life out of it. He swallowed it whole.

Gregor closed his eyes, savoring the morsel, fearing it would be the last meal he would be eating for quite a while. "It isn't fair," he grumbled, realizing, he did not have anything to use for bait if another scrawny rat came along.

Gregor pushed himself off the floor. "I wait no longer," he growled, as the bones under his feet cracked from his weight.

A bubbling noise.

Suddenly Gregor was startled by a blast of light. He stared in fear as the pool he was standing in erupted into a boiling fury. "Oh, no! Not again," he groaned, as he recognized the flaming ball of lava now settling back into the steaming water. "I wish he would leave me alone!"

The water exploded around him, flames leaping from its center.

Gregor backed away as the Dark Ruler emerged from the molten ball of lava.

"I'm back," the Dark Ruler said, laughing upon seeing the redness of Gregor's skin and the singed hair from being too close to the flaming lava.

Gregor was furious and had not fully learned his lesson. "Why have you returned, oh, great Master? Are you not satisfied that you left me here to die of hunger?"

"If I wanted you to die, you'd be dead long ago," The Dark Ruler smiled benevolently.

"You warned me not to leave—"

"You brought this upon yourself again. I warned you not to let them see you. I warned you that what you did centuries ago would not be tolerated in this century by mankind—"

"I kill man if he gets in way." Gregor pounded his fist on his chest.

The Dark Ruler tried to appear sympathetic. "You, sadly, are no match for humans now. They have evolved and have new weapons."

"I not afraid of man."

"I heard how brave you were when the gun fired," snickered the Dark Ruler. "You ran like a scared rabbit."

Gregor was fuming. "Need food," He snarled, exposing his blackened teeth. "I starving!"

This whining creature disgusted the Dark Ruler. "Well, I have good news for you. My sentries inform me that men are no longer searching this area for you." He gave the beast a smile, completely fake. "You see, that is what comes when you obey me." He glared at Gregor to be sure he had gotten the message.

"I obey," the giant replied but was still furious.

"Well, now that you have followed my instructions, and there is no longer the threat of you being discovered, you have my permission to leave the cave." He gave the creature a kind smile. "See how simple life is when you are a good boy?"

Gregor was excited. "I may go anywhere?" He could almost taste fresh meat in his mouth.

"No. Absolutely not! My bats will show you where to go."

"Gregor need meat!"

"And you shall have it. The land here is arid, but the bats have told me there is ample game if you follow them. And you will follow them. Is that clear?"

Gregor nodded.

"Good. I do not wish to have to discipline you again." He waved his arm. "I shall soon have excellent news for you."

Gregor watched as the Dark Ruler stepped back into the fireball.

"Remember my orders, and you shall be rewarded." As the last words faded, the fireball burst into a massive explosion of noise, flame, and smoke, and then was gone.

The bright light turned back into a solid wall of blackness, but Gregor had already begun groping his way to the entrance of the cave. Stepping out into the cold night, he sniffed the air, searching for prey.

Gregor pulled himself up between two large granite boulders covered in thorny shrubs. The loose gravel under his feet caused him to slip and slide, struggling to reach the peak, wishing he could fly like the bats he was following.

Finally, hours later, reaching the summit, he looked out over the dark valley. "Where are these bats leading me?" he growled when he spied distant lights on the horizon. "Those are the lamps of the humans, so why are they bringing me here?"

The bats kept moving toward the lights.

"Must find food," Gregort mumbled, as he continued to follow the bats heading south. *If humans come, I crush them as easily as I did the rat,* he thought, as he hurried to keep up with the Dark Ruler's guides.

* * *

Shu had been blowing clouds across the mountain range when he saw Gregor reach the top of the ridge. *Oh, it's him again,* Shu muttered, disengaging himself from the cloud he was riding hoping to find Gregor.

Shu sailed above the beast for several hours until he realized that Gregor was heading toward Carlsbad Caverns. Wasn't that where Steven was heading to surprise the Guardian? Shu knew this could mean big trouble for Steven and the others, so he hurriedly flew back to Steven's home to spread the alarm. He hoped he wasn't too late.

* * *

"That settles that. We must take Gregor out of the equation," Steven said, determined not to have to face two monsters at the same time. "Shu, please go back? See if you can delay Gregor. Distract him. I'll warn The Seeker that we have to get to the cavern and free the Guardian before Gregor gets there. What a mess!"

"Steven, you are not going anywhere on your own," Aunt Celia said, crossing her arms in front of her chest.

"But, Aunt Celia–"

"No. No. No."

Steven sighed. "Aunt Celia, if we don't stop Gregor from reaching Carlsbad, it means we will have to face him and the Guardian together, not to mention the possibility of the Dark Ruler showing up while The Seeker and I are in the cavern. I see no other choice but to split the team up. You, Bastet and Morag will eliminate Gregor, while The Seeker and I take care of the Guardian. We have to keep them from joining together."

"I don't like dividing up the team," Aunt Celia protested.

"We have no choice. Morag and Bastet need to be full size to fight so they'll never fit in the cave. Having them work, with you, to eliminate Gregor before he can get to the cave, is our best strategy."

"I should be with you," Aunt Celia insisted.

Steven felt frustrated. "I understand how you feel. Once you eliminate Gregor, you can join me in the cavern."

"I still don't like it," Aunt Celia said.

Steven sighed. "Aunt Celia, you will only be about a half mile from the guardian's cave." He handed her a paintball gun. "Once you arrive, come down carefully until you find us, Keep this paintball gun loaded."

"Does The Seeker agree with dividing up the group?" Aunt Celia asked.

"We discussed this possibility and he agreed that it was my call if he wasn't around." Steven looked into his aunt's eyes. "I don't like dividing us like this either, but The Seeker also feels that it would be in our best interest to manage a 'surprise attack' on both of these targets at the same time, so they have no warning."

Aunt Celia still wasn't happy. *Was Steven's strategy the only option? At least Steven would be out of the way if something goes wrong with our attack on Gregor, but can I let him attack the Guardian without me?*

"It will be worse if those two join up," Steven repeated as if reading her mind.

Aunt Celia frowned. "I still don't like it, but okay, we'll your lead. I won't lie, I am very reluctant to do it your way, but I agree that if we tried to liberate the Guardian all together, we could end up fighting Gregor, the Guardian, and the Dark Ruler simultaneously. That would be very difficult, especially in a cavern where Morag can't help."

"That's why I don't see any other choice," Steven said, wishing he could think of another way. "Okay, Shu, you can go now. It's settled."

Aunt Celia stared out the window as Shu left. She wondered if she was doing the right thing, letting Steven go after the Guardian without her. Working with her nephew seemed to always present her with difficult decisions, but he appeared to make the right ones. She wondered if this was the right decision.

Steven tried to look confident, but inside, he wondered if the team could pull it off. He understood dividing up would weaken them, make them more vulnerable to being overpowered, but he also knew it gave them the advantage of possibly surprising the enemy. But could this enemy be surprised? Could a boy, his professor of an aunt, and four mismatched mythical creatures, really hope to defeat the vast collection of monsters the Dark Ruler had drafted for his army? Could they really pull it off?

Chapter 45

Aunt Celia, backpack strapped to her, waited anxiously for Steven to open the Portal. Next to her were Bastet and Morag.

"I have set the Portal to let you off in a small ravine about one mile from the cave. A large outcrop of fern and aspens cover the surrounding area, so hopefully, you won't be detected. When you climb out of the ravine, head north and move into the woods. The exact location of the cave has been entered in your GPS. I'm not sure if there are any smaller crevices or caves with wild animals in the area, so please be careful," Steven said.

Bastet and I will locate the best place to corner Gregor, Morag said. *Once we find a secure location for your Aunt, I will leave her and track him as he proceeds to the cave. Bastet, will you remain with Aunt Celia until I locate Gregor?*

"Please find him quickly. I don't want him suddenly bearing down on us," Aunt Celia said. "Let's go!" Aunt Celia commanded, eager to take out Gregor and rejoin Steven and The Seeker as soon as possible.

"Okay, but please, contact me after you identify a safe place to hole up," Steven said as he pressed the enter button on the computer opening the Portal. "I don't want to worry about you."

"Now, who sounds like a worried parent?" Aunt Celia smiled at Steven.

Several minutes later, Steven heard a low ding on his smartphone telling him his aunt had arrived safely. He transcribed the new location to the computer and waited. The Phone chirped, indicating a message had just been received. Steven looked down at the screen.

"Having a wonderful time. The weather is hot and I am hot! Need I say more?"

Steven smiled and typed a response, 'will send sunscreen.' He laughed but realized someone was looking over his shoulder. Turning, he came face-to-face with The Seeker. "Holy cow! You scared the life out of me, sneaking up like that!"

"You must always be on your guard and fully alert, Steven. Are you confident that Aunt Celia, Morag, and Bastet can eliminate Gregor?" The Seeker asked.

"We really have no choice. We know by eliminating Gregor, the Dark Ruler will be alerted that we are onto him. Dividing up will allow us to enter the cave and free the Guardian's spirit before the Dark Ruler has any idea of what's happening. Once they eliminate Gregor, I believe The Dark Ruler will know in a short time, which means we need to eliminate Gregor and remove the evil spirit from the Guardian before the Dark Ruler becomes aware. Splitting up is the only option."

"You're right. We do not want to have to face all three at the same time, and with Gregor heading for Carlsbad, we must eliminate both him and the Guardian, almost at the same instant. Not an easy job," The Seeker said.

Steven nodded. "Gregor moving in on us here did complicate things. After Aunt Celia eliminates Gregor, she will contact me by phone, our signal to ambush the Guardian. She will then travel to our location and join us. You must free the Guardian's spirit quickly. No telling how fast the Dark Ruler will react to the news of Gregor."

"*The Dark Ruler, as I have observed, seems to have two methods to track his slaves. One is the bats we have seen around the Carlsbad Cavern. The second is some type of mental telepathy,*" The Seeker said, deep in thought.

"Yeah, I think you're right. The bats are a kind of warning system, but he must also have at least your ability to pick up thoughts," Steven replied.

"And that means he could rush to the cave to defend the Guardian a lot faster," The Seeker said.

"I didn't think of that," Steven muttered. "Another complication."

"And here's one more," The Seeker said, still voicing his thoughts, "Once I release the spirit of the Guardian, how will you and your aunt know when the Dark Ruler arrives?"

Steven smiled. "I've got that covered. From your description, we know The Guardian's cave is protected by a large pool of water. Correct?"

"Yes," responded The Seeker.

"You said the Dark Ruler jumps from place to place using a fireball."

"That's correct," replied The Seeker. "I have seen him do this many times while I was his captive."

Steven nodded. "So, when he sets the fireball down into the pool of water, the molten lava will cause a loud noise and the steam will alert Aunt Celia and me of his arrival. While you contain the Dark Ruler in the cave, Aunt Celia and I will blast him with the guns loaded with incense-filled powder balls. It worked before on the Guardians, and stopped the Dark Ruler when you fought him in the tomb of Seti I."

The Seeker nodded. "What if the incense doesn't work on the Dark Ruler this time?"

"Then we have a major problem," Steven said.

"Yes, we do," The Seeker replied.

Chapter 46

Aunt Celia's GPS screen indicated she was two miles from the cave entrance. The night was quiet, with an occasional mournful howl from a coyote, in the distance.

Bastet and Morag sat next to Celia between two scrub bushes. Bastet sniffed the hot air and listened with her keen ears for any threatening sounds.

Bastet and I sense you are safe here, Morag relayed telepathically.

Let's communicate this way to eliminate being detected by unwanted guests, Aunt Celia said telepathically in a whisper. *Is there a limit to the distance I will be able to hear you?*

Yes, Morag replied, *Bastet and I will stay as close as possible.*

Thank you, Aunt Celia answered, surveying the area.

Morag let out a puff of smoke. *I'll see how close Gregor is. We might have to move you to intercept him.* She leaped into the night and headed north.

While you search the area around the cave, Bastet, I think you should take on your lioness form. There may be coyotes, jaguars, wolves, and even lions in the New Mexican desert. You would be a tasty meal as a small cat, Aunt Celia said.

Let them try, growled Bastet, as she reverted to the shape of a lioness.

Aunt Celia placed her hand upon Bastet's back, rubbing the soft tawny fur. *You are beautiful,* she said. *I never thought I'd be petting a lion.*

Would you like to see me as a woman? Bastet asked.

That would be wonderful, but maybe some other time. Us girls could sit and talk over a glass of wine, Aunt Celia replied, a broad grin on her face.

I will hold you to that, purred Bastet, as she silently padded into the night.

Aunt Celia laughed, covering her mouth to stifle the noise.

Bastet turned, smiled, and continued until she was out of sight.

Aunt Celia's grin was quickly replaced with a look of worry as she realized she might never see her new friend again if things went wrong.

I've got to focus, she told herself, straining to hear any sound of movement in the area around her.

At first, all seemed peaceful, but suddenly, Aunt Celia froze. She had felt the air move. Something was fanning it. She felt it getting close. *Thank goodness, it's you,* she exclaimed as Morag landed.

There is no threat that I can detect, Morag said. *I did find Gregor, though. He is still several miles from here, but moving fast. Stay where you are for now, but be prepared to move should the situation change.*

Thank you, Morag, Aunt Celia said. *Next time, make some noise when you get close.*

Morag leaped back into the dark night to continue her vigil.

Aunt Celia leaned back against her backpack, gazing up at the starry sky. She searched for Pegasus, the winged horse from Greek mythology, but found it challenging to find among the millions of stars. The anxiety of preparing to confront Gregor was wearing on her. She closed her eyes and dreamt her face was being warmed by the sun. As she dozed, she suddenly felt a few drops of water. *What is that?* Startled awake, it took her several seconds to focus on what was staring her in the face.

The yellow eyes of a large mountain lion loomed over her. Its mouth was open, revealing sharp teeth. A droplet of saliva sat on the tip of its tongue.

Aunt Celia held her breath as the cat sniffed her face. A foul odor reached her nose each time the cat exhaled. Panic gripped her like a vice. I mustn't move. Don't move, she repeated in her brain. Her fingers dug into the sand as she desperately tried to force down the scream of terror building in her lungs. I can't show fear, she told herself. Her mind screamed for Bastet or Morag's help before it was too late...was it too late already?

The tan lion sniffed at Aunt Celia's neck. He was just below the jugular vein. His tongue whipped across her flesh.

The seconds ticked away. Aunt Celia tried desperately not to panic. Can animals sense fear? Mine is growing with each second, she thought,

Yes, a cat can sense human fear, Bastet said in a telepathic reply. *Stay still.* She ran up onto the embankment, several feet above Aunt Celia's head. *Keep still,* she ordered.

Aunt Celia held as still as she could manage with a lion in her face. Out of a corner of her eye, she saw Bastet's front paws had become long and sharp with nails jutting from the fur. She heard low, menacing growls. She felt the lion tense. *Would it attack her?* She closed her eyes.

Bastet hissed.

Aunt Celia squeezed her eyes tight, not knowing the sound came from Bastet. *Oh, please,* she begged silently.

Long seconds passed.

Aunt Celia opened her eyes just a crack. She was relieved to see she was no longer face to face with the voracious predator. But he was still inches away, his head turned away from her.

Stay where you are, my fellow feline, Bastet said, trying to sound friendly.

The human is mine, the lion rasped. *Mind your own business, my fellow feline.*

I understood him, Aunt Celia exclaimed *telepathically. How is that possible?*

Never mind that. The lion wants his dinner, Bastet said.

Do you mean me? Aunt Celia asked.

A thunderous roar exploded from Bastet.

Aunt Celia felt sand striking her face as Bastet's paws dug deep into the sand. With eyes narrowed for combat, Bastet issued a final warning to the other lion, also poised for battle. *Move away, lion. I don't want to hurt you. This human is my friend. I will not let her be harmed by you. This is my last warning! I am Bastet, an Egyptian god! Move away, or I will have to destroy you.*

Aunt Celia was surprised Bastet had called her a friend. She wondered if that was true, but now was not a good time to ask.

Do you think I am afraid of you? The lion roared, standing over Aunt Celia, and eyeing her throat which was, even more tantalizing with beads of sweat. *Back off, and I'll let you go on your merry way.*

Aunt Celia shivered as a hot drop of saliva landed on her face again. *It isn't working, Bastet.*

Without hesitating another second, Bastet leaped down upon the lion, surprising him with her ferocious attack.

The lion, startled by the speed of the attack, was thrown backward, but he recovered quickly and lunged at Bastet.

The two cats screamed and clawed at each other, each trying to tear the other's flesh with teeth and nails.

Aunt Celia was terrified as the two animals rolled over and over on the sand, their screams sending chills down her spine. She realized that Bastet in physical form could be hurt, perhaps even killed, by the lion. She was surprised the cat was willing to risk that for her.

The two large creatures were still seeking advantage over each other, rolling in the sand, and screaming out their fury.

The lion saw an opening and tried to bite into Bastet's neck.

Bastet ducked and clamped her powerful jaws down on the cat's throat. She locked her teeth around the struggling lion's neck, refusing to let go. She shook her head violently, and the lion screamed in agony.

"Don't kill him," Aunt Celia shouted. "Let him go? Please?"

Bastet released her grip and backed away, panting hard. *Are you sure you want to spare this miserable creature?* Bastet roared still prepared to kill her adversary.

Aunt Celia was still shaking. "I hate killing animals. Please, Bastet? He was doing what comes naturally."

I'll never understand humans, Bastet muttered but nodded. *You! Consider yourself fortunate. This human has saved you. If I see you again, I will kill you.*

The lion struggled to stand and started backing away, not taking his eyes off the strange lioness that had almost ripped his throat in half. Once he was a short distance from Bastet, he turned and ran as quickly as he could to get far away from the demonic cat that had almost killed him.

Bastet sniffed the air to ensure the lion was not circling back.

"Thanks, Bastet for being here for me. I'd prefer not to have dinner plans with a lion," Aunt Celia said, her voice and hands still quivering.

We girls must stick together. Bastet replied, already cleaning herself off.

"Thump!"

Aunt Celia and Bastet jumped when Morag dropped between them.

192

What did I miss? Morag asked. *"Bastet, you look terrible!"*

"Nothing." Aunt Celia said, "We have work to do." She gave Bastet a wink. *What are you two up to?* Morag asked.

"Should I tell her, or will you?" Aunt Celia asked.

Let me, Bastet responded. *"I love sharing war stories."*

You know what? Morag replied. *We have no time for fooling around. Gregor is heading here fast. I have found a crevice in the mountain where you can hide, but you need to get there as quickly as you can. He is almost on top of you! And he is hungry!*

"Fine. Bastet, let's get going? Morag go aloft and keep tracking Gregor. We don't want any more surprises. One unwanted 'guest' is too many." Aunt Celia was already waddling away.

Morag shrugged her wings. *I have no idea what you are talking about, but I'll let you know when Gregor gets closer.* She spread her wings and quickly soared back into the sky, sand flying everywhere.

Show off. Bastet shouted, smiling at Aunt Celia and then leaping up the hill.

Aunt Celia was relieved to see Bastet was remaining in her lioness form. It's safer, she thought, still unable to get over Bastet's transformation from a harmless house cat to a full-grown lioness whenever she wanted. I wish I could do that, she thought, as she started up the trail.

Follow me, Aunt Celia, Bastet called, as they headed for the location Morag had described as being an excellent place to trap Gregor.

It was a long, hard walk over rocks and shifting sand. Arriving at the designated spot, Aunt Celia dropped her pack. She placed her rifle on top of it. "This time, I'm ready," she announced, but wondered if she really was, especially after the lion's attack. "Are you sure that the lion is gone? He was pretty scary." She assumed a ready position on the ground.

Bastet saw Aunt Celia was still shaking and was worried about her. *I will search the area again, but you need to prepare yourself, to face Gregor. Are you okay to do that?*

Go on. I will be fine. I have my Beretta and rifle to keep me company, Aunt Celia replied, as she pulled a handgun from the holster fastened around her waist.

I'll be back soon, Bastet said, and quickly disappeared, running across the sand.

* * *

Gregor stopped and sniffed the air. The desert was dead quiet, too quiet, he thought. He stood motionless, not wanting to give his location away if any humans happened to be near. Was he being watched?

Gregor searched the surrounding area again. The desert was empty. In centuries gone by, Gregor had always been able to rely on his senses, but captivity had made him less attuned to nature. Spending more time in the wild again, he realized his ability to detect noises, smells, danger, was slowly returning but was still weak.

Morag was flying high above Gregor. She watched with interest as he seemed to be searching the sandy desert. Flying away before he spotted her, she sent a telepathic message to Aunt Celia, *Gregor is about a mile ahead of your location. Remain where you are, but get ready. I am prepared to swoop down if anything goes wrong. Oh my gosh! He is starting to move toward your hiding place. Get down! Get down!*

Chapter 47

Aunt Celia was huddled down on the rocks. An unnatural quiet blanketed the area around her. Nothing moved, not even the air, as she searched the horizon for any clue that Gregor was somewhere in front of her. Pressing her eye against the rifle's scope, she searched for Gregor through the infrared lens.

Morag, I don't see him. Is he still moving toward me? Aunt Celia asked telepathically.

No, he has stopped. He appears to be searching for something. I will contact you when he is on the move again. Stay low, and please be quiet?

Bastet, hearing the discussion between Aunt Celia and Morag, returned to Aunt Celia and crouched down next to her. Her keen eyes were looking far out into the desert.

A buzz startled Aunt Celia. She picked up a message Steven had texted, then raised her head and frowned at Bastet. *Steven and The Seeker are ready to enter the cavern once we send word that Gregor has been killed.* Aunt Celia sighed. *I hope he is going to be safe, and they succeed at freeing the Guardian.*

Let's hope this time it is for eternity. Bastet replied, still searching for any sign of Gregor.

It will be light in about two hours. Gregor has got to head to the cavern soon, or he will be out in the open for all to see, Aunt Celia said, becoming more edgier as time passed.

Morag, what is Gregor doing now? She asked, wishing this whole thing was over and she could get Steven back to the lab and safety.

As if on cue, Morag settled down next to Bastet. *Gregor has not moved. In*

195

fact, he sat down next to a boulder and appears to be napping.

What? Napping? Aunt Celia let slip out, wishing she could have taken back the sound. She quickly checked the scope for any movement along the sand. After several minutes, she sighed. *Nothing yet. I hate all this waiting.*

It is better than doing battle with these demons, Morag said.

What about the three bats that were leading him to the cave? Any sight of them? Bastet asked, eyes still staring far ahead.

Those pests are still with him, Morag replied. *"Once you eliminate Gregor, I will roast them. Yummy!"*

Always thinking of your stomach, Bastet grumbled.

"He has got to move soon! Time is running out," Aunt Celia muttered. "I have an idea. Bastet, maybe you can get him to chase you over to here? This waiting is getting on my nerves."

I agree. Anything is better than all this useless waiting, Bastet replied. *Morag, you keep an eye on me and swoop down if you see that monster about to chomp down on my beautiful tail.*

Oh, brother, Morag said, as she leaped into the sky to follow Bastet, who was headed in the direction where Gregor was last seen.

Aunt Celia settled down to wait. I only hope I haven't put my new friend in danger, she thought, regretting her decision to use Bastet as bait.

Long minutes passed. Aunt Celia, bored and tired, started to doze off. She thought she was dreaming when she realized Gregor was on the ridge right in front of her. "Oh no, no," she moaned.

A thunderous roar bellowed from Gregor's mouth as he descended toward her, scrambling over the rocks.

Seeing this monster almost upon her, Aunt Celia let out a blood-curdling scream and made a grab for her rifle.

Gregor let out another terrible roar.

Aunt Celia was surprised at the speed of the enormous beast's attack. Seeing a giant hairy arm rising to strike her, she raised the rifle.

Gregor knocked it out of her hands.

Aunt Celia was lying on her back, looking right up at the monster. Her face ached and was covered with sand from Gregor's charge. "I can't see," she cried, covering her face with her hands. One more attack and she knew she was finished. Her last thought was who would protect Steven.

A loud roar reached her ears. It did not sound like the monster.

Bastet leaped in front of Aunt Celia and was now facing Gregor. Her fierce eyes and bared teeth warned him not to advance toward his fallen prey. But would it be enough?

"Why are you protecting this human?" Gregor demanded, wondering if this cat was trying to keep the fat, juicy human, for her own dinner.

Still, on her back, Aunt Celia was trying to wipe the sand from her eyes, knowing she had seconds before the monster might attack again.

Stay still, Bastet commanded. *Maybe he'll think you're dead.*

Aunt Celia lay still, praying Bastet would be able to save her. Suddenly she heard another voice.

Bastet, get Gregor to move away from Aunt Celia, Morag said telepathically. *I will come up from behind and burn him to a crisp.*

He's too close to her, Bastet said. *If you miss, Aunt Celia will also be cooked.*

If we don't try, Aunt Celia will soon be in that monster's stomach, Morag replied. *Now hurry!*

Bastet nodded her head. She knew she would be risking her life to save Steven's aunt, her new friend.

Aunt Celia, her eyes still blurry, watched helplessly as Bastet let out a loud howl and launched herself at the monster's throat. She aimed her teeth at Gregor's neck, but Gregor dodged, preventing Bastet from locking her massive jaws around her target. She felt a huge hand hammer into her side, knocking her into the sand yards away.

Gregor stomped toward Bastet, picking up a large bone to use as a club. He raised the bone high over his head and let out a ferocious roar.

Bastet, still weakened, jumped away at the last second from the killing blow of Gregor's club.

"Aw! Are you hurt, little kitten?" Gregor taunted, raising the club again. "It won't hurt much longer. Just stand still, and I'll do it fast."

Bastet backed away, growling at the beast with all her fury.

Morag circled above, prepared to launch herself down on Gregor, but knowing the flames would be too close to Aunt Celia. Steven would never forgive her if something happened to his aunt. *A little more, Bastet...just a little—*

Are you kidding? Bastet shot back telepathically. She braced herself for what she feared would be the last blow. "This guy is no cream-puff!"

Gregor advanced toward the fallen cat, thinking how good she would taste once he tore her apart.

Bastet, wobbly on her feet, backed away from where Aunt Celia was in the sand. *Morag, where are you?*

A little further, Bastet, Morag said. *He is almost far enough away from Aunt Celia. Just a little more...*

Suddenly, Gregor stopped moving. He turned toward Aunt Celia. "Why am I settling for a mangy cat when I can have a nice juicy human?"

Bastet knew there was no time left. *Morag, he's not going for the bait. You've got to get him now.* Without thinking of her own safety, she ran between Gregor's legs and ripped his calf open with her sharp teeth.

Gregor let out a howl of pain. "Why you!" He turned back to Bastet. "You want to be my dinner that badly?" He swung the dense bone around his head. "Crushed cat chops it is!"

Bastet backed up again, drawing Gregor a few steps further away from Aunt Celia. *Come on, Morag,* Bastet urged, *where are you? She's never here when I need her.*

Aunt Celia, eyes still blurry, moved her hand slowly down to her holster, afraid the monster would see. She pulled out the pistol and cocked the hammer. Still unable to see clearly, she was scared to fire for fear of hitting Bastet.

Bastet couldn't move any farther away. Her back was against the rock wall, waiting for Gregor to charge.

Gregor, sensing the kill, roared in triumph and prepared to lunge at Bastet and kill her with one mighty blow of his club.

A ferocious roar erupted from above.

Gregor turned just as Morag dropped down in front of him.

It's about time, Bastet said, panting at how close she had come to be dinner.

Morag let out another roar. *Surrender now, and I shall spare your miserable life.* Her face was inches from Gregor. *I do not kill for pleasure, as does your Master, and you–*

Burn him, Bastet shouted.

Aunt Celia is still too close, Morag replied.

Gregor charged at Morag with his club raised. "I will enjoy killing you," he snarled. "It has been centuries since I have tasted dragon."

You will never get the chance in this life! Morag growled. Infuriated, Morag lashed out with her tail, catching Gregor on the side of his head. The blow knocked Gregor backward, unfortunately, straight toward Aunt Celia.

"Not again," Aunt Celia cried out, wishing she had not dropped her gun.

Morag leaped in front of Aunt Celia.

Bastet moved to her side.

Step aside, Bastet. I want him for myself, Morag said.

Bastet backed up, happy to give her wounds a chance to heal, but ready to jump in if needed.

Aunt Celia remained behind Morag, trying to reach the rifle.

I've waited for you to show up again, Morag hissed, the fury building up the fire inside her.

"I'll kill you and enjoy feasting on your bones," Gregor replied, about to put all his strength into a killing blow of the club.

Morag belched out an enormous flame.

There was a terrible scream.

Aunt Celia dropped her arm, which she had raised instinctively to protect her face from the fire and intense heat. She saw Gregor standing in the middle of a massive ball of fire. She winced at the sound of his agonized screams as flames danced on his furry arms. The smell of burning hair and flesh caused her to gag. She wished she could spare him, but knew that would put Steven's life in danger. She turned away, not wanting to see even this vicious beast suffer such pain.

I like my meat well done, Morag roared and released the second ball of flame.

Gregor was totally engulfed in fire. He screamed in agony, beating his arms against his body, desperately trying to extinguish the flame all over him.

Morag leaped into the predawn sky.

Aunt Celia thought it was over until Morag let out another roar and shot like a rocket toward the ground.

"Everyone down and cover your eyes," Aunt Celia shouted.

Morag dove at Gregor. Rearing back just inches from Gregor's burning form, her talon's cut deep into the flesh around the beast's flaming midsection.

"Enough!" Aunt Celia tried calling Morag, but the dragon stretched her wings, and took off, lifting Gregor into the sky.

"Where is she taking him," Aunt Celia asked, watching Morag fight to gain altitude, with Gregor as an unwilling passenger.

It doesn't matter. That beast is done, Bastet said. *Good riddance.*

"How long will Morag be able to carry him? He must weigh a ton," Aunt Celia said, still upset at the echo of Gregor's cries of pain.

As long as it takes, Bastet replied. *You don't mess with angry dragons.*

"Maybe, if it's far enough away, Morag could spare him? He is a living creature, after all." Aunt Celia tried to communicate telepathically with Morag, but there was no response. She tried again and again. "She isn't answering. Are we too far away?"

She doesn't want to talk to us, Bastet said.

"Why not?" Aunt Celia was exhausted and still covered with sand. She sat down on a rock, and Bastet dropped down next to her. Neither said a word. Aunt Celia kept thinking that Gregor may have been a monster, but he had also been a living and feeling being. She wished the Dark Ruler had not made him his tool. "Will Morag be alright," she asked. "I've never seen her so consumed by anger. She was quite frightening."

Bastet didn't reply. She was staring at the night sky, wishing she could spot her friend flying back. She would know then that Morag was safe.

Out of the corner of her eye, Aunt Celia watched the three vampire bats hovering over the spot were Gregor had stood. "Bastet," she said, looking off in the distance. "I just saw the three bats fly off. Our time is short. The Guardian inside this cave must be eliminated quickly. Those bats are going to report to the Dark Ruler. We have no time to lose!"

* * *

Morag struggled to keep a tight lock on the heavy beast clutched between her talons. She saw the mountain peaks just ahead. *Can I make it?* The weight of the struggling beast, flames that had been cooking his body had been extinguished by the rushing air, was sapping her strength. She glared down at Gregor. *I have a score to settle with you, she said, But how?*

A few minutes later, finally satisfied she was high enough, Morag released her grip. She circled the screaming monster as he tumbled down toward the jagged rocks below.

She smiled as she saw Gregor's body smash against the rocks. *That is for all the death and destruction you have inflicted,* Morag said, the taste of methane gas still active in her mouth.

In the silence of the mountains, only the sound of her wings could be heard as Morag floated down to inspect Gregor's corpse. She circled several times over his smoldering remains until satisfied the beast was finally dead. *And that is for my mother, she said.*

Aunt Celia, Morag called telepathically as she flew back to where she had left her friends. *The beast is dead. You can contact Steven and The Seeker that they are free to eliminate the Guardian.*

Are you okay? Aunt Celia asked telepathically.

Morag felt tired. The tension of these last months, the constant fear of attack by the Dark Ruler's dark forces, and now the battle with Gregor, had taken its toll. Making the fire that had finally defeated Gregor had sapped a lot of her energy, but there was something else that was causing her even more pain.

Morag, Aunt Celia called again and again, with no answer.

The dragon was frightened. She hadn't expected her violent reaction when she finally saw Gregor after so much anticipation, and remembered what he had done to her mother centuries ago. She hadn't planned to set him on fire and was shocked at how much she enjoyed his agony, his screams, his thrashing against the murderous flames. And yes, she enjoyed it. As horrible as it was, the lust for revenge for her mother's ordeal had overcome everything. She realized she had lost control and the violence so often attributed to her species, had taken over. It disturbed her to know she had enjoyed watching Gregor suffer. She had loved every painful second of it. I am a beast like he was, she thought, now hating the way she felt. All my years of controlling my dragon rage did not help.

Morag landed on a mountain peak and looked to where she knew her friends were waiting for her. She was afraid if she joined the others, she would want to experience that brute power again. The memory of Gregor's terrified eyes, the joy she felt at his screams...the taste of methane gas still in her mouth. What power that had been. *To have such an ability and not use it?* She thought of Steven, and could almost see his face. Would he have been terrified to see her true vicious self? She wanted desperately to go back and help him, but could she risk it? Could she risk unleashing the beast inside her again? Smoke streaming from her nostrils answered her questions. She wondered if somewhere in the world there was another of her species. The loneliness was overwhelming.

Chapter 48

The lair was black, pitch black, except for the occasional flash of flames erupting behind the Rulers throne. The silhouette of a hooded figure moved back and forth, pacing angrily. The sound of molten lava bubbling in the pools went well with his increasing rage at not finding the boy. Thick steam filled the cavern as a bat descended. "Why are you back again? Have you found that boy? Tell me you have."

The bat, shivering at the rage of his master reported that Gregor was traveling south, away from the Mammoth Caverns.

"Who told him to leave the mountains? I commanded him to remain," the Ruler bellowed. "I told myself he was not to be trusted. Anger and hatred of the boy have again clouded my judgment. Gregor will pay for his disobedience. Get back and find that boy!"

The bat was grateful to be able to leave the hellish cavern, glad to be alive.

The Dark Ruler stared glumly after the bat. "When and where will they strike next? It was that boy and the priest who freed the dragon." He let out a deep sigh. "I gave that priest a chance to join me before I imprisoned him." He laughed cruelly, "He calls himself a man of God? A Guardian of mankind? He needs a small boy to do his bidding." An evil laugh erupted from his throat. "Your time is short, my friend. And that boy? Oh, how he will suffer when I have my hooks in him. It's just a matter of time until my servants' find you, and then..." He touched the tarnished medallion on his neck, the image of a human figure being consumed by fire, his arms raised to heaven. He raised his eyes and summoned his lava ball.

The specter of molded rock and flame rose from the depths of the abyss.

The Ruler stepped inside and let the flames engulf him. In seconds, he was standing in the Guardian's cave. The Ruler called his name. "Ripper of Death, arise and honor your Master."

"I am here master," a ghostly voice replied.

The Ruler smiled as he gazed upon a human form, now deformed by his hand. The Guardian was tall, more than six feet tall, clad in chain mail, partly covered by a torn, blood-spattered white cloak. His red beard, what was left of it, hung down to his belt. Protruding from his chest was a dagger. He walked unsteadily toward his master.

The Dark Ruler felt proud of his creation. "The boy and The Seeker will be here soon. Have you prepared for their arrival as I instructed?"

"All is ready."

"Remember, don't chase the boy. Allow them to enter your cave. I will then arrive and block the entrance and capture the boy," the Ruler hissed.

The Knight watched with hollow eyes as the Ruler disappeared in the molten rock and flame. Within seconds the light in the cavern faded, the steam diminished, and the cavern began to cool down.

The Knight, once a heralded warrior, returned to his cave and darkness.

Chapter 49

S teven heard the whoosh as the Portal vanished. It took several seconds for him to realize he was standing in the dark. Dark is not the word for it, he thought. I can't see my hand even. He pressed the toggle switch in his LED flashlight, and then his helmet light, and stepped out of the cold spring in which the Portal had landed. He shot the flashlight beam around the cavern walls in search of any stray prehistoric squirrels that might have survived. He did not want them to alert the Guardian. Detecting no sign of the rodents, Steven said to The Seeker, "Let's go."

"*I have been waiting. Gregor is dead?*" The Seeker asked.

"*Yes, Aunt Celia just sent me a text.*"

Hurrying, Steven followed The Seeker heading for the Guardian's cave. He panned the flashlight around him, wondering if all the rodents had joined the bar-b-que. Without the prehistoric squirrels to warn the Guardian, he hoped to take the evil servant of the Dark Ruler by surprise. He felt more confident after hearing from Aunt Celia that Gregor was no longer a threat. He was sure they could free the Guardian before the Dark Ruler heard of it.

The sound of steadily dripping water echoed off the limestone walls, as Steven slogged down into the tunnel. *We must be getting close,* Steven said telepathically, not wanting to alert the Guardian or any sentries that might still be lurking nearby.

Stepping out of the narrow tunnel, Steven gazed up at the stalactites hanging down from the vaulted ceiling. Draperies of gray-white calcium deposits clung to the limestone walls. His flashlight reflected off the surface of the walls formed by rushing water eons ago.

"*I feel we are close,*" The Seeker said, wishing he didn't need to put Steven in such danger.

Steven slowed his pace, trying to step around the pools of water to cut down the splashing noises.

"We must be silent," The Seeker cautioned.

Steven felt the amulet around his neck become warm. *We're very close. Strange, I don't believe I've ever felt the charm get warm when I came near other Guardian's caves. I still don't know what powers this amulet possesses or how to use them. I wonder if The Seeker knows.*

I sense no movement, The Seeker said, gliding ahead.

Steven directed the beam just above what he felt had to be the entrance to the Guardian's cave.

A shrill, terrifying, scream filled his ears.

Steven jerked the flashlight toward the source of the piercing noise and spotted a saber-toothed squirrel standing in front of an opening directly to his right. "What big fangs you have," he muttered, as long, razor-sharp nails extended from the prehistoric squirrel's front paws.

The startled squirrel arched its back and snarled menacingly.

"He's going to alert the Guardian," Steven warned The Seeker.

The squirrel, stunned by this intruder, hesitated one second too long.

Steven's instincts kicked in. He aimed the flashlight into the rodent's eyes.

The squirrel, not used to bright light, averted his eyes. He trembled as if the brightness was hurting him.

Looks like not all the rodents joined the roast, Steven said, keeping his flashlight on the squirrel, wondering if it might charge. *I thought they were all gone,* he said to The Seeker.

There is always someone who doesn't get the word, The Seeker responded from somewhere ahead.

He's going to warn the Guardian if we don't stop him, Steven shouted, still controlling the menacing creature with his light. *Go after the Guardian. I'll hold off this annoying creature.*

Your aunt will kill me if something happens to you, The Seeker said, thinking of turning back, but knowing if he didn't act fact, the Guardian might be alerted by all the noise.

We'll all be in deep trouble if you don't free the Guardian fast, Steven replied. *I can take care of one little squirrel. He* gripped his hand tighter around the large flashlight.

I don't like leaving you, The Seeker said.

I'll clobber him with this thing if I have to, Steven replied.

Just don't take any chances. Please? The Seeker reluctantly headed toward the entrance of the chamber.

Steven turned his attention back to the toothsome squirrel. "You, Mister Prehistoric Squirrel, better be good. I'm not going to allow you to enter the Guardian's cave to alert him." He said, and moved along the wall, using his body to block the entrance. "Come on, little squirrel," he coaxed, using his flashlight to force the squirrel to back away. "Why don't you and I become friends?" He lowered the torch to see if the squirrel would appreciate that gesture of friendship.

The saber-tooth squirrel hissed and jumped down on the cave floor. It paused for a moment before leaping on the outcrop of stones several feet above the pool. From his high perch, he seemed to be studying Steven, perhaps never having seen a human before.

See? I'm not going to hurt you, Steven said, his eyes on the sharp white teeth. *Be a good squirrel now, and we'll get along fine.*

The rodent let out a roar and charged.

Steven aimed the light directly into the attacker's eyes.

The squirrel was still coming, his face turned away from the light.

Steven squeezed the flashlight tightly in his hand and braced for the attack.

The squirrel jumped from stone tower to stone tower jutting above the water. Only a few feet from Steven, the rodent paused, teeth bared and hissed furiously.

Steven tried one last time to win his enemy over with a friendly smile. '"*Come, little guy, let's play?* He held the heavy flashlight ready just in case. *I have some nice prehistoric nuts at home for you.*

A shrill cry burst from the squirrel's throat again and he leaped at Steven's throat.

Steven quickly estimated the speed as the Saber-tooth squirrel hurled himself into the air, mouth open, sharp fangs ready to bite into flesh. Stupid squirrel, Steven thought, as he lifted the flashlight above his head.

As the squirrel sailed through the air, his attack cry was cut short when the heavy flashlight smashed hard against his head, hurling him against the cavern wall. A loud thud and the sound of breaking bones echoed in the cave.

Steven, ready for a second attack, saw the squirrel slide to the cavern floor. A trail of blood followed. He felt sad as the squirrel quivered several times and then stopped moving. He approached the animal cautiously, suspecting a trap.

The squirrel didn't even twitch.

"I'm sorry. I really didn't want to hurt you," Steven whispered, lowering the flashlight. *How does the Dark Ruler turn so many creatures into mindless killers? I wish I knew.* He kicked the dirt next to the body, wishing again that the creature had not attacked.

Steven stepped closer to the entrance of the vault that led into the Guardian's chamber. He listened for The Seeker's voice, but except for the water continually dripping, all was quiet. Too quiet, but Steven was exhausted from the long night and the unexpectedly tricky battle with the killer squirrel. He sagged against the cave wall, trying to catch his breath in the thin atmosphere deep underground. He wished he had x-ray vision so he could see if The Seeker had already freed the spirit of the Guardian. *Where the hell is my aunt?* Steven thought, realizing that at any moment the Dark Ruler might materialize right in front of him. If the squirrel had been so vicious, imagine what the Dark Ruler would be like if he shows up.

Chapter 50

The Seeker was poised over the sleeping Guardian, hoping he made the right decision in leaving Steven to battle the prehistoric rodent on his own. He thought about the Dark Ruler and wondered how a priest from the highest Egyptian priestly order could turn on his fellow men and create the monsters he had placed throughout the world. He studied the body of the Knight Templar, embedded standing up, in the cave wall, as if waiting to be called into battle, unfortunately, on the side of evil. He was grateful no rodents were around to awake the knight.

There was a loud scream from the outer chamber.

It had to be the prehistoric squirrel, The Seeker thought, hoping the cry would not wake the Guardian. He hurriedly prepared to spread the incense he'd brought with him over the knight.

The Guardian stirred, his arm lifting slowly, as if in pain.

Steven, I need you here to assist me, to free the Guardian's spirit according to the prophecy. Hurry, he is starting to stir! The Seeker called telepathically, hoping the Guardian could not pick up the mental messages, but unsure of the powers of these supernatural beings.

Coming, Steven replied, getting up to his feet, even though he felt exhausted and light-headed. He moved as quickly as he could through the shallow pool of water and entered the Guardian's cave. He removed the paintball gun from his backpack and loaded the incense-filled pellets into the chamber.

Thank goodness, you're safe, The Seeker said telepathically.

You should have seen that crazy squirrel, Steven began.

The Guardian is waking. Get ready. I will hold him down while you sprinkle the incense over his entire body. The Seeker said, his eyes never leaving the Guardian's face.

"Cover your eyes," Steven shouted, pointing the gun at the Guardian and squeezing the trigger.

The blast of compressed air sent the paintball exploding against the Guardian's body.

The recoil knocked Steven off-balance and a second shot bounced off the cavern walls. The cavern filled with powder, burning Steven's eyes.

A low moan rose from the Guardian's throat.

It was difficult to see, but Steven squeezed the trigger, firing again. Can't take any chances, he thought, as he watched the powdery tentacles of incense wind around the Guardian.

"Good shooting," The Seeker said.

The Guardian screamed and bucked high into the air.

Steven aimed his gun again. Frightened by the screams and thrashing of the Guardian.

The Guardian's body twisted and quivered, incense tentacles tightening.

Steven was still pointing the gun at the Guardian, but realized that three shots were enough. "The recoil made me miss the second time. I must remember this when it comes time to shoot at the Dark Ruler." He coughed, the cloud of incense choking him. "I hate this stuff," he muttered, wiping his eyes with his shirt sleeve.

"It is done," The Seeker said. "You don't need to remain for the rest."

The smell of the decaying body turned Steven's stomach. He wanted to leave but was afraid the knight might still break free of the incense tentacles now slithering like snakes over his body.

The skeleton-like creature let out another hideous scream and bucked hard against the grip of the tentacles. The creature's arms and legs tried to kick free. The unearthly cries were shrill and endless.

Steven covered his ears. The pain must be awful, he thought.

The Seeker was staring in silence, a sad look on his face.

There was another keening wail.

Steven leaned forward, about to fire at the creature again when he saw the bucking stop, and the Guardian's body settle back into the wall.

"I think it's over," Steven said, placing the paintball gun into his backpack. "That was terrible. Did you hear the screams?" He shook his head. "Do you think he suffered much?"

The Seeker, tucking the good bag of incense under his belt, pointed to the ceiling. *"That thin ribbon of blue above us is his soul. He has been freed. He is at peace."*

"Sadly, a brave knight could be made into a ghoulish monster by the Dark Ruler," Steven said, wondering if he would ever have peace.

"You should feel happy that you have set him free of his slavery to the Dark Ruler, Steven. You are fulfilling the prophecy."

Steven pulled his smartphone from his pocket and informed Aunt Celia that the Guardian had been freed, his mind still hearing the agonized cries of the once noble knight. Well, it won't be long now before we can head for home, he thought, feeling incredibly tired.

"Let's prepare for the Dark Ruler's arrival," The Seeker said. "My guess is he already knows we are here."

"That was the plan," Steven replied, wondering if he would be brave enough to face the monster of all monsters. This was bad enough, he thought. "Maybe we can do this another day," he wanted to ask, but knew the answer, so he didn't bother.

The Seeker was silently studying the cave. "This cave would make a good trap for our foe. I will remain hidden up there." He pointed to a deep hole in the limestone ceiling. "I suggest you move over to the other side of the cave and hide in the small opening under the stalactites. From now on, we will communicate telepathically. He could be here at any time once he realizes his Guardian is no longer under his control."

Aunt Celia should be arriving soon too, Steven said and waded over to the hiding place. Still tired, he removed his pack and crawled back into the cavity, pulling the bag behind him to cover the small entrance. *It smells awful in here,* he complained, sneezing from the incense in his nose.

Steven, you must stop that noise. And your light! You must douse it. Remember, only communicate telepathically.

The cavern turned black after Steven shut off his flashlight. Huddled in the small hole, he felt frightened. The battle with the squirrel and with the Guardian had been much more difficult than he'd expected. The Dark Ruler was a terrible enemy. He took a deep breath, trying to control his fear, hoping his trembling would not give him away. Steven felt as if the walls were pressing in on him, but held perfectly still. Two down, and one heck of a monster to go, he thought, about to fight the most sinister monster in the world.

Chapter 51

The Dark Ruler sprang awake when he sensed the loss of one of his Guardians. "No!" he roared, jumping from his chair, eyes glowing a fiery red. "I lost another slave? Impossible! I want answers!"

At the sound of his shouting, the gargoyles near his feet cowered in terror.

"Which of my slaves is lost to me this time?" The Dark Ruler grumbled as he searched throughout the world into those caverns where he had concealed his secret soldiers of death. He breathed a huge sigh of relief when after sending telepathic messages he received puzzled replies from each of his sentries. "Maybe I was wrong," he muttered, checking off each location after his sentries responded. He stopped cold when he didn't receive a response from the sentries guarding the Knight Templar, whose tomb lay deep within Carlsbad Caverns. He tried again to find his sentry. "You must be kidding. That knight was one of my favorites," he fumed. A dark expression filled his face. Somehow The Seeker and the boy must have found his Guardian.

The Dark Ruler's temper exploded. He had been cheated of the soul of a knight who had once been a man of bravery and virtue, but who he had taken great pride in transforming into one of his slaves. The brave knight had become a mindless slave with no purpose other than to kill upon his command. "I will destroy that priest, the boy. I will destroy them all," he screamed.

The gargoyles came to attention. Their mouths open, teeth gleaming.

"I didn't summon you," The Ruler roared, flames shooting from his eyes. "You're all useless! A mere boy is worth more than all of you together!"

The beasts cowered in fear behind the throne, afraid to lay eyes on the Dark

Ruler's grotesque features when he was in such a rage.

The chamber's rock walls glimmered with an orange-reddish glow as the Dark Ruler's fury was building to an explosion of immense magnitude. "Where is that idiot Gregor?" The Dark Ruler screamed, making the entire mountain shake. Stalactites that had hung for centuries shattered on the floor. Small pools surrounding the chamber wall bubbled and then burst upward, throwing hot molten lava into the air. The heat in the chamber reached over three thousand degrees from his volcanic fury.

"How could that Priest have known about him?" The Dark Ruler asked over and over, glaring at the gargoyles and hog servants, who were shivering with fear that they might become the target of his fiery temper. Not one dared to confront him. Not one dared to say one word to calm him. Not when he was like this.

Suddenly, the sound of flapping leathery wings caught the Dark Ruler's attention. He glanced up just as three squawking bats flew out of a nearby tunnel and into his cavern. "They'd better have good news for me," he growled to his gruesome servants.

"Master. Master," the bats squealed.

"Speak, my loyal spies," The Dark Ruler ordered, hoping they had news that he'd been mistaken about the loss of his knight.

Dropping to the floor, the largest of the three bats waddled toward the Dark Ruler, bowed, and began squealing his message.

"Gor atk," he squealed. "Gorgor ded."

The Dark Ruler leaned down and said in forced calm, "Will you please repeat what you said?"

The bat gulped, sensing he was in real danger. The other bats had already backed away. "Sor to reprt...Sire..." He swallowed again, knowing he was about to be bar-b-qued by the master's blazing hot eyes. "Gorgor ded."

"What?" The Dark Ruler roared, the bats thrown into the air by the burst of energy from his mouth. "Dead? Did you say, DEAD?"

"He ded. Gorgor ded," the bat squeaked, crawling on the ground before his enraged Master. "I sor to reprt. I ver sor–"

"Get out!" Dark Ruler yelled. "Get out of my sight!"

The bats scrambled away on their stomachs.

"Wait!" The Dark Ruler's command froze the bats in place. "You must be mistaken," he said, eyeing them with menace. "There is nothing on this earth that can kill Gregor."

"A tiny voice from behind the chair whispered, drag-on."

The Dark Ruler needed nothing more to set him off. "Get out! Get out and warn the others," he screamed at the bats who were already fleeing from the cavern. "You will warn me if any of my other slaves are attacked. Otherwise, I will enjoy dining on your well-done carcasses."

The bats squealed and raced into the night.

The Dark Ruler tried to control his temper, so he could think about his next actions logically. "Darn fool bats! I can't trust anyone." He shot a fiery look at the hogs and gargoyles cowering in fear. "If something is to be done, I must do it myself. You're all useless to me. I should cook every one of you."

"No, master! No!" They begged, groveling on their knees, ready to run for cover.

The Dark Ruler shook his head. "Maybe later. For now, I must see for myself what happened to my knight. You are lucky I have no time to waste on the likes of you." With that, the Dark Ruler hurried over to the lava pool and summoned the ball of fire.

The pool erupted into hot bubbles as the flaming sphere rose from its depths.

Within seconds, the Dark Ruler was concealed by the molten lava, and the flaming ball dropped down into the furnace of hell. "I will avenge the loss of my Guardian, and settle the score with that boy and The Seeker, once and for all!" he roared, as the ball carrying the Dark Ruler sped to the Guardian's location.

In the depths of his lair, the hogs and gargoyles trembled at what they thought the Dark Ruler would do to them if he did not find The Seeker and the boy. They were glad they were not the boy. Oh, what their Master was going to do to him! Their mouths salivated at the thought.

Chapter 52

Steven squirmed uncomfortably trying to fit in a narrow opening in the jagged walls. He rolled onto his side and pulled out two limestone rocks that had been pressing against him. I hate the dark, Steven thought. His aunt had told him to breathe deeply and exhale slowly. He tried it several times, then gave up. Not working this time, he thought. The wall seemed to squeeze tighter around him. How long would he have to wait pressed in this tiny space? "I don't know what I am more scared of, the darkness of this cave or the Dark Ruler," he mumbled, wondering if The Seeker could pick up his thoughts.

Time passed, and Steven, still tense, tried to relax by concentrating on the sound of dripping water.

"Drip. Drip. Drip."

"This is ridiculous," Steven said, pulling the black paintball pistol from the side pocket of his backpack. He held it close to his eyes to be sure it wasn't damaged, and then placed it in front of him, where it would be within reach. He then slid his hand into the right pocket of the pack to double-check on the second magazine and the three spare CO_2 cartridges. From experience, Steven knew there was plenty of CO_2 in the current cartridge, but his nervousness made him recheck everything. He clicked off the number of incense balls he had fired at the Guardian and reckoned five remained in the chamber. *More than enough to immobilize the Dark Ruler...if they work at all?* Steven realized The Seeker was counting on him once the battle began. It was all in the prophecy. *Seeker!* Steven called telepathically.

I am here, Steven. Are you okay? The Seeker asked.

Yes, but I hate the darkness! I can't see my hand in front of my face. Steven held up his hand.

You must not use your light. It will give us away, The Seeker cautioned. *I know you are afraid. That is natural, but you must wait here, or all is lost. If 'our friend' does not show by morning, or if you do not hear from me, I want you to return home.*

What do you mean, not hear from you? Steven did not like the sound of that.

Do not worry. Now we must remain silent. I do not want to risk the Ruler overhearing our thoughts. You must get some rest, so you are at your best when the time comes.

Steven rested his head on his folded arms. The rhythm of the dripping water echoing in his ears began to lull him. In minutes, his eyes closed from exhaustion.

The Seeker was grateful when Steven drifted off to sleep. He remembered not long ago that Steven had been an innocent boy, a boy who like any other child, enjoyed sports, watching television, spending time with friends. Those days are over, The Seeker thought sadly, knowing the boy was about to face a battle that could change the world forever. He gazed over to where Steven was sleeping and wished he could turn back the clock and give him back that wonderful childhood he would no longer know.

* * *

Steven awoke abruptly. Something strange was happening. He was blind-folded so he couldn't see. He was suspended in air, his body swaying, arms and ankles tied to a pole by thick straps. He felt as if he was being carried up a steep incline. He detected the sound of sandals scuffing against a sandy floor. Steven heard voices but could not understand what was being said.

"Where am I?" he shouted as he wanted to remove the covering from his eyes. His arms and hands would not move. He strained against the bindings securing his arms and legs, but they would not give. He turned his head, trying to peak under the blindfold tied tightly across his eyes. Then he saw a flickering light pass over his head. As quickly as it had appeared, he was thrust back into darkness. *Was that a candle?*

The swaying stopped. Steven felt as if he was still suspended in the air.

The smell of rotten meat reached his nose, making him gag. His stomach churned. He was hot, very hot, sweating. *How could that be?* The last he remembered, he had been lying in a cold, damp cave waiting for the Dark Ruler. *I remember that now. So how did I get here? Where is here?*

Steven tried to speak, but something was stuffed into his mouth. He decided to move his tongue, but the cloth gag prevented it. Steven strained, twisted and pulled against the tight straps wrapped around his arms and legs. He rocked violently back and forth, fighting against his bindings. "Let go of me," his brain screamed. "Let me go?"

There was a loud, snapping sound, followed by searing pain across Steven's arm and chest.

Steven cried out, his voice muted from the gag in his mouth, as the pain coursed through his body. "Stop!" he cried, but no sounds escaped.

There was a second loud snap.

Steven's back exploded with pain. Tears welled up in his eyes and ran down into the wound. "What do you want from me?"

"Stop struggling," a voice growled from somewhere above.

Steven stopped moving.

"Put him here next to the pit," the voice commanded.

Steven was thrown to the stone floor by invisible hands. Banging his head against the hard rock floor, he blacked out.

Some time later, Steven was jerked awake when he felt someone pulling his bindings. Sharp nails cut into his skin as his tormentor grabbed the rancid cloth that had been tied tightly over his eyes. The sudden light blinding him, he blinked, trying to focus.

A nightmare face was staring down at him.

"No," Steven moaned, closing his eyes, trying to push the sinister dark face back into the nightmare from which it had come. *This can't be true. I'm dreaming,* he screamed in his mind. *This is just a dream...just a dream.*

Banging his head against the opening in the cave wall, woke Steven from what had been a terrifying nightmare. He took a deep breath, trying to calm himself. "That was a bad one," he said aloud, letting his eyes check around, to make sure it had been only a dream.

"What woke me? Where's The Seeker?" Steven heard loud hissing and saw an enormous flash of light. The chamber was becoming incredibly hot as a cloud of steam rose in the cavern.

Steven froze. His face was illuminated by a strange orange light as he peered over his backpack.

A massive ball of flame was rising from the depths of the pond.

Steven watched in fascination as a man dressed in a long black robe stepped from inside the heart of the ball of flaming lava. That has to be him, he thought, as his eyes were drawn to the long, gnarled fingers hanging down from the over-sized sleeves of the stranger's robe. The man's back was turned to him.

The Dark Ruler is here. Steven sent a telepathic message to The Seeker. *He's here!*

The robed figure stood still, his eyes on the ball of lava.

Steven watched, barely breathing as the Dark Ruler turned slowly toward him. He shivered, as the ghoulish red eyes appeared to be studying the wall only a few feet from where he was hiding. An icy chill raced through Steven's body. This was the monster.

The Dark Ruler's pulsating red eyes panned the cavern floor in front of Steven.

Steven didn't move. Had the Ruler sensed something as he emerged from the ball of molten lava? *What will I do if he sees me? Where is The Seeker?* Steven searched for the paintball gun resting on his backpack. Moving his finger to the trigger, he was prepared to fire the weapon loaded with incense balls, if the Ruler walked toward his hiding place. He hoped that wouldn't happen. Though he looked like an ordinary man in a robe, Steven couldn't stop shivering. This creature was terrifying. *Please, don't let him see me?*

After what seemed like hours of scrutinizing every corner of the cave with his eyes, the Dark Ruler turned his head back toward the entrance to the Guardian's tomb. He walked toward the small opening. Suddenly, the Ruler paused again, still sensing something was wrong...something was near.

Search the chamber again, he told himself.

Steven felt sweat building on his forehead. He could fire the gun but might miss. *Where is The Seeker when I need him?*

The Dark Ruler shook his head and sighed. Then he bent his tall body and squeezed through the small opening in the limestone wall that Steven knew led to the tomb of the knight whose soul they had freed.

He's getting away, Steven shouted.

The Seeker, sensing the Dark Ruler, was just outside the Guardian's cave prepared to attack.

My turn, The Seeker said, as he slipped from his hiding place and floated down toward the entrance of the Guardian's cave.

Be careful, Steven said.

You too, my brave friend, The Seeker replied, knowing this might be the last time he would see Steven if things didn't work as planned.

Steven waited in suspense, knowing the two titans would clash. He could feel every bone in his body tensing with fear.

Suddenly Steven was pressed back into the tube he was hiding in by a deafening explosion.

The cave shook violently as a plume of smoke and fire shot out of the Guardian's cave.

Oh no! Steven exclaimed. Has The Seeker been destroyed by the Dark Ruler?

To his surprise, Steven saw the Dark Ruler had been hurled out of the cave so hard he hit the wall. It's over, Steven thought. The Seeker won!

The Dark Ruler fell to the ground.

That was easy, Steven mused. It looked as if his worst enemy was unable to move. He prepared to crawl out from his hiding place, to check on The Seeker, but decided to wait just a bit longer.

As the smoke of the explosion cleared, Steven finally saw The Seeker emerge from the Guardian's cave, a slight smile on his face. *It's over, Steven. He never stood a chance against good.*

Finish him. Steven urged telepathically. *Don't give him a chance to stand up. Don't stop —*

Chapter 53

Steven watched helplessly as the Dark Ruler launched himself through the air toward the startled Seeker.

"Did you really think I could be defeated that easily? I swore I'd destroy you," The Dark Ruler screamed, as he flew through the air. "And I will!"

The Seeker, unprepared for the charge, hurriedly raised his wooden staff and it threw up a deflector shield, bouncing his attacker back against the far wall. "You and what army?" He challenged, ready for another charge.

"You are stronger than I thought," The Dark Ruler said, shaking his head, the hood falling for an instant.

It was enough. Steven saw the twisted, grotesque, face of the monster for the first time up close. He shivered at the pure evil. No skull Steven had ever seen had such terrifying pits and cracks, but the eyes frightened him more than anything else. He had never seen eyes so full of hate. He worried for his friend as The Dark Ruler stood again, looking fully recovered.

"It is nice to see you again Sonchis," The Dark Ruler said, a sinister smile on his gray lips.

"I Can't say I share the same feeling," The Seeker replied, taking the measure of his opponent.

The Dark Ruler extended his hand. "I have no quarrel with you, my old friend. I come here only for the boy. Give him to me, and I will spare you. Where is he?"

The Seeker sighed. He'd hoped his foe might not know about Steven. "The boy from the prophecy, the boy you fear, will arrive shortly. We are both making ready to send you back to hell."

A blood-curdling laugh rang off the cavern walls. "Send me back?" The Dark Ruler released another gale of laughter. Then he grew serious again. "How do you propose to do that, you weakling? You have never been able to overpower me. I see no reason to believe that you can do so now."

"Are you forgetting our 'meeting' in Seti I?" The Seeker asked.

"I haven't forgotten, and neither will you, once you have been returned to the cube where you were my prisoner. Except this time, you will not be offered the sublime pleasure to witness my destruction of mankind. You will be confined in a windowless cell filled with tormented souls, ravenous spirits, to keep you company through all eternity!" The Dark Ruler raised his arms and wiry threads shot out from under the sleeves of his robe. The steel threads formed into the heads of twin snakes. They shot like arrows at The Seeker. Their jaws open, and long fangs extended like sharp knives.

Steven gasped as The Seeker countered by spinning the staff held in his right hand. Acting like a shield, the spinning staff twisted the venomous snake bodies around each other. The serpents hissed angrily as they were vaporized after biting each other with their venom. Gray particles, the last remnants of the snakes were flung through the air, as The Seeker returned the staff to his side. "Snakes? Really? Can you think of nothing more deadly?"

"Well done," The Dark Ruler sneered.

"It's my turn now." The Seeker launched a bolt of lightning straight at the Dark Ruler before he could fire some other weapon.

"Is that the best you can do?" The Dark Ruler shouted as a glimmering shield materialized to protect him.

The lightning bolt hit the shield and flew toward the opposite wall, striking a few inches from where Steven was hiding. It was challenging to keep still when the lightning crashed near him, but he managed.

The Dark Ruler roared with laughter, the walls quivering as his voice resonated through the cavern. "My turn again," he said and thrust the head of his staff toward The Seeker. "I like this game, but sadly I must end it soon."

The shaft flew straight to its target, The Seeker's heart. It would tear through flesh and bone, carve out its victim's heart and bring it back to its owner after it did its bloody task.

The Seeker saw the deadly projectile and transformed into a white vapor just before the blade hit.

Steven watched the shaft travel through the air and embed itself deep into the wall behind where The Seeker had stood. He wondered if his friend had escaped the attack.

The Seeker reverted to his original form and immediately launched his own spear.

The spear was deflected by the Dark Ruler's shield.

"You appear to be slowing down. Has old age caught up with you?" The Dark Ruler taunted.

"I'm just getting started," The Seeker replied, as he stealthily drew the bag of incense from the belt hidden by his robe. Once in his hand, he hurled it at his enemy.

The Dark Ruler side-stepped the bag with ease. He watched with amusement as the bag smashed against the cavern wall and splattered into a dark powder. "A canvas bag? That is your secret weapon?" He shook his head and laughed. "My dear friend, why are we fighting? I am impressed. You are stronger than I remember. Why not join forces with me? Together, we will conquer the humans. We will rule this planet as we wish, as the gods we are."

"That is a tempting offer," The Seeker said, trying to catch a glimpse of where Steven was hidden.

The incense was spreading across the wall and floor. Its fumes were reaching out in all directions.

The Dark Ruler barely noticed. While the smell of the incense singed his nose slightly and forced him to move farther out toward the center of the cave, it was more a nuisance than a threat. "Is that incense?" He shook his head, disdainfully. "Did you really think one bag of that junk would finish me? You should know better by now." He let out a deep sigh.

Steven realized The Seeker was in serious trouble. The incense wasn't working the way they thought it would. He also realized that the only way to immobilize the Dark Ruler might be a joint attack. But The Seeker had warned him to stay hidden, no matter what happened. Could he disobey his friend?

"Yes, it is an interesting offer," The Seeker said, leading the Dark Ruler further and further away from where Steven was hiding.

He's sacrificing himself for me, Steven thought, wishing his Aunt would hurry and show up to join the fight before it was too late.

"You see, Sonchis, my old friend, even your precious incense, has no effect on me. I have become much too powerful. Evil does that to one, don't you know?" He waved his arm in a large circle. "Come, join me? Feel the power of evil with me."

"Nothing is more powerful than good," The Seeker suddenly shouted, and spinning around before the Dark Ruler could protect himself, he swung his staff as hard as he could up against the Dark Ruler's head, knocking his foe backward. "I could never join you. You disgust me."

Stunned by the blow, the Dark Ruler staggered and slid into the pool of water still hot from the lava ball. "You hit me," he shouted, sitting in the water, surprised by an attack that was not magic, but a physical blow. He shook his head and raised his hand in a sign of surrender. "I give up. You win." He shook his head again. "Let's talk out our differences? Surely two reasonable beings cano settle these minor disputes peacefully?"

The Seeker stepped back slightly but moved his hand down to his belt to retrieve the second bag of incense to finish off this evil entity, once and for all. *Gone?* He searched his robe, hiding his concern so the Dark Ruler would not guess that the incense had disappeared.

Steven guessed what had happened. He had seen The Seeker place his hand by his belt and noted his mentor's facial expression once he realized the other bag of incense was no longer there. He ordered me to stay here, Steven reminded himself but wished he didn't have to obey.

"Go ahead. Talk. I'm listening," The Seeker said, stalling for time while searching the ground with his eyes for the missing bag.

Steven couldn't believe it. Was The Seeker going to take the deal?

Chapter 54

Although Steven suspected The Seeker was acting as if he could be persuaded, to delay The Dark Ruler while he searched for the missing bag of incense, he feared it was a bad mistake. He had been told many times by his father that if an attacker is down, make sure they stay down. Don't back away until you are sure they aren't able to attack again. He wished he could shout that message to his friend. He hoped he could tell him to forget about the other bag of incense and just use the staff to pound his foe into a pulp.

"Still a 'gentleman fighter' I see," The Dark Ruler said, wondering why The Seeker hadn't attacked, sensing something had gone wrong. "That is most admirable." He smiled his sharkish, best-toothy smile, "But you should have finished me off when you had the chance." Pushing himself up like a rocket, out of the boiling water, the Dark Ruler flung himself at The Seeker, the blade on the end of his shaft aimed at his enemy's heart.

The Seeker rallied quickly but barely deflected the attack with his staff, knocking the Dark Ruler to the right.

The Dark Ruler regained his stance and swung his staff again.

Blocking the attack, The Seeker spun around hard, his shaft knocking the Dark Ruler's weapon to the floor. He then spun around and smashed his pole hard against his enemy's head.

The blow would have killed a human, but neither fighter was human. The Dark Ruler jumped up, and the fighting continued furiously.

Steven could do nothing but watch in fear as the battle between good and evil raged on. Neither one was gaining ground. How long can they keep this up? He wondered. Suddenly, he realized his arms were soaked. *Water! Where is the water coming from?* His eyes were searching the cave when a loud sinister laugh brought him back to the battle.

Steven saw the Dark Ruler was holding The Seeker up in the air and spinning him around and around. The vicious Ruler grimaced grotesquely and threw The Seeker with deadly force against the rough cave wall.

"No," Steven stifled his cry when he saw his friend lying crumpled on the floor.

The Dark Ruler rushed over to The Seeker, his shaft held high above his head. "You are mine now!" he screeched and brought the rod down powerfully toward The Seeker's head.

The Seeker, eyes opening wide, swung his shaft up, blocking the downward thrust of the Dark Ruler's pole. He couldn't stand, felt weak, but knew he had to keep fighting. He twisted his shaft and lodged it in the rock between the Dark Ruler's legs.

"Too tired to fight? Don't expect mercy from me," the Dark Ruler taunted, glaring down at The Seeker with venomous eyes.

Steven shivered, seeing his friend unable to rise. He wanted to help, but he had been ordered to save himself for the prophecy. But if he didn't do something now, The Seeker was doomed, and then it would be his turn to face the unleashed wrath of his enemy, on his own. *What should I do?*

"And now the happy ending," the Dark Ruler declared. He raised his shaft, his heart, and demon soul filled with rage.

Steven burst from the narrow chasm where he had been hiding. I'm too late, he thought, frozen to the spot.

As The Dark Ruler stepped forward, blinded by his fury, prepared to deliver the fatal blow, distracted by Steven's noise, he tripped over The Seeker's shaft embedded into the ground and fell to the hard earth.

Boy, stay back. The Seeker summoned his last ounce of strength and pulled himself up, leaning on the wall. He stepped toward the Dark Ruler and raised his shaft over his head and....

"Spare me?" The Dark Ruler begged. "You are not a killer."

The Seeker hesitated but a second.

Steven shouted a warning telepathically as he saw the Dark Ruler reach into his robe and throw a blazing red ball of fire at The Seeker's face.

The ball exploded instantly, knocking The Seeker into the air. He landed, stunned, face-up in the pool of water, eyes closed. He was motionless.

Steven kept his cries to himself, afraid the Dark Ruler would find him, as he saw the demon pick himself up and wade over to where The Seeker was floating. He could barely breathe as the Dark Ruler raised up his blade-tipped staff for the fatal blow.

Laughter rang off the walls of the cavern as the monster looked down at The Seeker. "As I said, Sonchis, you are mine now, and nothing can stop me."

Steven was standing on shaky legs, the paintball gun pointed at the Dark Ruler's back.

Sensing someone behind him, the Dark Ruler started to turn around.

"Let me correct you. You are mine now," Steven said and squeezed off five incense balls in rapid succession at the Dark Ruler.

"Who are you?" The Dark Ruler lifted his staff to block the pellets. "I can't see you."

Too late! The five balls exploded over The Dark Ruler's head, spraying incense all over his body.

At first, the Dark Ruler laughed at what he thought were mere bullets. "You're the boy! You're so little I couldn't even see you!" The Dark Ruler laughed at the idea of a boy trying to defeat him when he had beaten the mighty Seeker. "Your weapons can't hurt me, foolish boy," he gloated, walking toward Steven. "I'm your friend. You'll soon see, once I take you home with me."

Aunt Celia, who had just arrived, was now standing on the opposite side of the Dark Ruler. "I'm here, Steven." She raised her gun and fired off five more incense balls.

Powder filled the air as the incense smashed all over the demon's body.

The Dark Ruler, caught off-guard by the concerted attacks, was now feeling the effect of the incense. He dropped his staff and raised his hands to cover his face. Blinded by the powder in his eyes, he was struggling to brush away the tiny particles as the incense tentacles began to choke off his breathing.

"A boy and an old lady? The prophecy?"

Aunt Celia reloaded her gun. "That's for ordering your slaves to kill my brother and sister-in-law, and trying to capture my nephew and his friends. May your cursed soul burn for eternity," she said, firing her gun.

A hideous scream rang out, high, and piercing, as the balls of incense splattered against the Dark Ruler and spread like slithering snakes over his writhing body. No matter how he tried to wipe them off with his hands, the powder seemed to be hardening into more wiry tentacles, gripping every part of his arms and legs.

Steven heard the inhuman cries become louder as the razor sharp thin strands of incense, like barbed wire, shredded the black robe and tore into the Dark Ruler's skin.

"What have you done?" the monster wailed, as the pain forced him to his knees. "I am all-powerful!" he cried out, trying to rise, but being held down by the excruciating pain of the ever-tightening wires of incense.

"This is terrible," Aunt Celia said, holding her ears to block out the screams.

"It is unfortunately what he brought on himself," The Seeker replied, rising from where he fell.

The Dark Ruler was still thrashing against the incense cords that were binding him. He was writhing on the cave floor like a trapped wild animal, but the ties were continually getting tighter. The incense was a weapon he could not fight.

Within seconds, the powerful tentacles covered every inch of The Dark Ruler's body. The piercing screams became muffled pleas for mercy as the threads formed a translucent cocoon, finally covering even his mouth and nose. His eyes still were blazing red fire until they too disappeared under the incense web. Then all movement stopped. No sound.

Steven and Aunt Celia scurried over to The Seeker. "Are you hurt?" they asked.

The Seeker shook his head, still recovering from the terrible battle. "I wouldn't be here if you both hadn't risked your lives and jumped into the fight. Thank you."

"Well, I thought while you were 'resting,' I would dive into the fray for round two," said Steven, smiling now that he knew his friend was okay. "Besides, it was all part of the prophecy."

"I didn't know if you and your Aunt would be a match for his evil," The Seeker said, coming to his senses.

"Good always triumphs over evil. Isn't that what you always say?"

The Seeker smiled. "I do. I just didn't know if you were listening."

"Steven, now that we are finished with the Dark Ruler, there will be a rematch with you and the paintballs. And may the best aunt win," Aunt Celia said with a broad smile.

"I'm sorry, dear Lady," The Seeker said. "The fun will have to wait. We still have work to do. Steven, open the Portal. Let's get this monster secured in his vault before he causes any more trouble."

Aunt Celia looked anxious. "Do you think he still can?"

The Seeker sighed. "You never know. He is the vilest creature ever, but we've got him now."

Aunt Celia nodded, but her eyes were fixed on the cocoon, wondering if it was strong enough to keep evil locked away forever.

Chapter 55

The Seeker gazed down at the Dark Ruler stretched out in the cocoon on the ground. "Steven, it is regrettable when a soul that could have been a beacon for others becomes lost in the darkness. I truly wish we could have saved him." He sighed and bent down to lift the Dark Ruler, wrapped in the cocoon, into his arms.

The Dark Ruler squirmed and tried to break free from the cocoon as The Seeker, holding him in his arms, stepped through the open door of the Portal. "It is time, Steven. We must hurry."

Steven felt sad as he entered next. He wasn't sure if he was tired or if he shared the Seeker's sadness that nothing could save this fallen priest from his evil side.

Aunt Celia watched Steven with concern, prepared to follow. "I still can't believe Steven, and I have the means to travel the globe using the Portal," she said, as she entered the whirling pool of light.

"I'm glad you are enjoying it," The Seeker replied, wondering if she finally understood just how vital a part Steven played in the battle against evil, and that the war was not over.

Once they entered the Portal, they were bathed in swirling lights and rainbow colors. Even Aunt Celia was no longer afraid as the Portal speeded them across the globe.

"We're here," Steven announced.

Stepping out of the Portal, Aunt Celia's eyes grew wide. "Where are we?" She asked, panning her flashlight on the stone floor and walls. "Is this the Dark Ruler's home?"

"We're in the lowest section of the Seti I pyramid," Steven responded.

"I don't see a door anywhere," Aunt Celia said, feeling a little worried, as she scanned the stone walls with her flashlight.

"This area is unknown to humans. Even you, Steven, have never been this deep," The Seeker said, looking down at the body of the Dark Ruler to be sure the cocoon was holding.

"What door?" Aunt Celia asked, searching for a doorway. "I still don't see any door."

"That's what I said many times when we searched for other Guardians. It took me a while to locate the keys to open the sealed doors," Steven said.

"I don't understand," Aunt Celia said, beginning to feel closed in.

"Let me show you where the door to the vault lies." Steven stepped toward the stones in front of him. Moving the flashlight to the top of one of the rocks, Steven slid his right hand across the top right corner.

Aunt Celia watched Steven remove something from his backpack and start picking at the dark filler between the two stones. "Steven, what are you doing?" She hoped whatever it was, would be completed before the cocoon was weakened by the still struggling Dark Ruler. She found her eyes drifting to the shrouded body squirming on the ground.

Steven shifted to the opposite corner of the wall and proceeded to remove the filler there with a small pickaxe. He repeated this process at the bottom edges of the stone as well.

"I wish you would hurry," Aunt Celia said, her hand resting nervously on her pistol as she eyed the increasingly active cocoon. She released the snap on the back of the magazine chamber and inserted five paintballs just in case she needed to fire another layer of incense on the Dark Ruler. "Steven, refill your magazine too. I don't like the way he is still trying to get loose," she said, taking no chances.

"Who is getting loose?" The Seeker asked, satisfied none of the Dark Ruler's Guardians had followed them into the tomb.

Steven refilled his magazine and removed the Amulet from around his neck. "Are we ready to enter the vault?" He asked The Seeker.

"Almost, but first, you must hear the rules."

"Rules? I'll have you know I'm a grown woman and—" Aunt Celia was indignant that he was dictating rules to her as if she was a child.

"Silence!" The Seeker shouted. "You are about to enter the evilest place you have ever seen, so, yes, you must obey the rules, or we are all lost." He glared at Aunt Celia. "You are the most stubborn woman—"

Aunt Celia frowned right back at him. "And you're a stubborn ghost."

It was up to Steven to break the impasse. "Aunt Celia, this isn't the time for war. Let's get this over with before 'you-know-who' breaks free again, and all our work will be for nothing."

The Seeker sighed. "Perhaps I should be more tactful. I apologize, but I am very concerned for your safety, my friends."

"I'm sorry too," Aunt Celia said. "By now, I should trust you."

"Thank you. As I was saying, both of you, for your safety, must never place your hands, or any part of your body, on the coffins, and you must stay clear of the pools."

"Not that I'm in any mood for a swim," Aunt Celia said, "But what is wrong with the pools?"

"Dear Lady, they are filled with the souls of the damned. They will try and grab you if you get too near."

"Souls of the damned? I don't like the sound of that."

"Speaking of sound, as soon as I open the door, you will hear a terrible wailing. It will sound as if a thousand beings are in pain—"

"Oh, wonderful," Aunt Celia said. "And can we do nothing to help them?"

"No. You must be on your guard, for they will plead and beg that you help them by pulling them out of the pool. Each tortured soul will exert their supernatural mental powers to control you...Steven too."

Aunt Celia placed a protective hand on Steven's shoulder. "Over my dead body." She quickly realized she shouldn't have said that.

"You must fight the kindly urge to help free them from their captivity. Be warned. Touch the souls, and you will be doomed to their plight. Do you both understand?"

Steven nodded.

"Must Steven go with us?" Aunt Celia asked.

"You know the answer to that already," The Seeker replied. "While I wish it were not so, the prophecy demands his presence, or all will be lost."

Aunt Celia nodded.

The Seeker admired her for caring so much about Steven. "I will do everything to protect him."

"I know you will." Aunt Celia gave him a rare smile.

"Stop worrying about me. What else do we have to do?" Steven asked.

The Seeker smiled at Steven. "You are very brave, my young friend. But please, obey what I have said." He peered deep into Steven's eyes and then continued. "I will carry the Dark Ruler through the secret door, and then you will follow. You will stay close while I place him securely in his vault. You are not to touch him. Is that understood? Steven, Celia, I can't say this enough. Touch nothing! Please?"

"Yes," Steven answered, holding his hands in the air.

Aunt Celia was deep in thought.

"*Aunt Celia, I mean you as well,*" The Seeker said.

"If you think I want to touch anything in this place, you are crazy," she replied but knew if Steven were threatened, she would do whatever it took, even touching the devil himself, to keep him from harm.

"Ok, as long as we are agreed on the rules, Steven, place the Amulet on this stone and let us begin."

Steven stepped up to the stone and pressed the Amulet on the hard surface.

"Nothing is happening. What are we waiting for?" Aunt Celia asked clearly nervous.

"Just watch, Aunt," Steven replied, still pressing the Amulet against the rock.

Nothing happened for several seconds, and then the walls started to shake. Sand from the thick wood joints in the ceiling was falling. A loud grinding noise soon filled the room as the massive granite stone was being pushed by an invisible force inward. As the corner of the stone door cleared the wall, Steven and Aunt Celia were instantly engulfed in the most horrible wailing sounds either had ever heard.

"The lost souls," Steven said.

"Aunt Celia nodded," panic building inside her at the agonized cries of the dead.

The Seeker picked up the Dark Ruler's cocoon and entered the vault. "Remember what I said. Touch nothing!"

Steven entered next, followed by his aunt. They stepped, carefully, as if afraid the ground would explode into an earthquake at each footstep.

The wailing appeared to be coming from a pool of reddish water, steam rising to the ceiling. It was bubbling with a thousand trapped souls, eyes fixed on the humans entering their realm. A putrid smell carried by the steam filled the vault and made Steven's stomach churn.

"This is disgusting," Aunt Celia said, holding her nose. "It smells like blood."

"It is blood," The Seeker replied, finding a path between the pools of lost souls and the coffins a distance ahead. As he led them past the bubbling water, scorched arms reached toward them. He shook his head and mumbled words of prayer before moving away.

When the souls realized they were not being set free, the wailing, screaming, and pleading erupted into an even more unbearable crescendo. The noise of their desperation was deafening.

Steven and Aunt Celia pressed their hands against their ears to block-out the heart-breaking wails.

"Watch out, Steven!" Aunt Celia yelled.

Steven jumped as a hand lifted out of the pool and attempted to grab his leg. He ducked but was confronted by another hand reaching up for him, threatening to pull him off the narrow walkway.

Aunt Celia doubled back and pulled Steven toward her. "Not today," she shot at the frustrated spirits that sank back into the turbulent water.

"You saved me," Steven gasped, the hands and faces lifting out of the boiling red pools filled him with terror.

"That's what aunts do," Aunt Celia said.

For once, Steven was glad to hold her hand. He let go only after they were past the frothing pools and near the tombs.

Steven did not like the looks of the sarcophagi, but at least he was away from the pools. He turned to see what The Seeker was doing.

Steven did not see a ravaged face peering hungrily at him as it emerged out of the nearby coffin.

Aunt Celia yelled at Steven to move back, but he couldn't hear her. He was still watching The Seeker, oblivious to the danger next to him.

"Damn!" Aunt Celia rushed toward Steven and pulled his arm away just as the monster was about to bite down on it.

"What's wrong?" Steven asked, wondering why she was holding his arm so tightly.

"Look," Aunt Celia said, her shaky finger pointing to the twisted face and skeletal arm that was reaching across the coffin where Steven had stood a second ago.

"That was a close call," Steven said.

"Too close," Aunt Celia replied, holding Steven's arm and moving him away from the coffin.

"Thanks, Aunt Celia, again."

"Please, don't make this a habit," she replied, watching every step he took.

The Seeker frowned. "You two have to be more careful," he said. "I have my hands full...but not much longer." He scanned the room and found what he was looking for.

Both watched in silence as The Seeker gently placed the Dark Ruler in an open sarcophagus. "This is where he belongs."

Aunt Celia shook her head sadly. "I would not want to be here."

"That could never happen to you," Steven said. "You're way too good."

Aunt Celia beamed at him.

"And now, Steven, you must help me. The prophecy says only you can seal the coffin. You must push it closed."

"It looks too heavy," Steven said.

"Your faith will make all things possible," The Seeker replied.

"I believe him," Aunt Celia added.

Steven stared at the heavy coffin lid. It was made of stone, its carvings almost faded from age. He could see the still squirming thing that had been called The Dark Ruler and knew he had to find the faith and strength to fulfill the prophecy or this evil creature would be free again. He smiled at his aunt and leaned against the large stone slab. All his logic told him he would never be able to budge the heavy lid, but The Seeker had said it was his destiny. He mustered all his will, all his strength, and pushed hard against the stone. Was it his imagination? The lid seemed to be inching forward. He felt his muscles aching, but refused to stop until he heard The Seeker say, "Steven, we are done at long last."

"Are we really?" Steven, still pressed against the lid, looked doubtfully at the now sealed coffin.

The Seeker sighed. "Yes, it is over. We must leave now and secure the door, so no one can ever release this monster again."

Steven, Aunt Celia, and The Seeker hurried out of the vault, the wails of the dead still echoing in their ears.

No sooner had they stepped into the small outer room when they heard the grinding sound of the large stone wall sliding across the stone floor, sealing the vault, hopefully forever.

Steven felt strange, disorientated, after surviving the horrors of the now sealed chamber. He found it difficult to believe the long battle was finally over. Steven could go back and be a typical boy again. That would be incredible, he thought, looking forward to a time when he would not feel pressured to do anything. He was shocked out of his growing hope for peace and quiet when he heard, "Steven, get us out of here! I want to get you home, so you can take a nice, warm bath, catch up on all your homework, and get ready for school."

"And you thought you were done with the Dark Ruler?" The Seeker burst into laughter, as Aunt Celia grabbed Steven's arm and dragged him toward the Portal and a healthy life?

Chapter 56

The team, in single file, stepped out of the Portal and into the lab. Aunt Celia and Steven dragged their tired bodies over to the two black leather chairs and flopped down. The Seeker floated next to Steven. They had just returned from placing the Dark Ruler into a sarcophagus in an underground vault containing the souls of the damned. It had been a terrible experience, hearing the cries of thousands of tormented souls desperately struggling to leave the swirling pools of blood in which they were imprisoned for eternity. Although painful to listen to their calls for help, they had to bear them for several long minutes to ensure that the Dark Ruler was indeed locked in his vault securely.

Steven remembered that The Seeker had said that tormented souls, such as those in the Vault of the Damned, would never be truly free. He could not imagine how anyone could want an eternity like that. He had a lot of questions about that for his aunt, but a noise startled him.

Bastet and Morag jumped onto the computer table.

"I'm so tired," Steven muttered. "Where were you two?"

After we took care of Gregor, we were guarding the entrance to the Caverns. We were protecting you, Bastet and Morag said as if one.

"I knew that," Steven said. "Thanks."

Morag began to tell her story of how she had been afraid of losing control of her violent nature, but how she had conquered that fear because she knew she had to help Steven.

Aunt Celia and Steven rested their heads back against the chair and closed their eyes. Soon they were both asleep.

That didn't last long, Morag said.

Shu came rushing into the lab. He was excited at hearing from The Seeker that the Dark Ruler had been secured in the chamber of tormented souls. *I have been searching for that storm that is still hunting you, Steven.*

Steven yawned, so tired he ignored the fluttering papers flying all over the lab.

"I thought we were finished with all this?" Aunt Celia said, staring helplessly at the whirlwind of papers.

I wish, Shu said. *Do not fool yourself, dear, Aunt Celia, we may never be completely done. But I will be here when you need me.*

"Thank you," Steven said.

As suddenly as he appeared, Shu vanished. But not before setting the usual piles of paper whirling around in the air a second time.

"Not again?" Aunt Celia grumbled, scrambling to catch the sheets of paper flying around the lab.

Steven remained slumped in his father's chair. The anguish from hearing the cries and pleas of the damned in the vault haunted him.

The Seeker placed a hand gently upon Steven's shoulder. "You did well, Steven...for a human." He let out a little laugh.

Steven looked up and said, "I can't get it out of my head. I felt the pain and torment of each soul in that awful place. There must have been a thousand hands reaching up, trying to pull me down into...."

"Dante's Inferno?" Aunt Celia interrupted, quivering at the image of all those lost souls. "My dear nephew, you were not alone. I felt the same way. It was an inferno."

"Dante's Inferno?" The Seeker asked. "I've never heard of it. Is it a place?"

Aunt Celia put on her best professor's look. "It was a poem written by Dante Alighieri, an Italian poet, hundreds of years ago. It is considered one of the masterpieces of world literature."

"I never heard of it either," Steven said. "I'm not crazy about poetry."

Aunt Celia shook her head. "You should be. Dante's poem describes what he claims he saw when he was guided through the nine circles of hell. Now if we–"

"Aunt Celia, do you think we could review Dante's poem later?" Steven interrupted, eager to go over the final details of their mission. "It sounds interesting, but we still have a lot to talk about."

"Yes, please do finish later? I am extremely interested," added The Seeker.

"I'm surprised, Mr. Spirit, you haven't heard of it before. I'll be happy to teach you, and 'anyone' else who wants to learn." Aunt Celia eyed Steven, so he knew she meant him.

Steven shrugged. "Okay. Later you can tell me all about this poet guy. But for now, I just want to say thanks to everyone. I think we turned out to be a pretty good team...even our newest member." He smiled at Aunt Celia.

Aunt Celia turned to Bastet and Morag. "Both of you saved my life. I'm not sure what I can do to repay you?"

Breakfast would do for a start, Bastet meowed.

I'll take a sizeable raw piece of red meat, Morag said, showing her teeth blazing white and razor sharp.

"Do the two of you ever think of anything but eating?" Steven asked, giving Morag and Bastet a playful look.

I'm a growing dragon, Morag said, and let out a small puff of smoke.

And I am a god and require pampering, Bastet meowed.

"What happens now?" Aunt Celia asked. "Will we have to free all the Guardians the Dark Ruler concealed across the world?"

"I guess that with their Ruler gone, all their souls are now with him in hell. You will have to wait for Shu and me to check that out," The Seeker said.

But for now, I think we should all get some sleep, Bastet said, yawning loudly. *I, for one, can't wait for a 'cat nap.'*

"Great idea!" said Aunt Celia, as she got up from her chair, sand dropping to the floor. "Oh, by the way, Steven, as I said earlier, I still demand a Paintball rematch tomorrow night, just with you, and without the help of Bastet and Morag."

Can't wait to watch this, Steven, Morag said. *You're on your own this time. No help from any of us.*

Aunt Celia, you're going down, as you humans say, Bastet teased, flicking her tail. *It will be like a game of cat and mouse.*

"We'll see about that," Aunt Celia said, and burst into laughter.

Steven laughed too, but in the back of his brain, he thought he could hear long sharp nails scratching at the thin threads of a cocoon.

The strange thing was The Seeker heard it too.

THE END

Can Steven fight his fear and defeat the Dark Ruler again? What is Morag's secret that will force her to risk her life? The next exciting adventure for Steven will take him to China, to a massive tomb where rows of clay soldiers amaze visitors and become his next terrifying challenge. Are they a secret army waiting for the Dark Ruler's command? Can Steven stop them?

Find out in Steven's next adventure: The Guardian of Mount Li.

Visit AimHiPress.com for more books and other products from AimHi Press and the rest of the Newhouse Creative Group family!

About the Author

William S. Russell and his wife live in The Villages, Florida. He is a member of the Writers 4 Kids and the Writers League of the Villages. Although he has never traveled to Egypt, the Egyptian architecture, inscriptions, language and culture have always intrigued him.

Made in the USA
Columbia, SC
07 January 2020